ANITA McANDREWS

MARCO'S GIFT

outskirtspress
DENVER, COLORADO

For my seven children

A hunch, *a powerful hunch, Elizabeth could no longer resist it.* Not the island itself but its history—the marvelous possibility of Gauguin paintings hidden there.

More than a possibility, yes. Elizabeth had done some research and convinced herself that Taboga Island, ten miles off the Pacific coast of Panama, concealed an art treasure beyond her imagining.

Elizabeth Rogers denied herself most impulses. She did not question this one. "If those paintings exist, I will have them," she told Janice, her gallery assistant.

Janice grinned. "If you want them, they're yours—that's your style, Elizabeth." She was thinking how perfectly this Boston art gallery framed its owner. The pastel walls, hung with the small paintings of Elizabeth's personal collection, enclosed the office space with a grace inherent to Elizabeth herself. Slim, full breasted, two years past thirty now, Elizabeth's bloom of skin and hair softened her stubborn tilt of chin, the intensity of her gaze. No one must guess the depth of Elizabeth's unease in a world she considered rife with pitfalls.

Her posture evidenced an arrogance she had earned. She had named her gallery Numero Uno and, like Elizabeth herself, it was a work of art and artifice.

"We're almost top of the heap, Janice," Elizabeth said. "We have our sea legs now. It's been a hectic year, and I need a diversion. Those Gauguins haunt me."

"You and how many other collectors?" Janice asked.

"You're right, it's always been more than a rumor." Elizabeth put her hand on a well-thumbed book on her desk. It was Gauguin's *The Writings of a Savage*, a journal in which Gauguin wrote of Panama in 1887 and his stint there as a laborer on the French Canal. He had been ill with malaria and had been twice hospitalized in the French sanitarium on Taboga Island. He had wanted to settle there. He had not recorded work accomplished, but Elizabeth could not imagine Gauguin not painting. She had no use for idleness, and Gauguin was an artist she admired. He had chucked all pretense, made the grand escape. Elizabeth, too, would unbind her hair, mount a purple pony, find the moon in a jungle pool. She would shout aloud those words she had forbid herself to speak.

Janice noted the sudden flush of Elizabeth's cheeks. "Are you okay?"

"I'm excited," Elizabeth admitted. "But finding those paintings will not be easy."

Janice grinned. "That's you, Elizabeth. Even a vacation must have its difficulties."

Elizabeth leaned back in her chair. "I need an adventure. I like a new place, especially if the setting is solitude. I'm burned out, Janice. That February slush out there," she pointed at the window, "is getting to me. I want to lie under a palm tree, build castles from the sand."

Like a child with a secret, Elizabeth hugged herself. "Gauguin. What a challenge! Not a whiff of this must reach the art world. If anyone asks, just say I'm on vacation. And Panama mustn't know what I'm after. I'll tell the authorities there that I'm checking out tourist possibilities. I've a friend in the tourist business; he'll give me the correct protocol. That fat cat dictator they have down there—he's greedy, he'll spread the proverbial red carpet."

Janice nodded. "For U.S. dollars? I guess so."

"Imagine, Janice, what those Gauguins will do for this gallery."

Elizabeth's gaze caressed her present treasures. Those two small Pissarros bought from a drug dealer in Barbados, were not for sale. Neither was the Magritte sketch discovered in Barcelona in a back alley antique shop—courtesy of a Brazilian needing his fix. It had been the last of the seventies and the art market had been glutted with drug money and contraband art.

"You'll go alone?" Janice asked. "Kind of scary, isn't it? Armed thugs patrolling the streets, student riots. Why must you take such risks, Elizabeth? You tempt fate."

"I don't believe in fate," replied Elizabeth. "And you forget our Canal. It's still ours. Our own boys stand guard. I'll play safe, I always do. I like life by myself."

She did. On her own, she could wander where she wished. She spoke Spanish; it was her favorite other language. Her knowledge of art history impressed the dealers. She was known for her quick decisions; she drove a sharp bargain.

"Alone is fun," she said. "A Latin lover maybe? Janice, have you ever—I mean a dark one?"

Janice shook her head. "I don't trust Latinos."

"Trust?" Elizabeth shrugged. "You know I don't do that. Or love either."

It was the sex she liked. It relaxed her, lent a sheen to her skin and hair. Sex cleared her mind, tamping down demons she had no desire to entertain. "No, I don't do love," she repeated.

"You're too hard on yourself," Janice said.

"I call it saving my life," Elizabeth replied.

Like Gauguin, she had buried her past. Her life now was neat as her wealth of white-blond hair, coiled and pinned above the nape of her neck. Heavy, yes, and the combs scratched. At night, alone, she shook down that hair, breathed deep for a moment, then—because loose hair induced crazy dreams—she braided it up again, scraping it back until her eyes widened, twin blue pools that tempted a stranger to look deeper. He would meet with a cool rebuff. Compliments lied, so Elizabeth believed. Beauty was only skin deep; what lay below was a darkness she had learned not to explore.

"Life is one hell of a climb," Elizabeth told Janice now. "I've earned these Gauguins."

"And all by your lonesome," Janice said, thinking it was not often her employer revealed this much of herself.

"I don't depend on anyone," Elizabeth said. "I learned that early on."

Only once, very young, had she depended on another—and known betrayal. In Elizabeth's reckoning, the sum total of love was death. She would not give herself again—not to man nor woman, or whatever, whoever was God. A ward of the state, she had done her time in Catholic orphanages; the rituals had fascinated her, but that ultimate offering of herself they urged upon her, that she refused.

No, she was not about to entrust body or soul—if she had one, and Elizabeth doubted that—to anyone else's care. The eighties now and people were shopping for salvation, too often on their knees to some-one or something. *Mea culpa*. It was a position Elizabeth considered ridiculous for those endowed with a capacity for reason.

"One primary rule, Janice," she said now. "No trespassers, ever. Nobody steps on my shadow."

She pushed to her feet. "This trip—I am definitely psyched. Make my flight reservations for Boston to Panama this coming March, a month before Easter. Not the island hotel, I hear it's impossible. Find an agency and rent me something on the beach. And I'll need to know how to get to Taboga Island from Panama City."

"Yes," Elizabeth said, "I'd sell my soul for those paintings." She laughed. "An easy trade, that! Something I don't believe in for some-thing I very much do."

*E*lizabeth's conviction that the Gauguins did exist had been confirmed from cruising friends recently from the Caribbean. They told Elizabeth about an island, Taboga, forty-five minutes by ferry from Panama City. "A pretty place," they said; they'd anchored there. "Full of stories," they said. They had heard one wild tale of several early Gauguins kept secret in one of the houses there.

"We knew you'd be interested and we did a little sleuthing," Elizabeth's friends told her. "A woman in the village, Mrs. Amado, is said to own the paintings. We knocked, but she wouldn't open her door. We tried several times. I wish we'd had more time.

"You, Elizabeth," they had urged, "this is your cup of tea. We think you should give this a try."

"I just might," she'd answered, pretending a disinterest she did not feel.

"It's getting those paintings out of Panama," someone said.

"If they don't know they have them, they won't know they're gone," Elizabeth had replied.

"That old woman," someone remarked, "her house is a shack, pitiful. These are simple fisher folk, Elizabeth. If that woman has Gauguins, chances are she doesn't know it."

"And wouldn't understand if we did tell her," Elizabeth had answered. "There's no need to mention Gauguin at all." Then, realizing she sounded somewhat cruel, she added, "I would pay her something of course—a sum she could comprehend. A monthly stipend maybe?"

"But no money to Panama," her friends had insisted. "Nothing to the military dictatorship there. The General was a city cop. When his murders and mayhem were done, he promoted himself—four gold stars no less! Don't cross him, he's a nasty bastard. Drugs are a real problem. Taboga's harbor is full of pirates. It's a known fact the General works hand-in-glove with the Colombian cartel. Taking something like those Gauguins out from under his nose would be most satisfying!"

And it could create an international incident, Elizabeth knew that. She had enlisted the aid of a writer friend traveling in Central America. At Elizabeth's request, this friend had visited Taboga and was able to confirm that a woman in the village there was said to own several French paintings.

"Paintings from the French colonial years, so goes the rumor," Elizabeth's friend said. "Gauguin is just a name, and there's nothing left of the French sanatorium where he was twice a patient. The stones of that area were used by the Americans when they built the Canal; later that area was occupied by our military. It is all rubble now. The village, fisher families mostly, is its own ruin. No night life, except for the drunks in the plaza. There's just one run-down hotel, government owned. Unpaved streets, tin cans and tomato sauce. Not your kind of scene, Elizabeth."

"I'm not so sure," Elizabeth had answered. "There's an old travel book I found. It has a photo of a Spanish colonial church, its roof still layered with mother-of-pearl. And the Spanish had another name for the island. They called it *La Isla Morada*. The wine-colored one. That's pure poetry!"

"That's Greece, not Panama," her friend said. "What's cool is the island witch. El Brujo, they call him: Devil Man. I didn't meet him. He lives by himself, top of the highest hill. The people speak of him like he is some kind of god. They told me he turns water into rum. Acres of high grass where he lives. You know what that means. Clever fellow!"

"What else?" Elizabeth had pressed.

"The island has a weird kind of magic, I felt it," her friend had admitted. "It could be a setting for a gothic novel, or a hot romance. There's a haunted convent—a Spanish ruin where the ghosts of nuns wander. And, full moon, a headless bishop rides the hilltops. The action's in the plaza where the village idiot hangs out—just he and his drum. Pirates there, too, swapping sea stories. And a fortune teller; she owns the one grocery store. It cost me a dollar to learn I could have what I wish for—if I really want it, that is."

"And the Gauguins?" Elizabeth insisted.

"I honestly don't know. You're on a wild goose chase, I think."

"I like a chase," Elizabeth said. "I don't know why, but that island is standing on its heels, shouting my name."

*P*anama City. Traffic snarls, a nightmare of delays, red tape. Guns. The taste of fear in her mouth. She had not expected such heat.

The need to extend her tourist visa kept Elizabeth two extra nights in the city. A bureaucratic tangle, wearying to an extreme. One government building to another, elevators stalled, a million marble stairs. It was the thought of the proximity of the Gauguins that enabled Elizabeth to keep her temper in check.

Two days until her papers arrived on the right desk. Hours more before the General picked up the scent of American dollars. Elizabeth, ushered at last by two into the inner sanctum, sensed immediately the power inherent to that room. Its occupant, the General, was a real spook. A short man, stubby. Lost somehow behind his acres of green formica. He did not rise to greet Elizabeth. His eyes appraised her with an arrogance that told her this was the kind who would take whatever he wanted.

The huge black-and-white abstracts on his office wall unsettled her. She did not recognize the artist.

Brusque, pretending an indifference to her American presence, the General did not address her by name or title. He waited for her to speak.

The back of the chair in front of Elizabeth was greasy. She did not sit down. "I've come to ask a favor," she said. "You have given me a week on the island. I expected longer. I planned a month. I must get to know the place, its possibilities."

"Nothing is definite?" He was petulant.

Elizabeth shook her head. "The talking stage."

Standing opposite him, she must look down on him. He gestured at the chair. "Please." Gingerly, Elizabeth perched, keeping her hand-bag on her lap.

"Not everyone sees me this easily," the General said. "Boston?" he asked, in English. "A frigid climate." His snicker was suggestive.

"We have lovely summers," she said, in Spanish.

"Your destination is Taboga?" He insisted on her language. "It is an is-land with something for everyone, yes. It should be developed. But there is—how you say it?—an obstacle. This island does not belong to me."

"Belong to you?" Elizabeth could not resist. She gestured at the map of Panama on the wall behind him. "All that is yours?"

He smiled. "Panama is mine, yes. In the sense that my word is law." He leaned back in his chair, plump fingers tip-tapping his puffed belly. "The world invests now in our little country."

"The Canal, of course," Elizabeth murmured.

"But we are more than a Canal."

"Are you?" she asked. And saw his cheek twitch and knew she had overstepped.

"I must tell you, Taboga is a cursed island, señora."

She was not sure she had heard him correctly. "Cursed?" The word was almost medieval.

"It is owned by one who calls himself a Devil Man. Of course he is mad," the General tapped his forehead. "But the *Taboganos*, so we call them, are ignorant, superstitious. They are frightened of this man, they do his bidding. He will not tolerate any intrusion of what he in-sists is his territory. It is he who will stop you." The General leaned forward. "I tell you now, be careful. The man has real power. No one is immune."

"Meaning?" Elizabeth asked.

"We are a Catholic country," he said. "Satan worship is forbidden. We must catch this Devil, and put him where he belongs." He slammed his desktop. "I will commit him to the public asylum. An infamous place, I assure you."

Elizabeth shook her head. "I don't understand."

"Of course not. You are American." He dusted his hands. "Not to worry. We will see you come to no harm. You have only to telephone and my men will be there. You may go where you wish. No one,"—and he crossed himself, medals included—"not Satan himself, will dare make trouble."

Bending to his desk, he scribbled an order and slid the paper in Elizabeth's direction. "I give you your month, *doña*. And," he held out his hand, "in exchange, your passport."

On her feet then, clutching her handbag to her, "No. I don't think so."

He shrugged. "Your passport would be safer with us. Taboga is a pretty place, yes, but primitive. A woman alone...you are alone?"

She kept her voice even. "Hardly alone. You are aware I represent several large US agencies." With all the dignity she could muster, she picked up the official order, folded it, and tucked it into her handbag beside her passport.

He shrugged, and inclined his head, a gesture of dismissal. "I will not detain you."

"Detain me?" She knew her voice slid high.

He laughed. "You gringas—you see too many movies."

He bent to the work on his desk. She turned, too quickly, colliding with the orderly behind her. "Oh, I am sorry."

The General raised his head. "Sorry?" He gestured impatiently, erasing that word which Elizabeth knew had no meaning for him.

"You have my permission to remain on the island one month, se-ñora. Any longer, and you must visit me again. You will remember that."

Yes, she would remember. His permission! Like he was God. Off with their heads! Yes, he did that too.

*N*ow, *checking her watch, Elizabeth saw she was less than an hour from her destination.* This ferry was beginning to feel one-dimensional. It hung, seeming motionless, caught between a flat blue sky and a flatter sea. Overhead, the tropic sun simmered like an egg in hot oil. The stink was urine, sweat, and stale beer. Pelicans and terns trailed the ferry wake.

Watching the receding towers of Panama City's buildings, Elizabeth likened them to alabaster minarets. From here, out in the bay, the city appeared tranquil. But it wasn't, she reminded herself; it was studded with guns, a cesspool of treachery. The National Museum had been closed, doors barred, as was the Archeological Museum, robbed this month, she was told, of the last of its gold relics from a pre-Colombian past. It was said, tongue-in-cheek, that the present dictator, the General, collected fine art.

Elizabeth squirmed, netted in the stares of fellow passengers. It did not occur to her that perhaps she was a curiosity. She had forgotten that she was, after all, the one white person aboard this ferry. She could not know that these islanders believed blue eyes revealed a lack of soul. The women shrank from Elizabeth, fingered their plastic rosaries. Men pursed their lips, tickled their crotches.

Elizabeth tugged on her hat brim, pushed to her feet. She walked forward, picking her way between plastic baskets and swaddled infants. A drunk shoved his bare foot in front of her and she tripped, and had to catch his calloused hand not to fall.

Somebody giggled.

Reaching the bow, Elizabeth gripped the railing. Just ahead, she saw her Island, so she called it now, her own. It ballooned, a giant tangle of green and gold bursting from a lavender sea. Fresh air, fresh water, the air had a different taste, sweet odors. Elizabeth clutched the ship's railing and, impatient as a child, pulled herself up on her toes.

Slowly the island floated center stage. Its green hills were eyelids, closed. Sky and sea were blue comforters, wrapping themselves around Elizabeth until her tension eased. Yes, she told herself, she would be welcome here. Surely Gauguin had felt this same release.

Adjusting her sunglasses, the better to see the harbor now, the sweep of the green hills, down. "So," Elizabeth whispered, "so does this story begin."

And when the paintings are public knowledge, she thought, Taboga will jump. Another Hilton Heaven, and Elizabeth smiled, imagining a Gauguin Hotel, or maybe Paul's Overnight. A Gauguin Museum, of course, a gift shop with the inevitable postcards. Panama would have a field day. The General would purr, take all credit for himself.

Lifting her head, Elizabeth watched the island cut the afternoon with Gauguin's colors: reds, blues, the purple splash of jacaranda.

Two tall hills leaned towards her, their shadows cupping a village, and a harbor smooth as a china bowl. At the heart of it all Elizabeth saw the sparkle (surely mother-of-pearl) of a church spire. Tipsy houses, roofed with aluminum or tile climbed from an ocher beach where multicolored dinghies sprawled the sand.

Tracing the contours of the highest hill, Elizabeth glimpsed a large house at the top. She wondered who lived there, separate, apart from all others.

The ferry whistle sounded, bouncing off the island hills. Jesu, caretaker of the big house on the top of the hill, raised his head and sniffed the air. Had Don Marco returned? Jesu bent to quiet the three hounds at his feet. He roughed their nudging heads, whispered secrets in their ears. When they were still, Jesu stood straight again, and watched the ferry ease into the harbor. That slim figure in the bow? Jesu squinted, could see only a woman in a straw hat, the glint of her sunglasses. The American tourist? Jesu knew his master's house in the village was readied for someone. The girl Flore had told him that. It was she who cleaned that house, took care of its tenants.

She was standing in front of him now, her pregnant belly pushing like a round root against the worn cotton of her dress. She had come to purchase a bottle of love potion. "Too late for that," Jesu told her, eyeing her bulge. "Perhaps another kind of medicine?"

Flore shook her head, spread her hands protectively across her stomach. "I carry Marco Rodriguez's son. This time, when he returns, I will tell him."

His master's child? Jesu doubted that. Flore opened her legs to every *bandido* who fished the waters here. For a price, of course: Flore was poor and greedy. She was pretty enough, and young. It was possible, Jesu conceded, that his master had shared this girl's hammock. Marco seldom turned down the gift of pleasure. Devil Man or no—and Jesu crossed himself—there were times a man thirsted for what he could not find.

"The love potion," Flore insisted, and Jesu went into the house and returned with a tall bottle. Uncorking it, Flore shook the liquid over her black hair, rubbed it between her breasts, and stroked it on her thighs.

"What is it? Does it work?" she asked.

"*Muy caro,* too expensive," she said, shaking out the last precious drops.

It was the juice of pressed hummingbirds, an ancient recipe, and who knew if it worked or not, but Jesu never told anyone that.

"Love costs high," he said. "And you'd better hurry. The ferry is in, I see a *gringa* aboard. You must ready the house."

"Yes, Marco told me," Flore said. These *gringos* puzzled her. They had money to go anywhere, so why did they come to Taboga? Flore hated this island—its dirt, the stink of fish—it was her prison, she would never escape it. The baby, now, was it really Marco's? It could be, yes, it could be. Because once, not too many months ago—*Dios!*— she had prayed it would happen: Marco had been lonely, groggy with too much sweet Sangria. She'd been cleaning the house, scrubbing out the last vestige of the recent gringo tenants, and he'd come to pay her for her work. The bed unmade, and he'd taken her right there, without a word. He'd been angry at himself afterwards.

"It means nothing—*es nada,*" he'd told her, his eyes so black they burned. Flore had wanted to slap him, make him see her. Yes, make him love her once again! Ever since that time, she had imagined Marco's loving her, willing it so real she could almost tell herself that it had happened, yes—again, and again.

"The señor will be back soon," she told Jesu now.

When Marco returned, she would tell him about the child. He would not abandon her. She had told her family this was Marco's baby, and they wanted to believe her. Because the *brujo* would take care of them all. They would be rich beyond their imagining.

Flore never told Marco about the American husbands who took her right there, in that house. One had given her a silver necklace, another a pair of stockings. Their chest hair tickled Flore's nose; their pale stomachs reminded her of yeast bread rising. Their wives, the prettiest ones anyway, fell in love with Marco. If they offered themselves, he took his pleasure. It was getting rid of them that bothered him. "They cling like ticks," he told Flore. "Pinch them off," she had replied.

A woman never forgot a Devil Man's lovemaking. That was part of his legend, and Flore must believe it because Marco had left her with an insatiable hunger.

The ferry whistle sounded. Flore set down her empty bottle. "Your magic better work," she said.

"If you believe so," and Jesu turned, dismissing the girl.

He whistled for the dogs. He doubted his master was on this ferry. But he would make a *sancocho,* just in case, and lay a fire. Dry season now, the wind blew dust through every crack. This cursed weather— three months now without rain and the sky so smooth it weighed like a flat stone on a man. Times Jesu could not get his breath.

The big house brooded, empty without its master, gone from it too often lately. Looking for something, Jesu guessed, Don Marco was restless, short-tempered too. What is he wanting? Jesu knew the answer. Marco wanted what he couldn't have. And he couldn't ask for it either. Prayer was forbidden Satan's man.

It was Jesu who prayed Marco's prayers. Lately he asked God for a woman, a special kind of woman. Jesu imagined her clearly: small and dark, her brown fingers weeding the herb garden, her voice like bird song through the house. Yes, every day Jesu prayed for this miracle from God. Imagining the girl, he felt her presence stronger, stronger...

Except for the ghost now, a pale figure always intruding. Try as he might, Jesu could not rid his meditation of this uninvited one.

Gazing downhill, he saw a crowd on the dock now, the ferry passengers disembarking. The figure in the bow sat still. When at last she lifted her head, Jesu felt her gaze brush him light as a breeze, and gone. She raised her hand, as if in greeting. She straightened her hat.

A chill in the air. Rainy season around the corner now. Jesu rubbed his hands. Don Marco would need a fire tonight.

The ferry nudged the dock and people crowded, shouting greet- ings. Island boys shoved each other, grabbing at boxes, sacks and luggage, tossing it all dockside. Elizabeth watched two crates of cack- ling chickens dumped, followed by her own suitcases. Hand to hand the cargo tumbled. Milk cartons, cases of beer, a floor fan, two lamps, a television, and more beer.

Elizabeth remained seated in the bow. Janice had assured her someone would meet her. Looking to her right, Elizabeth saw a stretch of beach, palm trees, and a low building which must be the one hotel. On her left stretched another beach lined by an old brick wall, a path above it, and the village then, pinpointed by the church tower.

A drift of white caught Elizabeth's eye, and she raised a hand to a white butterfly. It dipped, circled her, and settled on the ferry railing in front of her.

"You pretty thing," Elizabeth said. She rose to her feet.

Butterflies are yesterday's ghosts, someone had told her that.

Those on the dock watching the stranger, the white woman, saw her smile. They noted her tidy sandals, the crisp straw brim of her hat, escaped wisps of blonde hair against her cheek.

"Fair as the Virgin...," somebody whispered.

"Those blue eyes freeze my blood..."

"A beauty, yes—has Marco seen her?"

"The General's new whore perhaps?"

Loco, the village idiot, stretched his hands to Elizabeth. Fair as his Holy Mother! Had She come at last? Loco jiggled and burbled, spittle dribbling his chin.

"*Señora?*" The voice, just behind her, startled Elizabeth. "You are Mrs. Rogers?"

"Miss," she corrected the stranger. "Miss Rogers."

"Noel Reynard," and he bowed with an old-world courtesy. "I am here to help you." He spoke a clipped English. "You will come to my hotel. Your bags are safe, do not worry."

He stood too close, his belly grazing her arm—something sticky about him. "The hotel? But I have rented a house here, Mr. Reynard, it is all arranged."

He shrugged with that Latin helplessness that says nothing is ever quite arranged. "Let us begin with my hotel. I am manager here."

It was a short walk from the dock, in a brilliant sunshine, and she was grateful for the shade of the hotel verandah and the iced tea served her. She settled back in the frayed wicker chair. "Thank you, Mr. Reynard."

He sat opposite her. "Noel," he said, and raised his glass. "*Salud!*"

"*Salud,*" Elizabeth replied. Blown sand everywhere. Scuffed furniture, pillows spotted with mold. "I feel I've made a real crossing," she said. She removed her hat. "Night into day. From winter into summer."

"End of the season now," Noel said, "rain coming." He eyed Elizabeth over the rim of his glass. "It is not often such a pretty woman comes our way."

"Oh?" Compliments ruffled Elizabeth. "You are too kind." She fumbled in her handbag for a tissue. "I must admit it is hot. Will I get used to it?"

"We suffer," Noel confessed. He was wondering if all that blonde hair was real, and what on earth a woman like this was doing traveling alone. He slid his chair nearer to the table and folded his arms, somewhat concealing his paunch.

"What can we do for you, Miss Rogers?"

"Very little," she said coolly, guessing his assumption concerning herself. It angered her that men always assumed they could do for her;

they offered their maleness, convinced she needed it. She set down her glass. "I have rented a house here, for a month at least."

He nodded. "We were advised from the mainland." He grinned wryly. "The government runs the tourist business now; your reservation came down like a military order. And your house is charming—for two, really. A place for a honeymoon," Noel winked. "Will you be alone?"

"Why not?" Elizabeth asked, and knew she was rude, and softened her tone. "What are you doing here, at the edge of nowhere? Is your wife with you?"

Noel's eyes darkened. "She was," he said, shortly.

Seeing his fingers tighten round his glass, Elizabeth changed the subject. "Tell me about Taboga. I have read some of its history."

Noel settled back. "Before the present dictatorship, this hotel was always full. Panamanians, Americans, U.S. Canal workers; the U.S. military too. Centuries earlier, the Spanish settled here. They built their villas up the hills, behind the village—it is all jungle now. And the river that nurtured the island is no more than a filthy stream."

"The Spanish built the church?" Elizabeth asked.

Noel nodded. "Needing repairs now, like everything else. The islanders are ignorant, they don't know their history, don't give a damn. Centuries later, in 1882 to be exact, the French attempted a canal and kept vacation homes here, and a sanatorium for their canal workers. Malaria was vicious then."

Elizabeth waited. Perhaps he would mention Gauguin.

Noel continued. "Taboga has always been an escape from the heat of the mainland." He paused, then he asked, "May I call you Elizabeth?" She nodded.

"You may have noticed there are no cars on the island," he said. "We share one garbage truck. Rainy season gives us our water. It should be stored against the dry times, but the old Spanish aqueducts have not been maintained."

"Why not?" Elizabeth asked. Noel's bitterness irritated her. "Things can be fixed," she said. "It's a shame, a place like this..."

Noel shrugged. "Who's to care?"

He lit a cigar, inhaled, and blew the smoke toward the harbor. "No maintenance here, not now—this whole damn country suffers the same lack. It is said our General wants this island for his own dirty business." Noel shrugged. "He can have it for all I care."

"And your Devil Man?" And Elizabeth smiled. "The General told me about him. Just exactly what is a Devil Man?"

Noel drained his glass. "A desperate creature who has lent his soul to the Devil. It is superstition, the country reeks of such foolishness. The General himself...," Noel pulled himself short. "Black magic, I'm told." Noel looked behind him. "Spooks everywhere."

"Ridiculous!" Elizabeth exclaimed. "You're not going to tell me your *brujo* is for real? These are folk tales—you know these Latin countries."

"I, myself, am Latin. From Chile." Noel paused, noted Elizabeth's blush. He leaned forward, spoke softly. "I tell you, Marco Rodriguez is real as that ice in your glass. A devil of a man. You'll meet him soon enough. It is his house you're renting."

Elizabeth frowned, collected herself. She pretended a shudder. "You mean I'm to live in a real witch's house?"

Crushing his cigar butt in a saucer, Noel wondered how to explain.

"A pretty woman like yourself, you stay clear of our *brujo*. It is he runs this island."

How to warn this gringa? Noel wondered. What could he say without sounding deranged? How to explain in ordinary words this extraordinary man? Marco Rodriguez. The name alone cramped Noel's guts. He shoved from his chair. "You will excuse me a moment?"

*N**oel slammed the bathroom door shut behind him.* Squatting in a stall, he cursed his cramped stomach.

Marco Rodriguez, yes—the man held this whole island impotent. Impotent was Noel's word for it because that's what Rodriguez had done to him. The Devil Man's curse, Noel must believe it.

But how to phrase it in civilized terms that this Miss Rogers, an American and obviously a lady, would not laugh in his face?

Noel drew a deep breath and swallowed the shout that choked, stuck in his throat: Marco Rodriguez destroyed my life!

He got to his feet, yanked up his trousers, flushed the toilet.

Peering into the stained mirror, he fingered his jaw. Even his teeth ached. No, this tight-assed Yankee woman wouldn't understand. He hadn't either, not at first. Noel rinsed his hands, reached for a towel, found none and wiped his hands on his trousers.

He and his wife Veronica had come here from Chile last year. Noel, a small-time drug dealer, had had to choose between a Chilean prison or asylum in Panama. The General liked favors owed; it was he who had bailed Noel out, put him in charge of this hotel. And taken his passport.

Bored with island life, Veronica had begun a lazy flirtation with Rodriguez. Noel had protested, but Veronica had insisted the *brujo* was her only amusement. "The only real man around," she had taunted Noel.

In less than a month her bravura had vanished, she'd become hopelessly infatuated. When Rodriguez put her aside, she'd trailed him, provoking him. Noel was certain it was Rodriguez who had arranged Veronica's meeting with the General.

She was captive now, so Noel wanted to believe, despite the gossip drifting back to the island: Veronica playing queen whore to the military brass. Noel must believe she was a prisoner. And it was the *brujo* who had done this, so Noel had convinced himself. Noel fed on his hatred of the Devil Man.

He had a stash of hard stuff now, fresh from Colombia and damn near big enough to meet Veronica's offer to return. She had telephoned, her voice teasing, soft as Noel remembered. She was not cheap. He didn't love the bitch, but he had to have her: Veronica was something other men wanted. It gave Noel a hard-on, pretending she was his.

He shot a last glance in the bathroom mirror and returned to hotel verandah.

He found Elizabeth where he had left her. She had turned her chair to look at the harbor. Her paleness of skin and hair, exaggerated by the afternoon light, lent her an air of vulnerability. If Rodriguez caught sight of her, he'd not let her be. Noel slid into his chair.

"Who lives up there, top of the hill?" Elizabeth asked.

"Our Devil Man. He enjoys playing top of the heap. Those of us below, we stay out of his way."

Noel didn't lie. He was scared of the Devil Man, he'd felt his curse, hadn't he? Noel was impotent as the day he was born and the only one who could have done that to him was Satan. He couldn't figure why the villagers weren't scared like himself. Everyone here loved Marco. Not a thing they wouldn't do for him; Marco had it made. He devoured life like the bridegroom at a wedding feast.

"I'm not sure I believe all this," Elizabeth said.

"Take care of yourself," Noel warned her. "This is not the paradise you think it is."

Elizabeth pressed her chilled glass to her temples. "The dictator and the devil," she teased. "It's a movie, Noel."

Noel shook his head. "I do not joke."

His gloom was catching, and Elizabeth rose from her chair, wanting to terminate the conversation. "It's been quite a day. I would like to see my house. Is my witchy landlord around?"

Noel shook his head. "The man's been gone for some time, cooling his heels in the mountains on the mainland. He comes from somewhere north of here."

More likely off whoring in the city, but Noel did not say that.

"Your house—it's a ten minute walk. Your bags are there now. I'll take you."

Noel hesitated, then he said, "Rodriguez told me to remind you there's a hundred-dollar deposit due." An outright lie, but Noel dared it. Americans had plenty of money, they didn't mind spreading it around.

"No," Elizabeth said, surprised by her sudden real dislike of this man. "My office took care of the rent before I left Boston. I signed the check myself."

Noel feigned surprise. "Rodriguez should have told me..."

"Perhaps he did, and you've forgotten."

*T*he *walkway, framed by tall hibiscus, was wide enough for two.* Impatient, Elizabeth walked ahead of Noel.

She ducked palm fronds, evaded cracks in the pavement. Stopping a moment, she caressed a wild rose. The petals fell loose into her hand and she tossed them playfully at the white butterfly that fluttered just steps ahead of her.

Sunlight sparkled, unfamiliar scents tickled Elizabeth's nose. More than enough color here for the painter she sought. A marvelous mix. On impulse she stopped and slipped off her sandals. The pavement warmed the soles of her feet. She remembered herself as a child, off on a summer holiday, pavement burning the soles of her feet, her mother's hand clasped loose around her own.

Noel spoke from behind her. "You can't get lost," he said, and that this one path followed the water straight through to the village, ending at the top of the hill by the old Spanish graveyard. "Where Loco, our village clown, sleeps. You saw him at the dock, I think—the old crazy with the giggles."

"He sleeps in a grave?"

"Anyone here would give him a cot, but he's made a sort of shelter in an old mausoleum. I've heard him there, praying to the moon."

"But you let him wander about? Isn't that dangerous?"

"Loco never hurt anyone. If he bothers you, Elizabeth, let me know. He thinks all blondes are the Virgin Mary."

"This is all absolutely unbelievable! I love it, Noel, I am falling in love."

"Not yet," Noel teased. He had never met a woman like this. What was her business here? What was she looking for? A good time? He could give her that. But her kind didn't give him a second glance. Thought they were better than he. They shit, didn't they—same as he did...

Elizabeth interrupted his thoughts. "Where are we?" she asked. "I must learn these streets."

"This is First Street," Noel explained. One block up, to her right, was Second Street. "Where you'll find the church. It faces the plaza. There's a small market there, you can't miss it. Juana's place. She will sell you whatever groceries you need. For a dollar more she will tell your fortune."

A witch, and a fortune teller? The plot was shaping up nicely. The lost Gauguins would fit right in. She picked a spray of jasmine, its scent was sweet, seductive, and she tucked the flowers behind her ear.

"If I were you," Noel said, "I'd stay on First and Second Streets. You'll be safe that way. The villagers are suspicious of strangers."

A vine snagged Elizabeth's bare toes. "They ought to prune this jungle."

"I told you. Maintenance doesn't exist here," Noel said. "Rodriguez doesn't give a damn."

"Why depend on him?"

"You're right. There's always God, I guess," Noel said, and laughed at his joke. "Taboga is a world by itself. You and I are the intruders, Elizabeth."

She halted, caught by the view on her left. A small tower, its stone stairway tumbling to the pale sand, to the darkening water. "Witches and crazies," she said, "they can't spoil this island."

"What brings you here?" Noel asked.

"Call it curiosity," Elizabeth said. She longed to mention Gauguin. Careful, she thought, word of her real mission here might get back to the General.

She said, "This island is near perfection."

He nodded. "You find it so. Everyone does—in the beginning. I did, and Veronica. . ."

"Veronica?"

Avoiding an answer, Noel pointed at the house on their left. "Here we are."

It was a brownstone cottage set back from the street. It crouched, cozy as a squat turtle, secret in a bower of jasmine. Two lime trees framed the carved arch of the doorway in front of her.

Her luggage sat on the steps. All was so perfect, it scared her. Elizabeth slipped on her sandals and raised her hand to knock.

*T*he door swung open, revealing a plump and curly girl, her eyes the color of burnt coal.

"I am Flore. I am the housekeeper. All is ready."

She spoke a careful English; her lipsticked mouth framed sharp, small teeth. She touched her tousled hair, twitched at her snug dress which bound her thighs tight as a layer of pink wax.

Putting her hand firmly on Elizabeth's arm, she said, "I show you all." She would have shut the door in Noel's face if he had not slipped quickly inside.

Flore's face glowed with pride. Yes, the señora should be pleased. Flore worked hard to keep this house perfect. Almost her house. Hadn't Marco himself told her nobody kept his house as she did? It might as well belong to her, he had said that.

Inside, Elizabeth stood still, held by the cool of the house, the glisten of the blue-tiled floors. The white wicker furniture appeared freshly painted. From the doorway, she saw through the open windows to the beach.

She touched the white roses in a blue vase on the kitchen table. "Thank you," she said.

"Make yourself at home," Noel said. "I'll get your bags."

Flore led Elizabeth to the bedroom. "Don Rodriguez," she said, "I keep this house for him."

Elizabeth sensed the girl's possessiveness. "And nicely too," she said in Spanish. She was hoping this girl would not be underfoot all the time.

"I welcome you," Flore said, in English because Marco wished her to behave "*como una doña*"—like a lady. She was pretending to a warmth she did not feel. She hated these mostly blonde and always rich *gringas*. They paid Marco good money, but he treated them like guests. Nothing Marco wouldn't do for them. And nothing they wouldn't do for him. At the end it was always like that. Rich women, pretending to be ladies—it wasn't long before each and every one of them lay down for Marco, right in this room, here, on the big bed...

"You like?" Flore asked.

Elizabeth set sunglasses and hat on the dressing table. "I like, yes!" Elizabeth replied. "Especially that sea outside my window."

Flore smoothed the already smooth bed covers. She saw how the oval mirror above the dresser reflected Elizabeth's bright hair.

Elizabeth touched the mirror. "A real antique," she said.

Flore dared a glance at her own reflection; she hoped her belly did not show too much. Marco would not want her if she was fat. If he didn't want her, she would die. Flore had lived so long as Marco's wife inside her dream, it had become her reality.

Elizabeth straightened the mirror. "My mother had one like this," she said, gazing at herself and Flore in the glass. The girl is pregnant, she guessed—but aren't they always? Why can't they learn to take care of themselves?

Absently, she touched the mirror glass. "My mother told me that old mirrors like this one hold hundreds of lives. If you try, you can see those ghosts." Elizabeth smiled. "I used to imagine people like fish, swimming under the glass."

The mirror reflected the bed, and Flore smiled, thinking it was lucky the señora couldn't see all that had happened there. Marco had made love to her on this bed. Could I see that again? Flore resolved that the first chance she had, she would look deep into this mirror. Now she saw herself and Elizabeth. The *señora* looked like the moon.

Gringas! Flore grimaced. Life was kind to them, money kept them safe. God's special blessing perhaps? Flore had always wondered: did He prefer white skins?

Flore's envy of Elizabeth weighed heavier than the child in her. She was ashamed of the dragging slap of her worn sandals.

"A playhouse," Elizabeth said. She returned to the living room, to Noel. "I am pleased."

"I'm glad you like it," he said. "Perhaps you'll have dinner with me this evening? When you are settled?"

Quickly Elizabeth refused. Too quickly, she thought then, reminding herself that no matter how much she disliked this man, she would need friends on this island. "Perhaps tomorrow night?" she suggested.

He agreed and beckoned Flore to follow him outside. "Take good care of the *señora*," he said. "When is Rodriguez expected?"

"Tonight, tomorrow," and Flore shrugged, pretending to an indifference she did not feel.

Noel touched her arm. "You busy later?" He ran his fingers upwards until his thumb pressed her damp armpit. Pigs, the lot of them, he thought. "I need a girl," he said. "Colombian shrimp boats in later, the men will be asking for you."

They'd be loaded with coke. He'd take it off their hands, add it to his stash. Shit! He had enough now to blow the Devil out of Hell! Noel ignored the sliver of warning that pricked his guts. The General had told him more than once: this island was off limits to dealers.

What puzzled Noel was that the Devil Man knew of the influx of drugs and other contraband—and chose to ignore it. Either Rodgriguez had something on the General, or Rodriguez trusted his own power to keep himself safe. Trouble brewed. The two men circled each other like fighting cocks.

Noel gave Flore's arm a cruel pinch. "You'll do what I want? There's money in it for you."

Flore hesitated, wondering if Marco would return tonight. But she was sick to her soul of waiting for that devil. Noel offered diversion and she craved that pair of gilt sandals she'd seen last week in the city. "I'll come," she said.

Noel grinned, patted her rump. Flore was a good girl, a tortilla with spice. The men paid well for a piece of her. She was a girl with tricks you wouldn't believe, the men told Noel. Which made him believe she'd fucked Marco. Marco's women—it was said they learned the Devil's own way to pleasure. He eyed Flore, thinking he'd like a piece of her himself. He prodded her belly. "How far along?"

"None of your business," she snapped.

Noel chuckled. "Don't let it spoil our business, that's all I care about." He lowered his voice. "You've got a real lady here now. Take care of her."

Flore clenched her fists. "She had better take care! I wish to God she'd never come!"

E *lizabeth was restless in the unfamiliar bed.*
She felt diminished, lonely spaces on every side of her. Stretching, she pushed at the darkness. Hot sticky air, and she kicked the sheet down and wished she liked sleeping naked. She did not. Always, before retiring, she brushed her hair and braided it, and slipped on a nightgown. The gown made her invulnerable. She was dressed to meet the dark.

A breeze at last, at the peaking of the tide, and Elizabeth drifted into a sleep that rattled of sea shells, the hissing of small waves. She floated above a glittering mass and wakened abruptly to a shout, the rumble of men's voices. She sat straight up, straining ears and eyes.

Someone on the beach. Had she locked her door?

Elizabeth slipped from the bed, crossed the chilly floor, and knelt in the recess of her window. Peering out into the dark, she saw a rowboat and the bulky shapes of two men. One man sat at the oars, the other jumped ashore. *"Gracias, buenas noches!"* he shouted, saluting the man in the boat.

Ankle-deep in the rising tide, the man turned and looked straight up at the house. Elizabeth drew back. She had seen only that his figure was tall, blurred black, rimmed with the gold haze of a distant street light.

She waited, then leaned forward again. He was still there, gazing at her window. He lifted his hand in greeting then, and walked slowly up the beach. Straight towards her. Elizabeth's heartbeat knocked loud in her ears.

Slowly her eyes grew accustomed to the dark. The sand paled, the inky water defined its limits. Starlight glazed sea and land. The stranger's figure thickened and Elizabeth saw it then, his shadow. No moon, one dim and distant street light. The shadow trailed the man's heels like a mourning cloak.

Slowly, he strode up the beach. Then the dark swallowed him.

Elizabeth waited. Crouched in the darkness Elizabeth held herself still.

Elizabeth...

She heard his voice plain. She knew she imagined it.

Her feet were cold. Her fingers fumbled the window, dragged it closed. There was no lock. She fled to her bed, lay down, pulling the sheet over her head. Sweat trickled between her breasts, behind her knees. Probably that old crazy, she thought, that one who sleeps in a grave. She waited. Slowly fear drained from her.

She got up from bed and went to the mirror. Standing there in her silk gown, she unpinned her hair. Her reflection floated, a ghost in the glass. She watched herself touch her breasts, lift them. Who had called her? Would he come again?

Damn him for waking her!

She must not let this island get her down. Concentrate on the Gauguins, she told herself. She twisted up her hair.

The night was warm. She was not going to let some spook of a drunk spoil her sleep. She pulled the curtain back, opened the window. Nothing there. Nobody. Leaving the window wide, Elizabeth returned to bed. She would count stars until she fell asleep.

*E*lizabeth slept late. She felt strangely refreshed. The stranger was gone. Erased. A dream, maybe? She remembered only counting stars. So many. Never before had she known a night so bright.

She tracked the smell of coffee into the kitchen. Flore had been here. The coffee maker steamed. Feeling nicely spoiled, Elizabeth poured herself a cup. She remembered it was Sunday; the church should be open and she wanted to explore it. Too, she could inquire as to the whereabouts of the Amado house, the family said to have the Gauguins. She must begin somewhere. Excitement lumped in her throat.

Looking out the window, she saw the tide was low, the beach washed clean. Then, and Elizabeth saw them clearly, the print of boots, dark above the high-water mark. She had not dreamed him then.

She spoke the name aloud: "Marco Rodriguez." She knew it had been he.

"Devil Man," she whispered. And had to laugh at herself. An old habit of hers, inventing terrors.

She showered and dressed. Slipped on a blue shift, the color of this morning, and flat-heeled sandals. Brushing her hair in front of the mirror, Elizabeth was, again, mesmerized by the smoky oval-shaped glass. She moved it up and down, remembering how, as a child, she had tipped her mother's mirror just this way. Hoping perhaps to change the world reflected there?

She turned away and, forgetting her hat, she let herself out the door. A limp bouquet of jasmine lay on her door step. The flowers, tied with fishing line, still breathed a faint perfume. The stranger's gift? Elizabeth carried the flowers into her house, and put them in a glass of water. This time, on her way out, she remembered her hat. She was careful to lock her door.

She walked briskly, looking for a turn up the hill. It was Sunday, and she thought it odd the church bell was not ringing. She followed a narrow cement path that twisted steeply to her left. The air was scented with oleander, bleached in sunlight. Dust everywhere. The wind stole layer after layer of powdered earth, blowing it downhill, towards the sea. Little by little, Elizabeth imagined, these dry months will strip, shrink the island until, at last, there will be nothing left but stone. Even the Gauguins turned to dust.

A cock's crow startled her and, far up the hill, she heard the baying of hounds.

Another turn, and she was on a dirt path winding between houses crowded close. Elizabeth caught glimpses of the island's past: hand-carved balustrades and lintels, handmade bricks, a cracked mosaic patio floor.

Roses bloomed from rusted cans. Plastic lace curtains crackled in tipsy doorways. Scuttling noises, rustlings. Driftwood people, Elizabeth sensed their presence, their eyes on her.

A few more steps uphill, and she stepped into the whitewashed glare of the plaza where the only thing that moved was the shadow of a basketball net dancing spider-like across the faded mosaic tiles. A radio wailed somewhere, its strident rock jarring Elizabeth's ears. She stood still, blinking in the hot sunlight, and saw the church directly across the plaza. It was shuttered, its massive doors closed and padlocked, its wide steps inviting pigeons and children. Violet shadows stained the whitewashed walls. Gauguin had painted this scene. How could he not? Somewhere, nearby, his paintings awaited her.

Elizabeth sat down on a bench opposite the church. Absently, she watched a black dog chase its shadow, then defecate on the church steps. He crossed the plaza to sniff at Elizabeth's ankles.

"I won't bite," she said, offering the back of her hand.

The dog grimaced, showed its yellow teeth. And lay down, his weight against her feet. She smelled his fetid odor. She was reluctant to move.

*I*t **was then she saw him.** Not clearly, because the sun was in her eyes.

Recalling this later, she knew it was this man's presence she had felt first. Then she saw him full, and recognized immediately that same tall figure that had paced her beach last night. The same long shadow at his heels.

She would know him anywhere: the shape of his head, the width of his shoulders and, yes, that broad smile; it prefaced an easy laughter.

He crossed the space between them. She sat still, waiting. Nearer her, he paused, standing between her and the sun. She stood, his name caught in her throat.

"It is you," she said, and knew, inside herself, a gathering of force as if he might assault her. She stepped backwards, away from him. She was aware she held her hands straight down at her sides.

High in the steeple, the church bell clanged, once only. One o'clock.

"It was you last night," she said, all in a breath. "You frightened me."

"Never." His voice was deep, his English perfect. "I wished to introduce myself. But it was late. I am Marco—Marco Rodriguez." He bowed slightly. "You are in my house. You are my guest. Why would I want to frighten you?"

"I...I don't know." She watched the black mongrel slink from sight.

"That one haunts my footsteps," Marco said.

So this was he, *El Brujo*.

But he looked too ordinary to be a witch. His white shirt was rolled past his elbows, revealing his skin, a rich cafe au lait. Clean shaven; his height, his casual speech—he could be from her own world. Only his

open admiration of her, the invitation in his black eyes—bold, sensual—
told her he was Latin. An aura to him, Elizabeth sensed him strongly. He
smelled of homemade soap, charcoal. She saw his feet were bare.

He stretched a hand to her. "Come, you want to see the church?
I'll show it to you. I'm the only one who can. I keep the key."

"But why do you lock the church?" she asked, refusing his hand,
cooling her instinctive response to his warmth. "It is Sunday," she said,
"doesn't a priest come to say Mass?"

"We've not had a priest for years. Church doesn't give these people a damn thing."

"It is you who decides that?"

He ignored her question. "My island welcomes you, Elizabeth
Rogers."

"Thank you," she said. "But is all this really yours?" She remembered she had asked this same question of a real devil, some days ago.

"This is where I live," Marco said. "Noel told you about me? He
wasn't kind, I'm sure. There's not a man here hates me as he does, he
swears I bewitched his wife." Marco chuckled. "Wives aren't magic-ed
unless they want to be."

He turned and looked straight at her. "Are you really needing
Sunday Mass, Elizabeth? Or is it this old church you want to see?"

He spoke her first name easily. "Just a look inside," she said.
"Spanish colonial history is a hobby of mine."

Unlocking the padlock, he pushed the doors open. His hands
against the blue of the doors, and Elizabeth remembered—she had
read it somewhere—the color blue kept evil out, a medieval belief.
She glanced at Marco. Did a Devil Man know about blue?

"*Doña*..." and he gestured her to precede him into the dim inte-
rior. He turned and locked the doors behind them, and sat down in a
pew.

"Take your time," he said. "This is Spain's cruelest export—late
1500s. Nothing left of it now but dust and bat shit."

He settled back, his hands behind his head and studied Elizabeth through half closed eyes. A seductive walk, he thought, but seeming without intent; this woman was not deliberately provocative. Marco was accustomed to a woman's backward glance and Elizabeth had clearly forgotten him.

He rubbed his eyes. He'd had no sleep for days. He had run from sleep, from this island, from bellyache and boredom—escaped to the city. Like a diver, he'd plunged to the rush of lights and let himself drift, to run aground at last on a tall mulatto girl. Not she, it was the city seduced Marco, helped him forget what he was meant to be. Only in the city was he anonymous, shed of his distemper—or so he could pretend.

Satisfaction—it sobered an ordinary man. Marco was not ordinary.

His limbs might ache now, and his eyes burn, but he was never drunk enough, never drained or pleasured full. Always the search, never the find. Peace of mind, to have and to hold—these are not Marco's happy endings, they are the Devil's bait. Marco could destroy himself chasing illusions.

He stretched, watched Elizabeth through half-closed eyes. She stood, not far from him, near the main altar. Studying her, Marco rehearsed that fair coil of hair, the set of those shoulders. Then, as Marco knew she must, it was that way with him, Elizabeth felt his gaze, and turned.

She sneezed. The sound rustled the bats in the rafters. Blew dust from the altar. She sneezed again.

"Bless me, St. Peter." Elizabeth said.

*T**he saint sat in a carved armchair.* A tiny man—his feet did not touch the platform, they swung out triumphantly as a child's high kick at a birthday party. He flourished a large key.

"Nice, isn't he?" Marco spoke from behind her. "I've always liked him. Do you see his slippers? He was barefooted until I put those shoes on him. I had them specially made."

He could touch this woman if he wished. That knot of hair—the color of new corn.

"You put those shoes on him?" Elizabeth asked. "You climbed all the way up there? Marco, don't lie to me!"

"Believe me, or not," Marco said. "I was younger then. That old man, he was lonely. An easy climb up from the altar using the angels as handholds. And out from that window ledge there—a jump to St. Peter's throne." He laughed and pointed. "That key he holds, I stole it."

"No!" Elizabeth shook her head.

"Yes," Marco insisted, "a party—that key unlocked the Hilton Hotel wine cellar." He had never admitted to this youthful escapade, and he wondered now if Elizabeth appreciated the joke. "St. Peter's key," he said, "it opens the door to a heaven most men pray for."

"Oh, but you lie!" Elizabeth's laughter echoed in the vaulted space. "A good story though, and this church, Marco, it is charming. Something should be done about it."

In her enthusiasm she reached for Marco but, seeing the scar on his left forearm, caught herself. The lips of the wound were raised. The scar ran from the inside of his wrist straight up his inner arm to the elbow.

"I am sorry," Elizabeth said. "You've had a bad accident?"

"My Devil's mark," he said, easily. "You should not touch it."

"Devil's mark? What on earth do you mean?"

"My mark," he said. He touched his scar. "Inside here, there's a Devil Stone. I'm what they call a Devil Man."

She stared at him. "You can't expect me to believe you."

"I seldom tease. Not on this subject anyway."

Elizabeth stared at this man. She saw he was quite serious. She was not ready for this, not now, and she looked about her. "Is there anything more to see in here? That Madonna," and she pointed at a nearby statue, "she is lovely."

She was wanting out, out into the bright sun of a normal day.

"You must believe me," Marco said. "If you do, you won't be frightened. It is what we can't accept—that's what scares us."

"But I am not scared," Elizabeth said. "What is there to frighten me?" She squared her shoulders, took a deep breath and walked slowly around Marco, pretending to examine him from every angle.

Confronting him again, she said, "I don't see a tail, or a cloven hoof. You are not what you pretend to be, Marco Rodriguez." His eyes darkened. Elizabeth knew she had gone too far.

"Don't ever laugh at me." His hands were heavy on her shoulders. His weight unbalanced her.

"Please... ," she whispered.

Abuptly, he released her. She stumbled, cried out, reached for him. But he was gone, halfway down the aisle. Forgetting her entirely. What sort of man is this?

She stared after him. What an ego! He is pure melodrama! Scary, though, the weight of him. Her shoulders hurt.

"Marco?" she called. But the shadows had swallowed him.

Silence closed in on Elizabeth. She crossed her arms, hugging herself. This church had welcomed her, now its grey space threatened. Shrouded statues leaned from the shadows. The Madonna smiled idiotically at nothing. Approaching her, Elizabeth saw the faded flowers placed at her feet, and candle stubs. Someone visited here. She called Marco's name. Shouted then, angrily, "Marco! Where the hell are you?"

Cobwebs and spiders. The mold and stink of this place sickened her. Bats floated in the rafters, drifting like disembodied spirits.

"Marco!" Her arms outstretched, Elizabeth stumbled down the aisle towards the doors. They were closed. The bastard had locked her in!

She beat her hands against the doors. They swung open, catapulting her into blinding sunlight, straight into Marco's outstretched arms.

She fought him. He held her tightly. "That was not funny!" she panted.

"You are beautiful," he said, quietly. And released her.

She raised her hand, wanting to strike him. He caught her wrist. "Don't," he said.

"I couldn't find you," she said. "Back in there, I didn't mean to hurt your feelings."

"I am cursed with an ugly temper," he said, his eyes following a small drop of perspiration as it slid down her throat and into the cleft between her breasts.

"I will never hurt you," he said. And, after a pause, "You do not know how lovely you are."

She knew she blushed. "No. I mean, I don't care, that's not the point," she stammered. "You just can't suddenly abandon someone. Not in a place like this!"

Marco nodded. "Forgive me." His words astonished him: he doubted he had ever apologized to a woman, especially a *gringa*.

Her anger drained. "I don't understand you," she said.

"Not if you don't want to," he answered her. His eyes held hers, his gaze confusing her. She was tangled, caught up in whatever it was she had to make clear to him.

"I can't…I don't want…," she began.

"It's all right," he said, gently. In Spanish. *Esta bien.*

The phrase soothed her and she touched her hair, set her hat straight on her head. "I'm going now."

"You will come and see me," Marco said, pointing to the hill behind the village. "I live up there. You can come when you like. You and I must talk."

"Why?" Did he really think she would climb all the way up there in this heat?

He answered her unspoken question. "You will."

He lifted her hand, bent above it. She felt the warmth of his breath, his lips. Despite herself, something deep in her responded. "Perhaps, yes," she murmured, "yes...some day I will visit you." He smiled then and, somehow, his smile exacted one of her own.

"I will wait for you," he said. "Whenever you like, Elizabeth. And don't worry about my dogs, they won't hurt you. If I'm not home, Jesu is there—he can always find me."

"Jesus?" she asked, giving the name its English pronunciation. "Jesus?" Was he teasing her again? How could a professional devil have a servant called Jesus? She had to laugh. "Marco, you've written yourself into a book!"

"Jose Maria Jesu, my caretaker," Marco said, not a glimmer of a smile. He bowed. "Adios, *doña*..."

She stood, gazing after him. His bare heels dragged his shadow. A dead give away, she thought, she had meant to tell him so. She had read it somewhere: the Devil did not have a shadow, that was how you recognized him.

The sun dazzled her. Absorbed in her thoughts, Elizabeth walked slowly. So that's the famous island *brujo*? A stone in his arm? Impossibly barbaric!

A rustle behind her. A red hibiscus fell, beheaded by an unseen hand. Elizabeth walked faster. The noon sunlight dizzied her. She would have a swim, she decided, and not to forget dinner with Noel tonight.

Climbing the front steps to her house—no, she reminded herself, not hers but Marco's house. It was his key lay on her open palm. She put it to her cheek, felt the heat of it.

She locked the door behind her.

*L*oco heard Elizabeth's door close, her key turn in the lock. He had followed her since early this morning. He had trailed her to the church and seen her meet with Marco, and waited then, until they had come out. He had followed her back here to Marco's house. She was carrying her hat and her blonde hair shone bright as an angel's halo. Truly, Loco believed his Holy Mother had come to him. He wanted no more than her blessing. Perhaps, if he brought her more flowers, a candle, she would speak to him?

Loco was the village pet, its clown. Nobody remembered his age. The oldest granny in the village—ninety-six, she claimed to be—said Loco was the child of the island's first midwife. A black-skinned girl, so the story went, a small bird of a girl, with hands strong enough to bring the most stubborn child into the world. Marco's father had brought her here for just that purpose. Some sailor had gotten hold of her—it happens you know—and she'd died giving birth to the man's child. Grateful for the lives she'd brought into the world, the island women had a statue made in her likeness. Its name erased now by years and weather, the statue stood forgotten in a corner of the park. Often, Loco napped in the park, in that statue's comforting shade.

Up the hill, past the village, in the old Spanish graveyard, Loco had made his nest. Over the years he had furnished the empty grave with bird feathers, shells, and candle stubs from those he burned to the Virgin in the church. Loco went for his supper to the village where the women fussed over him, feeding him, shaving him, cutting his toenails. There was more than one who pinched his buttocks, tickled his penis. Loco giggled, not understanding. He would seek out Marco who was always kind.

MARCO'S GIFT

Loco hummed to himself. Marco was back from the city, he had eaten breakfast with him early this morning. Marco always brought gifts. He had ice cream for the man who'd lost his legs to a shark last year. And chocolate syrup in paper cups for every island child. Glass beads, too, for the girl who was to be married soon.

Rain, Marco said, it was sure to come. He'd bought five calves in the city, they'd be here soon on the boat. New picture books too, for his schoolroom. This Easter would be one to remember—he had promised that. And the city now, he said, it was an oven, lucky we are to live here, Marco said, and he'd laughed. Just the presence of the man made everyone feel better.

*I*n her bedroom, in front of the mirror, Elizabeth saw her tumbled hair every which way and she unpinned it, let it fall to
her shoulders. She stared at herself in the glass.

She'd forgotten this morning's original purpose: the Gauguins.
Elizabeth frowned. This was not like her. She had wasted the whole
morning. A complete stranger, his ridiculous story—she had allowed
him to divert her.

In the kitchen, the jasmine drooped, and she swept the fallen petals from the table. Everything wilted in this heat. Quickly, in the bedroom, dropping her clothes on the floor, she slipped into a bathing suit
and was out her back door, down the steps on to the beach.

The cool water took her to itself and, holding her breath, she
burrowed into it. Beneath her, in her shadow, shoals of small flash
flashed. Elizabeth floated on her stomach, watching the fish, reaching to finger shells and old glass fragments on the bottom. Another
world here, and she lingered, not leaving the water until shadows
blued the beach.

Out of the water, she looked down at herself, wishing as always
that she was slender. She had been, once. Skin and bones, her stepfather had called her that, his large hands spanning her pelvic flatness.
How she had envied her mother's plumpness. But then, when her own
breasts had rounded, Elizabeth had bound them tightly, willing them to
stop growing. Not to be like her mother—no, never like her mother.
A cloud slid across the sun and Elizabeth shuddered, aware suddenly of
the fragility of this island. Did nobody care? she wondered. Certainly
not Noel. And not Marco, he was too caught up in his own story.
A breeze brushed her shoulders. Behind her, the tall grass rustled, a

stone rolled loose. A crab slid from its hole, it circled her, its black eyes popping. All the lovely feelings of her swim drained from her.

She had left her back door unlocked, and she entered the house on tip toe. Nobody here. Who did she expect?

In her bedroom , Elizabeth drew the curtains closed. Tugging off her wet suit, she stood naked in front of the mirror. She seldom looked at herself this way, didn't like to, didn't like herself that much. Others did—men, they liked her body and told her so. And sometimes, when she felt like it, she permitted them to caress her. That self she had created became real under their hands.

Elizabeth stepped nearer to the glass. If she could see into her image there, she would find wounds, scars, yes, marks ugly as Marco's own. Gazing at her own reflection, she glimpsed, behind it, Marco's face. He was too much on her mind: he and his ridiculous devil tale.

She showered, scrubbing herself clean. Never clean enough, and she toweled herself roughly. Her skin tingling, she stretched herself on the bed and pulled the cotton sheet across her. Flat on her back, she gave herself to the memories, to the pain. Living it again, it didn't hurt so much.

*E*lizabeth turned on her side, drew up her knees, tucked her *fists under her cheek.* She must go straight through this night-mare, reach the other side: sanity.

A summer house, like this one now, curtains like sails, the whis-per of the sea beyond the window. She, just a child then, sprawled naked, salty from her swim. He had entered without knocking. Rum on his breath. "Child—ah, child ..." His whispered words, his sharp intake of breath. He had knelt on the floor beside her bed. She had just turned eleven, was both curious and proud of her body's rounding.

Her stepfather. Round-shouldered, a bull of a man. He drank too much, but he made them laugh—Elizabeth and her mother. He was their playmate, their lover, their occasional provider. Elizabeth's moth-er, widowed early, a teacher, was the sole bread winner. She was grate-ful for this unexpected happiness.

Elizabeth was not alarmed when he entered her room. He had bathed her every evening, long as she could remember. Her mother had protested at first, but been overruled. And he had tucked her in at night. But that afternoon, the warmth of evening, a breeze like kisses on her bare knees...

She had lain still, trusting. Liking it, yes, and liking it more when his fingers slid between her thighs—yes, she had let him have his way. Why not? She had trusted him, her stepfather. Only when his breath came hard had she opened her eyes, seen his face contorted. He had looked near tears and she had asked him, "Are you sad?"

He had stopped her question with his mouth, and ordered her to sleep. "Our secret," he had ordered, "yours and mine. You must not tell your mother." Elizabeth had thought that was fun; she liked sharing a secret. It was exciting to keep something from her mother.

He had come to her room regularly. He had taught her to please him. It was not long until she'd she learned how to get the whole ugly business over with, fast. Because she didn't like it, not anymore—it was ugly, embarrassing, yes, and he hurt her. Not even when he pleasured her, that, too, was, somehow, shaming. She did not dare refuse him. Only Mother could stop this. She was too ashamed to tell her mother. This was a terrible thing to tell her mother.

All summer long, the guilt growing, intensifying. She would stare at her nude body in the oval mirror in her mother's room and touch herself, wondering if IT showed. It. She had no name for what was happening to her. Sometimes Elizabeth believed her mother looked back at her from the glass, her mouth wide, crying, "Shame!"

She had thought her mother a fool not to see the wickedness—she could smell it if she tried—happening in this, her mother's house. How could Mother *not* know? Because she didn't love her, that's why. Mother was blind to everything and everyone but this one man.

Elizabeth had hated her mother for not putting an end to that which she, the child, could not stop. Finally, she had pitied her mother, then scorned her. And come, at the end, to take a perverted pleasure in flaunting this man's desire for her in her mother's face.

Winter then, and he was gone. Not a word, he melted like the snow, not a trace of him anywhere. "Damn him! Leaving us to freeze to death!" That was all her mother said.

He had taken what little money there was. They had had to give up the summer house. A different apartment too: the edge of the city. Stark, ugly. Elizabeth had not known such a place existed. "It must do," her mother said.

Your fault! Elizabeth had wanted to scream those words. *You never cared, of course he left!*

She held silent, keeping the secret. Because he might come back. If she told, he would come after her. Scary, the nights then, when shadows moved about her bed.

She wanted him. Sometimes she did. It was not Mother, but I, I who did not please him—so Elizabeth accused herself—it is my fault he left. My fault my mother suffers now.

Elizabeth had watched her mother, heartbroken, succumb to despair and, finally, suicide. Elizabeth would not forget that bathroom she had stumbled into, calling her mother, finding her behind the shower curtain, the kitchen knife slid from her open hand. Steam, blood, and washed-out eyes.

Elizabeth could not forgive her mother this ultimate desertion. She did not mourn—how could she? One does not mourn someone who has not loved you, someone who has failed you.

You do not mourn that person you have murdered.

Yes, that summer house—it had begun there—in an afternoon sun, fading, like this one now. Elizabeth sighed, brushed at the tears hot on her cheeks. She was never finished with crying. Never done with a self-loathing that suffocated all other feelings.

Best not to feel at all, the twelve-year-old Elizabeth had decided that, in her first of many foster homes. "A difficult one," they had said of her. "Impossible to reach," they said. And, defeated, they pushed the child on, one to another.

Unlovable, this too tall teenager, clumsy in her height, her speech a mumble. Her blue eyes looked right through a person. You couldn't get to the girl, they said. Elizabeth kept it that way. Because they might find out who and what she was: her mother's murderer.

"Shame!" Elizabeth told herself. And the word sank heavy as a stone in her, settling deep.

Such control it took, in those early years, not to become attached to anyone kind to her. There, in the basement of herself all the shapes of love moved, gnawing at her. Beasts, she thought of them that way, and she shut them down tightly. If she walked carefully, quietly above them, they wouldn't hear her. Not to wake them...not ever to wake them!

For shame, Elizabeth, for shame!

She had learned at last a careful balance. Learned to keep to the top floor of herself. Still, moments like this one, the smell of the sea, her nudity, it was then memories surfaced, dragging her down into the old ragged nightmare.

Soon she must dress, walk to the hotel for dinner with Noel. Sitting up, Elizabeth forced herself into present time, thoughts of ordinary things. What to wear tonight? The white dress, she decided, the long jersey, it was perfect. She got out of bed and held the dress against herself, saw it fit that image of herself she most needed now. She picked up her hair brush.

Soon, her reflection returned her the look she wanted. If she wasn't careful, Elizabeth reminded herself, she'd be brown as an Indian. Like Marco. If she were having dinner with him tonight, would he put on shoes? She smiled. She could not imagine Marco in a suit and tie. Take him away from this island and what would he be?

Slipping on what she called her dancing slippers, red velvet, flat heeled, Elizabeth knew herself ready for whatever she might encounter.

Noel awaited Elizabeth on the steps of the hotel. He saw she was wearing something long, that she looked spectacular. He told her so, in a formal Spanish, that he was flattered she had dressed for dinner with him. He would have kissed her, but Elizabeth had turned to the view, pointing out the new moon.

Noel indicated a table set for two on the verandah. They would dine outside, he said, but first, a cool drink.

Settling herself, Elizabeth said, "I saw your church today. It is worth restoring. Such a shame it is closed."

"Yes," Noel agreed, "I heard you were up there."

He had heard also—gossip was the life blood of the island—that Elizabeth had met Marco and spent some time with him inside the church. He watched her carefully now as he asked, "You have met your Devil landlord?"

Elizabeth nodded. "If you mean Rodriguez, I have met him, yes." She hesitated. "He is a strange one, isn't he?" She was tempted to question Noel about Marco, but decided she did not want him to think she had the slightest interest in the man. "It's this island's history I want to learn, " she said. "There must be old families, wonderful stories here, not just the Spanish, but French too, perhaps?"

He knew very little, Noel replied. History was not his forte. It was common knowledge that the Spanish conquistadors, Pizarro in particular, had outfitted their ships here. They had left not only a strong Catholicism, Noel said, but a legacy of violence and superstition. "Our star ghost," he said, "is a Spanish bishop on horseback. He gallops across the hills, his severed head in his hands.

"And, up the hill, in the convent," Noel continued, "when the moon is full, you can hear the dead nuns singing. Both bishop and nuns are portents of doom. Like St. Elmo's fire. And that was seen a few nights ago. By our fortune teller, of course." Noel chuckled. "Juana is in charge of all our fates."

"I've stepped into a book," Elizabeth said, squeezing a lime into her drink. She sniffed at the rind. "Delicious! You have many fruit trees?"

Noel nodded. "Our pineapple is famous."

"Nobody here works too hard," Elizabeth guessed.

Noel nodded. "Why should they? There's fish, mangoes, coconuts."

"This place could be a paradise, Noel."

He gave her a sharp look; the General had not told him Elizabeth's business here. He sensed she was more than just a tourist.

"I suppose I should see the Canal," Elizabeth said. "But I'd rather loaf here, in the sunshine."

"You work hard?" Noel asked. "Boston, isn't it?" He drained his glass. "You do know that in the year 2000, it will be Panama's canal."

Elizabeth frowned. "Let us hope it will not become the General's personal waterway."

Noel shook his head and poured himself more gin, a dash of tonic. "You Americans will always be in charge here. It is your military who service the General's forces. And if you, a gringa, get into trouble anywhere in this country, they'll send US soldiers along with Panama's Guardia."

Elizabeth laughed. "Am I going to need armies?"

"Just a warning," Noel said. "If you call a cop, you'll get a battalion from the mainland. Which, by the way, would not please Rodriguez. He is policeman, judge, and jury here—does not tolerate interference."

"Look," Elizabeth pointed at the harbor, "a new sailboat in." She turned to the waiter at her shoulder. "It smells delicious," she said as he set a full plate in front of her.

"Dopers on that boat," Noel told her. He had met these kids earlier.

They had come up the beach to the hotel to ask him if it was okay if they anchored in the harbor. He had stated his anchorage fee which was exorbitant, and he knew it. The girl had paid grudgingly. Dopers, sure—Noel could smell them a mile away.

Elizabeth picked up her knife and fork. "I've read that the French painter, Paul Gauguin, lived here. Of course, any work he did, it would have been discovered long ago."

Noel sipped his wine. "I've always thought that a rumor. But, curious because you bring it up now, a couple of tourists from New York— they asked the same question. More wine?" He filled Elizabeth's glass.

"Gauguin was more than a rumor. He was here, several times," Elizabeth said. She sipped her wine, finished her fish. "There is nothing here of his, I suppose?"

"Not that I know of," Noel said. "Isn't it enough we've got our Devil Man? Tell me, what do you think of him? Most women are intrigued."

"But I am not most women," Elizabeth replied. "If you want the truth, I think your witch man is a fake. He would not be crazy enough to persist in this unlikely role unless he had evidence people believed him."

Noel nodded. "Rodriguez is his own invention."

"But why?" Elizabeth asked.

Noel shrugged. "He is a rich man."

"And a bore." Elizabeth set down her glass. "I need your help, Noel. Friends of mine in Boston, they asked me to look up a family here—Amado is the name. I believe an employee of theirs is related somehow. Small world, isn't it?"

"Amado?" Noel nodded. "There's a woman, quite old now, she lives by herself. It's a shack, painted bright yellow, you can't miss it. Up on Second Street, around the corner from the church."

The only reason Noel remembered the name was because another visitor, some months ago, had also asked for the Amado family. He'd thought little of it then, but now he was puzzled. He would have to find out what the old crone was hiding.

"I promised I'd pay her a call," Elizabeth said, folding her napkin. "By the way, that old loony, now he does disturb me. Wouldn't he be better off in a home of some kind?"

Noel shook his head. "The government asylum is a hellhole. There are no 'homes' here as you Americans have them. Loco is part of this island. Our Easter procession would not be complete without him and his drum. By the way, you should stay for that fiesta, it's unique, part of our Spanish heritage. Quite a show. The Devil attempts to steal Christ's body from a glass coffin."

Elizabeth laughed. "And guess who's the leading man in all this?" She raised her hands. "No, don't tell me."

"Would you like coffee?"

Elizabeth shook her head. "Not for me, thanks. You don't like Rodriguez, do you?"

"He is dangerous. Stay clear of him."

She shrugged. "I doubt Marco and I will run into each other that often."

Her sudden use of Rodriguez's first name surprised Noel. "Be careful," he said, "the man will have your soul."

She laughed. "He can't. I don't believe in souls."

Noel blotted his brow with his napkin. "The evening is too fine for talk like this. Perhaps a brandy?"

Elizabeth shook her head. "No, thank you. It's been lovely, Noel, but I must be getting back. I've had too much sun."

"I'll walk with you," he offered.

Suddenly, she was sorry for this man. "Another time," she said.

Noel watched until Elizabeth's white dress faded into the growing dark. He returned to his room. Locking his door, he opened a wall safe and fingered the growing pile of small bags containing the precious white powder. This, plus the load he had stashed in a cave near the hotel—it was damn near enough. A little more and he'd be ready for Veronica's transaction. He had only to get this stuff to the city. A boat like the one just come in—kids like that would do anything for cash.

Noel flung himself across his bed. Desire for a woman ached his groin. Elizabeth was the kind would crush him under her heel. Noel squirmed, feeling an old pain. Veronica now—the damned beautiful bitch! Fucking her, he'd be on top again.

*M*oonlight, and the path ahead of Elizabeth unrolled like a silver ribbon.

Did she ever look for stars in Boston? Elizabeth doubted she looked higher than the traffic lights. She could not recall a Boston moon. But then, why should she? In Boston she knew but one small universe: her gallery, Numero Uno. She shut her eyes and saw it clear. "Hey, lady?" A figure slid from the shadows. A young man, slim, his hair golden under the street lamp. "Wait up! Are you a Spanish ghost or something?"

"Eric, leave her be." The girl's voice came from the dark edge of the path. Elizabeth could just see her outline. She lay flat on the wall, the top of her pale naked. She slid to her feet, and approached Elizabeth. "Don't mind my Eric," she said.

The boat kids, Elizabeth guessed. What had Noel said of them? Dopers, that was it. "Good evening," she murmured, attempting to walk between the boy and girl.

"Not so fast," Eric said, "we'll go with you."

One on each side of Elizabeth, they seized her arms. They stank of wet hemp and garlic, and Elizabeth balked; they insisted, giggling, propelling her forward.

"He's Eric, I'm Dierdre," the girl said.

"We're off that boat out there," Eric confided. "We've come to see the Devil Man. Heard stories about him far away as the Bahamas, and we sailed on here. He's got the power—that's what people say. I've come to see."

Dierdre skipped, jolting Elizabeth. "He's come to learn, my Eric. He says there's stuff the whole world has to give us, we've just got to look for it." She eyed Elizabeth. "I bet you know the Devil Man?"

"You mean Marco?" Elizabeth managed to release herself. "But he's quite ordinary. And now, if you'll excuse me?"

"No, you don't! " Eric grabbed her arm. "What do you mean, he's ordinary? Are you one of those I call spoilers? Listen, Mrs. Squeaky Clean, just because you can't see the Devil doesn't mean he's not around." He grimaced, pushed his face near Elizabeth's. "Boo you, lady!"

Elizabeth stumbled backwards. Hands caught her from behind, steadied her. Eric was shoved one way, Dierdre another.

"Marco?" Elizabeth breathed, "How on earth?"

He put an arm around her. "Are you okay?"

Eric extended his hand. "She called you Marco! You must be the Devil Man? We're off a boat, wanting to meet you."

Marco bowed. "I am Señor Rodriguez," he said, his tone formal. "Is that your boat anchored in the harbor?"

Eric nodded. "My boat, sir. We've sailed a long way to see you, sir, *señor.*"

"And I'm Dierdre," the girl said, offering her hand, smiling so warmly Marco could not resist her. He grinned. "So you have come to meet a Devil Man?"

Eric was polite as a schoolboy. "It's your power we heard about, sir. People say you're one hell of a guy. Stories about you far as Jamaica."

Marco looked at the two of them. He'd seen so many, boys and girls like these—they sailed the ocean on boats Marco considered fit only for kindling wood. Stoned kids, dreamers, starved for something he couldn't give them. But always they asked. They came to sit at his feet, wanting a new kind of hero, thinking it was easy. They wanted to know how Marco did it, and could they make magic, too? Hey, witch man, what have you got to blow our minds?

Marco said now what he always said: "Go on back where you came from."

He was keenly aware of Elizabeth beside him—her fragrance, her disapproval. He was tired; he'd been walking aimlessly. Flore had come to his house asking for him, and he had escaped out the back, come down into the village by his own steep path. A moment ago he'd heard Elizabeth's voice, and gone looking for her. Marco had learned to trust what happened inside him: a whisper of something, a hint, a tug, and he obeyed.

Elizabeth had been on his mind most of the day. He must feel her need. Not magic, Marco would say, it was a matter of leaving himself wide open to whatever, whoever, called. Moon or tide—Marco sensed, inside himself, their pull and release. Many times he had predicted, to the day and hour, the first rainfall.

Women were no different from the elements. Desiring one, Marco would focus all his energies on her, intuiting her desires. Elizabeth now, he felt her alarm, it quickened her body under his hand. What he wanted was the why and wherefore of those lights and darks changing the blue of her eyes.

But these kids now—what to do with them? The boy was more man than kid, Marco thought, this one's been through some kind of hell, carries it with him. The girl was pretty, but she shouldn't walk around uncovered; those breasts might give even Loco a twinge.

Dierdre sensed Marco's scrutiny and she winked at him. He grinned, responding to the admiration in her eyes. Elizabeth caught the exchange. "It is late," she said.

Marco nodded. "Time you kids got back to your boat."

Eric would not be denied. "Dierdre and me, we thought your lady was some kind of angel, that white dress and all." He chuckled. "Hey, Dierdre girl, it's not for real, this scene. The Devil Man here, he's hot for an angel!"

Marco grabbed Eric's shoulder. "Enough!" He would have swung a blow if Dierdre had not stepped between them. "Don't mind my Eric," she whispered, reaching a small hand towards Marco. He scowled at her. He pitied these young—their search for a different life was dead serious.

Dierdre pressed close to him, her nipples brushed his arm. Feeling her warmth, he relented. "Okay, if you can find me, I'll see you tomorrow."

"Yes, sir—we'll be there, sir!" Eric touched Marco's shoulder. He linked arms with Dierdre and the two set off, heads close, down the path.

"Crazy kids," *Elizabeth said.* "They think life is a picnic." She tugged at a loosened strand of hair. Marco reached a hand.

"Leave it," he said, "you're lovely that way."

His voice was a caress and Elizabeth stepped back, away from him.

"I'll see you to the house if you like?" he offered.

She awarded him a faint smile. "Thank you."

They walked awhile in silence, then Elizabeth asked, "Do you like it, when people come looking for the Devil Man?"

"I'm used to it."

"Ah? Then you expect it?" He does like it, she guessed, he is flattered, proud of his reputation. Suddenly then, she remembered his shadow, and she glanced over her shoulder to see if it was there. It was, and darker than she remembered.

"I am never without my friend," Marco said.

"I don't understand you," she protested, angry at the way he read her thoughts before she spoke.

His voice deepened. "Do I frighten you?"

"No," she said. "Anyway, the Devil doesn't have a shadow."

Marco chuckled. "Then I am not what I think I am."

"Definitely not," Elizabeth said. Carefully, she was keeping space between them. He shortened his steps to hers. "We are going to know each other, Elizabeth."

"Know?" A nervous giggle escaped her. "Know? In the biblical sense?" It was not her kind of remark, and she blushed. "Now that was stupid."

Marco shook his head. "I doubt you could ever be that. I was certain we would meet again."

Elizabeth shrugged. "Taboga is a small island. We're bound to run into each other."

Marco halted. His gaze held her motionless. "I don't know who you are," he said. "Something between us, though."

She was almost his height. Tipping her head back, Elizabeth saw stars on his shoulders, in his eyes.

He leaned towards her. She drew a deep breath to steady herself. "Thanks for helping out. Now, I really think..."

"Don't think." His hands on her waist, he turned her so her back was against him and she faced the harbor. "Look, Elizabeth, look out there—at the sea, that moon."

She felt him, straight down the length of her. She knew she trembled. "Please," she said, not knowing what she asked.

She broke from him. "My house," she stammered, "it's a short walk, I can... "

He seized her hands. "Stay with me," he urged. "The night is lovely. Keep me company, Elizabeth." Marco could not remember when he had wanted a woman so.

She shook her head. "Thank you, but no."

She was tempted. If he touched her again?

"Elizabeth?"

She shook her head. "You are a real spellbinder, Marco Rodriguez. But I must say good night."

"You must? Do you always do what you must, Elizabeth?"

"Don't tease," she said, meaning don't spoil it all now with some silly line. She turned from him. "Goodnight again, Marco."

They had reached her house and, without another word, she climbed the steps, found her key in her hand bag and set it in the lock.

He did not detain her. If he wished, he could make her stay. She would be his if he insisted. That was his power. Absently, he rubbed his scar. How would it be, this kind of thing, without his Devil Stone? The question always gave him pause.

Above him, Elizabeth fumbled her key, and dropped it. She leaned, couldn't find it in the dark, and turned, her hands outstretched. "I need your help."

If he asks me now, I will stay...

Marco took a key from his pocket and tossed it up to her. *"Buenas noches, doña."* He was gone before she could protest.

Like cold water spilled down her back!

Elizabeth slammed her door behind her. She had thrown herself at him. And he had thrown her right back. She'd left herself wide open. Why? This wasn't like her at all. She knew better. Hadn't her mother taught her?

Elizabeth pulled her bedroom curtains tight across the moon's bewitchment, tight against the rush of the rising tide.

*T*he following morning Flore brought Elizabeth her coffee and a sealed envelope.

"The letter was on the front steps," Flore said, looking disdainfully at the clothes strewn everywhere.

"A mess, I'm sorry," Elizabeth said, "I had a late night." Yawning, she set the letter aside. A busy day, and she couldn't wait for it to start. This was the morning she would begin the search for the Gauguins. She was about to ask Flore to confirm the whereabouts of the Amado house when she saw the anger in the girl's face and asked in Spanish, *"Que pasa, niña?"* What's wrong?

"Why does Señor Rodriguez write you?" Flore demanded. "You must not have anything to do with him, señora!"

Elizabeth glanced at the envelope. "How do you know this letter is from him?"

"A letter from the Devil Man is unlucky," Flore insisted, and reached her hand. "I will throw it away."

"If you don't mind," Elizabeth said, in English, "I will read it first. Thank you," she said, her tone one of dismissal.

Flore did not move. Deciding to ignore her, Elizabeth opened the letter. He wrote an educated hand. Just a line or two: he expected her for lunch today. Not, would she come—no, he expected her!

"No," Elizabeth said, firmly. "I've too much to do." She spoke in Spanish, slowly, recovering her knowledge of the language.

She put down the letter. "No," she said, again.

Flore scratched an armpit. "He wants something?"

"Yes, he invites me to lunch." Elizabeth said. "I could go, I suppose…" Despite herself, she was tempted.

"But, señora , he lives far up the hill. It is a dangerous climb. You should not go alone."

Flore had not seen Marco to talk to since his return. She had heard the gossip. Marco and Elizabeth had been seen entering the church. Juana said they had been inside for hours. And that black dog, the Devil's own, it had licked the gringa's hand!

Elizabeth was out of bed, brushing her hair. "Flore, do you know the Amado house?"

"Si, señora, it is around the corner from the church. Shall I take you? I know the old lady."

"No, thanks, I'll find it. Now, *por favor,* please, I must get dressed."

"You are going to Señor Rodriguez?"

"I don't know!" Annoyed, Elizabeth spoke in English. "I will go if I feel like it. Now, please..."

She will feel like it, Flore thought, returning to the kitchen. Marco will make it so. Of course he wants her; she is beautiful, she is everything I am not. I hate her—her clothes on the floor and I must pick them up, wash them. It is I must make her bed, scrub the floor, put fresh flowers in the vase. Marco tells me to do this. Por Dios! When will I see him? And Flore cupped her hand under her stomach which was, every day, bigger, heavier.

Elizabeth dressed quickly, choosing the yellow cotton dress, hesitating between sandals or sneakers—reaching for the sneakers. She would head for the Amado house, do her business there, see how she felt then. Lunch? It was too much. After all, she had resolved not to see this man again. But if he knew about the Gauguins? She might need him.

Elizabeth stuffed a small notebook and pencil, sun lotion, and some loose bills into her string bag. She did not forget her hat.

"Flore, I won't be back for hours. Lock the door when you leave. And be careful, that old man, Loco—he is somewhere around."

Flore scowled. "Loco is good. He makes me laugh."

"I don't like him," Elizabeth said. "If he's really crazy, he should be locked up."

Yes, Flore thought, that's the American way—lock up the old people! Flore had heard about that. Everything they didn't like looking at, the gringos put away, out of sight. Loco never hurt anyone. And Marco loves him. Oh, this gringa—truly she has no soul! Flore wrung her mop until her knuckles whitened.

*O*utside, *Elizabeth walked briskly.* It was still early, moderately cool. Up the hill, on Second Street, she found the yellow house.

She knocked. The door opened slightly, revealing the face of an old woman.

"*Sí?*" The voice was a whisper.

"Señora Amado? I am Miss Rogers." Elizabeth smiled her best smile, spoke her best Spanish. "I am told you have many beautiful antiques?"

This was often her most successful ploy and it worked again, now. The old lady smiled and beckoned Elizabeth inside. "Many treasures," she said. "I have old bottles from the Spanish, and a sword. And lace, old lace from France." She pulled a rag from her waistband and dusted off the torn plastic seat of one of two chairs. She gestured. "Please," she said.

Elizabeth looked about her and saw nothing but bare scrubbed poverty. Two chairs, a table, an electric light bulb hanging dead center of the high peaked ceiling. Just this one room: an iron cot in one corner, a small gas cooker in another. On one wall, a lurid poster of a bleeding Christ crowned with thorns; and another poster, an old one, of the Nestle milk cow and a red-cheeked milkmaid. No paintings.

A shelf high on the wall, opposite her, caught Elizabeth's attention. Among the jumble of objects there she saw a long bundle wrapped in plastic, tied together with cord. Grey with dust, the bundle looked as if it had sat there for years.

"Señora?" The old woman hovered like a small bird.

"That Nestle poster," Elizabeth said, "is certainly an antique."

Mrs. Amado spoke eagerly, "You wish that?"

"Maybe. But beside it, that roll of plastic up there? Pictures, perhaps?"

The woman pointed at the poster. "Five dollars."

"Yes," and Elizabeth fumbled in her bag. The poster was placed in her lap.

"A Spanish sword, señora?" Mrs. Amado went to a small chest, opened it, and pulled out something wrapped in rags. "This was Pizarros's own." She unwrapped a long rusted blade. "My father found it *en la casa del conquistador.*" In the conquistador's house.

Gingerly Elizabeth touched what might have been…well, almost anything. "It is very old," she said, lamely.

"Twenty dollars. I sell this treasure because I am poor, I am hungry," the old woman said.

"I don't know…" Elizabeth hesitated, then reminded herself she must return again. "I'll take it," she said.

She got to her feet. "You have lovely things. If you are hungry, I could perhaps…next time?"

Mrs. Amado bobbed her head. "What I like," she said, "is tea. Tea, and ice cream." She stared at this new gringa, who, she knew, wanted only what others had asked—the Frenchman's paintings. Perching on the edge of her cot, crossing her small bare feet, she awaited the question she knew was coming.

"You wouldn't have any old paintings, would you?"

Mrs. Amado nodded, satisfied. "Up there," and she pointed to the bundle on the shelf. She liked the excitement in the gringa's face. "I do not touch them," she said, "I promised my grandson. This house, all that is in it, belongs to him."

"But I love paintings," Elizabeth insisted. "Perhaps your grandson will show them to me?"

Mrs. Amado shook her head. "He is far away, on a ship. I sell only little things—my own. What else now, señora?" How much would this gringa pay? Once, a man had offered her fifty dollars! Just for a look, he'd said. She had refused. Her grandson forbid her to touch that bundle. He would put her out of the house if she did, he said.

Mrs. Amado leaned towards Elizabeth. This was a lady who would bring her many sweets. Sometimes, when he remembered, the *brujo* brought her ice cream. "*Nina!*" he would exclaim, swinging her up in the air as if she were young again, calling her a girl too, making her giggle. He sat down with her and shared the ice cream, smacking his lips, rolling his eyes. Ah! Don Marco was a breath of life in this quiet house! She loved him like a son. Once, she had asked him to take those pictures down, unroll them so she could have a look. He had refused.

"Yes, cookies, and ice cream," Elizabeth said. "Now, I need a bag."

From the depths of a wooden chest, Mrs. Amado brought out a used plastic bag into which she slid Elizabeth's sword and poster. The sword point cut right through and clattered to the floor. Elizabeth laughed. "Another time for that one," she said. "I'll just take the poster now." She gave the old woman another five.

Mrs. Amado pocketed the money. "Come back soon, *doña.*"

"Yes, I promise," Elizabeth wondered how many tea parties she must provide? No matter. She would win the trust of this stubborn little woman.

Mrs. Amado unbolted the door, opened it just wide enough to let Elizabeth through. "Don't forget," she whispered. "Strawberry ice cream. And tea."

She trusts me, Elizabeth exulted; this is a beginning. She would wait a day or two, then come again. Strawberry ice cream? She must ask Marco where to buy it. The grocery store was near here, she could leave her bundle there. It was time she started up that hill.

*E*lizabeth *found the small market, and Juana, behind the counter, dozing in her hammock.*

Seeing Elizabeth, she rolled to her feet. "You want fortune?" she asked, tucking the swell of her breasts into her grimy bodice.

"My fortune is fine today," Elizabeth said, her Spanish coming easily now. "Do you sell ice cream?"

Juana leaned heavily on her counter top. "It is Don Marco who orders the ice cream. He brings it himself, from the city."

"I will ask him then," Elizabeth said. "I am on my way to his house. If you will direct me?"

Hungry for every detail of this gringa, Juana stared at Elizabeth. She had seen immediately that this lady was Marco's kind. She looks like she can't be had, Juana guessed, but she can—if a man has the patience. She's brittle as glass, and those eyes, they're dry as this season now. Yes, a drought in this gringa, Juana saw it clear. Like Marco, this one, too, nurtured a secret thirst.

Looking for that man you could make the wrong turn, Juana wanted to say. Instead, needing to see Elizabeth's hand, she said, "Let's look at your tomorrow."

"I make my own fortune," Elizabeth said, taking some bills from her wallet. "I need a dozen tea bags, and those cookies there. I'll pay for them now, and pick them up on my way back. With the rest of my stuff." She indicated the bag at her feet.

Her hands on her hips, Juana let out a hoot of laughter. "The old one sold you something?"

Elizabeth smiled. "I almost bought Pizarro's sword."

Juana shook her head. "What do you really want, doña? What can I give you? A love story perhaps?"

"One I won't believe, yes." Elizabeth decided she liked this woman. "Do you know Don Marco? Where does he live?"

Juana squirmed, hiding her giggle. Did she know Marco? What to tell? One carnival evening, too many years ago, Marco had carried Juana up the path to his house. She'd come down alone, later, changed forever. No man, after Marco, had satisfied her. She'd been so young; Marco too, and he'd clowned so, she had wept with laughter. And wept too, when it was over. Even now, years later, when she thought about it, her lips smarted from Marco's lovemaking. He had never come back to her; a Devil Man did not stay long. Flore now—that one was a fool—wanting what she couldn't have.

"Many ways to a Devil Man's house," Juana said. "Best to go straight up," and she pointed skyward. "One street, then another—always up." She slid Elizabeth's purchases under her counter.

"Take care," she warned, "the sun burns skin like yours. Don't forget me. I will wait." She must see this gringa's face, returning from the Devil Man's house.

Juana saw Elizabeth on her way, and closed her store. This heat was impossible. Hours now when there was no water to be had at all. Perhaps the Devil Man would make one long golden piss? And Juana chuckled: Marco was no miracle worker, that power he had, it was natural, born in him. Some people had it—a magic to make others do what they wished. Being a Devil Man helped, of course. People were scared of Marco, in awe of him. But he was a good man; he took no more of life than what he needed. And gave much more than he took. Marco was the heartbeat of this island. If his hungers were larger than most men's, so be it. Juana sighed, scratched the inside of her thighs. It was people who made Marco whatever they needed him to be. It was people, too, who made things happen. Good and evil, they brought it on themselves.

*T*he trail was steep and Elizabeth stopped often to catch her breath.

Soon she had climbed above the village. The sun baked the sky clear of color. Not a breeze, or a hint of shade. Pampas grass stood high as Elizabeth's waist. Her sweat streaked her dress, stung her eyes. Thorned bushes pitted the earth on either side. Coconut husks blocked the pathway. At last, gratefully, she entered a stand of bamboo.

The shade was a relief at first, then startling, alive with sounds. The bamboo creaked. A flock of parakeets swooped low, screeching. Elizabeth covered her ears. Her hair had come undone; she could not remember the way down.

Out of the shade then, up through a clump of Birds of Paradise, their red mouths gaping. Heaps of rotting mangos, slippery under her feet. When she thought she could climb no further, that she must turn back, the path leveled and she stepped into a field of sunburned grass. High as her knees, a sea of grass rippled in the wind that swept the crest of this hill.

Elizabeth stood still, drawing deep breaths. Forgotten now her long climb. This was the top of the world! And there, across the golden field, stood a large brick house. It sprawled, rosy in the sunlight, its red-tiled roof catching the shadows of the tree that spread its branches over all.

Elizabeth paused, breathing in the scent of the grass, the wind. Here were Gauguin's lights and darks. Had he, too, wandered here? Elizabeth stretched her hand to a small white butterfly. It stayed a moment on her wrist.

Then, and the sound rocked her—dogs barked, a darkness hurled itself towards her. Wet muzzles prodded, tails thumped.

A man's voice rang out: "Padre...Hijo...Santo!"

The hounds turned. He walked towards Elizabeth, a gnarled stick of a man. Hesitantly, she stepped forward. "I am Elizabeth Rogers. The señor—Don Rodriguez—invited me for lunch. This is his house?"

Sternly the man stood, blocking the path. "I am Jose Maria Jesu. My master has guests."

"Elizabeth..."

She turned. Marco strode towards her, pushing his dogs aside. "Welcome!" He was beside her, seizing her hands in his. "I am glad," he said. "Come, please. I've been expecting you." He pushed back the hound that persisted in licking Elizabeth's hand. "Down, *Santo!*"

"*Santo?*" she asked. "Don't tell me you've named them Father, Son, and Holy Ghost?"

Marco grinned. "Yes. Because they are blessed beasts. *Padre*"— and he pointed at the most grizzled dog—" and *Hijo* there, his Son. And"—Marco stroked the head of the last hound—"meet *Santo*, the very spirit of dog love."

"You're serious, aren't you?" Elizabeth asked. She took off her hat. "That climb," she said, "I thought I wouldn't make it." It was hard not to respond to the warm welcome in Marco's eyes. His ease suggested he had been expecting her.

Marco answered her thought: "You wanted to come," he said. "You and I—we knew you would be here."

He brought her inside, into a large room, the floor brick-tiled, tall windows; a summer room, its marvelous space splashed with bright-colored cushions, primitive paintings. Elizabeth paused to admire a small Frida Kahlo. "Marco, where did you find this?"

"Mexico, years ago. Once, I thought I might collect her work." He shrugged. "Suddenly she got expensive."

"You'll have to introduce me to these others," Elizabeth said, because the colors on the walls shocked her, but pleased too. Her own Impressionists were pale, too precious, compared to this brilliance. "You should have a Tame," she said, "a big one."

"If you say so," Marco said. His hand was under her elbow. "You remember Dierdre and Eric? They will join us for lunch."

*T*he two young people rose to greet Elizabeth. They held tall glasses of iced tea and seemed very much at home. Elizabeth, relieved to see that Dierdre had topped her jeans with a t-shirt, nodded coolly.

"We'll sit here," Marco said, pointing to a low couch. He offered Elizabeth a cigarette from a gold case.

"I don't smoke, thank you."

Santo curled himself at her feet. The couch was deep, forcing her knees up. She would not lean back because Marco's arm was stretched behind her. "I am sorry to interrupt," she said. She was piqued that she was not the only invited guest. Marco should have known that these two kids were people she had not wanted to meet again.

Eric, cross-legged on a pillow near Marco's feet, blew a smoke ring. "You should try this tobacco," he said. "It's Marco's own mix." His eyes did not leave Marco's face. "Whatever you've got, Witch Man, I want it too." He beckoned Dierdre, and she came like a puppy to lie on the floor, her head in his lap.

Marco grinned at the two of them. "We've been arguing most of the morning. Eric insists I have a secret power. He believes I can give it to him. I say I cannot. We are—how do you say it—stagnated?"

"Stymied," Elizabeth said, pressing her iced glass against her temple. "Like I felt on that hill I just climbed. I don't need argument right now."

Dierdre giggled. "Relax, lady. This is the Devil Man's house. The other side of the moon maybe." She pulled up her shirt, settled Eric's hands on her flat belly.

"I want to know all about the the Devil Stone," Eric said, "and how you get one."

Elizabeth raised her eyebrows. "For starters: why do we want one?"

Marco was looking benign as a guru. She was not going to be part of it, and she said, "Perhaps I'll come back some other time…"

"No, stay." Marco rose to his feet. "Jesu is fixing our lunch. You are all most welcome. I'll be back in a minute."

Marco gone, Eric addressed Elizabeth. "Cool it, lady, you're in a world you won't believe." He gestured widely. "Marco inherited this whole scene. It's the Stone, he says, gives everything to him."

"Unreal," Dierdre breathed. She plumped a red pillow and nestled into it.

Elizabeth frowned. "A house like this, it takes a lot of work. And money."

Eric contradicted her. "The Devil Man doesn't work. Never has, he doesn't need to."

"Marco is a prince," Dierdre said. "I don't know about his Devil thing, but Marco, himself—he's good, I can tell."

"If you say so," and Elizabeth shrugged. "I for one do not believe the man."

His shadow fell full then, across her lap. "You refuse to believe many things," he said, sitting close to her again. "Try not to think so much, Elizabeth."

She gazed about her. The room had an energy to it. She would like to explore the crowded bookcase, to have a closer look at a small etching hanging opposite her.

Dierdre broke the quiet. "Marco has what he wants. I feel good here, like things will work out for Eric and me. We're not sure what we want, that's the trouble. Except each other." She grinned and hugged Eric.

"My boat, too," Eric said, "She's what I want. *Gull*'s her name."

"Nice," Marco said. He was looking at Elizabeth.

"Sailing's all I know," Eric continued. "After Nam—well, I had money saved. I bought *Gull* in San Diego, and learned to sail her on the Sea of Cortez. I met Dierdre in Hawaii, and"—Eric spread his hands— "well, right now I've got more than I ever thought I'd have."

"Gauguin," Elizabeth said, out of the blue. And, quickly then, because they were looking at her, "I don't know what made me think of him but he's a favorite of mine. And he did visit this island. Twice, I believe."

"Sure, he was here," Eric said, "I read his diary in Tahiti. He wanted to live on Taboga."

Marco nodded. "A family in town is supposed to have some paintings of his. I'm not sure it's true."

"You've never checked it out?" Elizabeth asked.

Marco shrugged. "Why should I? Only the old woman there now, and she's near dying. Why bother her? A Gauguin find—it would bring the world down on us."

"And why not?" Elizabeth said. "This is a piece of paradise the world should know about. A little improvement, trash pickup, a good clean up, Marco, and Taboga would be what it should be."

Dierdre interrupted. "I hate words like should and improvement."

"So did Gauguin," Eric said. "If his work is here, leave it where it was born."

"No," Elizabeth said, "if the paintings are Gauguin's, they deserve to be seen by everyone."

Marco turned to Elizabeth. "Are you in the art business?"

"No," Elizabeth kept her voice steady, "I just happen to love Gauguin's work. I would like a look at those paintings."

"The old lady won't show them," Marco said. "Her grandson has forbidden her. And he left her in my care, I promised him she would not be disturbed. If those paintings are Gauguins, Elizabeth, somebody would have tracked them down by now. I'm told our General is an art lover. Think what the Butcher would do—to have a Gauguin!"

"Why is he called the Butcher?" Elizabeth asked.

"He cuts off heads, sends the bodies down-river in mail sacks."

"And you let him be?"

"He has the guns," Marco replied.

Elizabeth could not resist: "And who gave him such power in the first place?"

Eric hooted. "People don't give that kind of power. That kind snatches it!"

"If you want a Gauguin?" Marco went to the far corner of the room and returned with a carved stick in his hands. He offered it to Elizabeth. "Here—it's a fine piece of work."

Eagerly her hands closed on the polished wood. She caressed the lizard head, the long body, the tail winding its way down the stick.

"What makes you believe this is Gauguin's?" she asked.

Marco smiled. "Like you and those paintings, I like to think so. My father found this, under a pile of junk where the French Sanitarium used to be." Marco reached for the stick.

Reluctantly, Elizabeth released it. "Will you sell it to me?"

Marco shook his head. "Like Eric said, if it was made on this island, here it stays. Besides," and he stroked the animal depicted on the stick. "This is an iguana, one of my favorite creatures. They were close to becoming extinct. We are learning not to kill them. I plan to breed them, raise them like chickens, they're good eating."

"You eat iguana?" Her disbelief amused Marco

"We've many treasures here," he said. "Maybe you will let me show you? There's a waterfall. Sunken treasure too. And an old Spanish convent—a magic there you will not believe."

Eric stood and stretched. "Witch Man, tell us the story you promised."

*T*hese three, Marco thought, they won't understand.
Maybe the two kids—they are looking for something, they'll come part of my way with me. But Elizabeth—she grew up in a different world, there's a fence around her, a wall, shutting out what she doesn't want to feel. And feeling is what it's all about, Marco knew that. Miracles happen, sly as small breezes; good and evil quicken the blood, or bruise. To believe it, every happening must be acknowledged, felt to the bone.

Marco glanced at Eric and Dierdre. Kids like these were a dime a dozen, and the only puzzle to Marco was why they came so far. What happened at home to send them searching? They hungered after an old lost magic, blew their minds in the search for it. Who could tell them the magic lies inside of each?

Marco knew that not one of them here had the courage to take the Stone. It was to take the Devil square on your shoulders, absorb his evil into your guts. The death fear rode Marco day and night. Dying with the Stone in him, Marco knew his soul would go to Hell. So he had been taught. So he must believe.

On his feet, he faced his listeners squarely. "It was Grandfather who took the Stone first. My power has been handed down, father to son." Carefully then, he sat down on the opposite end of the couch, distancing himself from Elizabeth.

Eric asked, "What is the Stone? Did your family invent it?"

Marco smiled. "Men have bargained with the Devil since ancient times. You've got to be born rotten poor. Born in some dusty pueblo where the only way out of the hell you live in is to make a pact with the Devil."

Absently, Marco stroked his scar. "It's not easy," he said. "Think of it as the priest's way, only the other direction." He grinned, and gestured. "Down, instead of up."

Dierdre eyed Marco's scar. "The mark is cruel," she murmured. "Is there really a Stone in there, Marco?"

He nodded. "My Stone is a gold cross, small as your thumb nail. The Devil Stone can be any object stolen from a priest."

He tried to state it as simply as possible. "In the campo, where I come from, only the priests have power and wealth. That swine of a priest who visits the village once or twice a year—he is much envied, and feared. It is believed he has a talisman, a magic from God that gives him what he wants."

Marco threw back his head. "Those damned city priests! They feed on the people; take for themselves. Nothing but dirt, disease, starvation in the campo—a living hell! But it must be endured, the priest says, life is suffering, he insists—it is suffering will get a man to Heaven." Marco was on his feet, pacing the room.

"No," Elizabeth whispered, sensing Marco far away, back in that wretchedness he spoke of. "No," she said gently, unaware she stretched her hand to him.

He gripped her fingers, and sat down, close to her. "Yes, Elizabeth, a misery there you can't believe. In the campo, a man has nothing to look forward to but death and Heaven. He must believe the priests, that they speak God's truth. What else is there?

"That he reach Heaven, a man must pay, every step of the way. And Heaven's price is high. It costs real money to be baptized, to be married, to be buried in holy ground. The priest asks more than a man can afford: the last of the rice, a year's labor of corn, perhaps the loan of a young daughter for an hour or two.

"Holy Fathers?" Marco spat in his palms. "God's devils!"

Elizabeth shook her head. "A man doesn't have to believe everything he is told."

Sternly, Marco regarded her. "When the present is only suffering, how can a man endure without the promise of a better hereafter?"

Elizabeth insisted: "It is foolish to believe in a promise, even a priest's promise."

"When you are starving and someone throws you a crust, you must believe it is bread," Marco retorted.

"But the Stone, as you call it—stealing from a priest must be a sin?"

"Mortal sin, yes," Marco replied. "Steal the priest's talisman, and Satan has you by the balls. You must sit down with him, your soul between the two of you."

Dierdre inched closer, her eyes wide. "Your Stone, Marco? How did your grandfather get it?"

He flexed his left arm, massaged his scar. "The way my father told me—it was somebody's wedding day, and the priest had enjoyed the wine. Dead asleep he was, in the church, passed out on the altar steps. The cross was on a chain around his neck. Grandfather took it. He set that cross in his arm. To be passed on when he died, to his son, my father.

"There is always infection," Marco continued. "Most men—their bodies reject the Stone. I had fever, my arm was on fire. Jesu nursed me, as he did those two who went before me. The pain was so bad I believed I would die."

Eric shuddered. "And you saw the Devil, Marco? What does he look like?"

"However you imagine him. My fiend is darkness and cold. I faced him square. I told him if he would let me live, I'd lend him my soul until I died. I saw his shadow fall across my own.

"The Devil lives here, in my guts." Marco struck his stomach with his fist. He let his head fall back against the couch. He was damnably tired. These gringos here, their prying eyes: Marco knew they did not believe him. And why had he told this? He seldom did, it brought him no more than mockery.

"It is too much, your story," Elizabeth said. "This Stone of yours, Marco, it could kill you."

"It will not," Marco said. "For as long as I live, the Devil's power is mine. Before I die, someone will take the Stone from me, and my soul will go to Heaven."

"But you cannot truly believe these things," Elizabeth said.

Dierdre kneeled to Marco. "You are not a bad man!"

"I am careful, I ask no more than what I need."

"And when you die?" Dierdre persisted. "If there is no one there to take the Stone?"

Marco touched Dierdre's cheek, spoke reassuringly: "You forget Jesu. He will take my stone, just as he took it from my father and grandfather."

The room had grown warm and Elizabeth went to the open window. Outside the world was bright with sunlight. All this talk of heaven and hell—it stifled!

Marco was standing behind her. "If I have seen Satan, then I must believe in God."

Turning, Elizabeth felt an immense pity for this man. "Marco, Marco…you are no better off than the man in your campo. Devil or priest, they are one and the same. As your people served the priest, so do you now serve the other master.

"Tell me," she demanded, "have you found happiness?"

He wanted to tell her about his school. But it was against the law now to teach English; if the General got wind of it, he'd shut the place down.

Eric interrupted, "So, who's happy? What I want to know is how you got your Stone."

Marco's eyes challenged Elizabeth. "Have you the stomach for it?" He joined her on the couch.

"Of course!" she flared.

Dierdre stood and stretched. "I am an old soul," she said, "I'll listen to you," she said, cuddling down on the other side of Marco. He smiled, and stroked her hair.

Elizabeth frowned. Marco's eyes caught her own with a look that told her he read her jealousy. Gently, he pulled her back to rest against his shoulder. "Come with me now," he whispered.

"*It was Grandfather who took the stone first,*" Marco began.
"My village was in the campo, dead center of a stone wasteland. Las Piedras is its name. It prospers now, the Pan American Highway runs close by. But in grandfather's time it was no more than its name implies—stones." His words fell heavily into the silence.

The quiet in the room was almost palpable. Dierdre was gripping Eric's hand. Elizabeth watched the afternoon sunlight turn a red pillow into a crimson pool.

Marco's voice deepened. "Grandfather was the first Devil Man in our family. He took the Stone because he wanted land. He said he'd had a dream. Those rocks he'd known since he was born could be put to good purpose. He was a peasant farmer with no money to buy land, no learning as to how to take title to it. He wanted that dream so much he dared to take the Devil Stone. The villagers were scared of his new power and they did what he asked of them. The mayor of Piedras made out some papers, ceding Grandfather acres of stones. People laughed at him. But they built him the house he asked, found him the tools."

Marco's eyes were closed. "Grandfather was a born artist, a stone-cutter. It wasn't long before his gravestones sold everywhere. Panama City cemeteries are full of his angels. I put one here, on Papi's grave. Somebody stole her. Or she flew away," Marco said. A fat unholy angel, Marco remembered, Papi's kind of lady.

"'Are you a stone cutter too?" Dierdre asked.

Marco shook his head. "Grandfather's talent died with him. His stones are a working quarry now. My uncles run it. Today every man in Piedras is employed, shaping those same stones which, generations ago, broke backs and feet, and lives."

Eric sat up and applauded. "You turned the Devil's work upside down, Marco!"

"It can be done," Marco agreed. *"Mi abuelo*—Grandfather—" and Marco grinned, "the whole town called him that. He gave a calf to every child born in Piedras. And his name too, if the child needed a name. There's a Rodriguez around every corner now. Most of them own stock in the quarry. The Rodriguez Devil Men have never taken without giving. We have never abused our power. To use the stone—as we used those *piedras*—that's what I was taught.

"Then it was my father's turn. He'd always hated the campo. And he'd have none of books or schooling. Heaven on earth lay behind the mountains, he said, he'd seen pictures of the sea—he got a craving for it.

"When the Stone was set in his arm he left the quarry to his brothers and set out for the coast. He took my mother with him. I was in her belly. She cried, my father said, leaving her land. It was too much for her. She was young, a mountain girl and Indian to her bones.

"She died here, giving birth to me." Marco paused, wishing as always that he could recall his mother's face. Young and beautiful, they told him, hair below her waist and her hips too narrow for birthing. A brave girl, they said, with a gift for reading people's thoughts before they spoke them.

"This island was a backwater then," Marco continued. "The rich visited on holidays. The island folk were poor. Most of what they had they gave to the church here, to the priest. He had a fine house, and servants—people from the island—to wait on him. He paid them in candles, and prayers for their souls. He had dogs, too, mean and hungry ones that kept ordinary folk from stealing the vegetables from his garden.

"Ordinary hungry people," Marco said, his tone bitter, "they must give a day's catch to the priest. He had his own boat, and he sold the fish on the mainland, kept the money for himself."

"No!" Elizabeth was unbelieving.

"Yes," Marco told her. "Papi told me how it was. The people here, Papi said, when he first came, they were scared of their own shadow. He changed all that. He wanted everyone happy as he was."

Marco paused, remembering that large booming man, his black moustache thick on his ruddy lips. Papi's kiss was rough, but the boy Marco had hungered for it.

"First thing, Papi chased the priest off and closed the church. People were scared, but Papi was kind in his way. He was generous with his rum. Food and drink—he made a fiesta every day until this house was built. His dream was to live up here, the sea below him. Horizons—Papi said a man needs horizons."

Dierdre interrupted. "Just you and him up here? How did you grow up? Wasn't it lonely?"

Marco shrugged. "I didn't think so. And Jesu was here, he was both friend and teacher. Grandfather had adopted him when he was a baby, picked him off a city garbage heap, and brought him home to Piedras. Jesu was sent to a Jesuit school. Grandfather named him Jose Maria Jesu. He said he must be guardian angel to the Devil Men. A joke in the beginning, but it worked out as Grandfather predicted. Jesu takes care of me and my soul. He is a good man. It is he who has taught me to read the silences behind things."

Pausing, Marco looked at his listeners. "But you have heard enough?"

Dierdre pushed back her hair. Her eyes, on Marco, were wide, adoring. "You have turned what was evil into good!"

Marco smiled at her. "I do what I can. But the Devil is always near. Speak his name and and his presence is felt." Marco raised a hand. "Listen..."

Eric and Dierdre were still. Elizabeth moved uneasily, feeling a chill, light as a shawl across her shoulders.

"No!" It was Dierdre who broke the silence. She made the sign of the Cross.

Eric was on his feet. "Tell me about evil!" he said, such a bitterness in his voice that Elizabeth huddled into herself. She shut her eyes not to see the shadow sliding one to the other of those sitting there. She saw a wetness on Eric's cheeks. She saw Dierdre wipe his tears, and lick them from her fingers.

"*I* have told enough," Marco said.
"No," Dierdre said, "there is more."

"Not much else," Marco said. He wanted to finish this now. It was Papi lay at the heart of this part of the story. Marco's throat tightened and he recognized that hot anger he had felt back then. Anger at that man he had called Papi, the shame he, Marco, not yet twenty, had felt.

"Jesu," Marco said, shortly, "it was he pushed me to study. Those two years in the States, at the University of Miami, I was lonely. It was Jesu who wrote me."

Jesu's letters had meant a great deal. Marco had been homesick. He'd boasted, that first year, of his island home. He had hinted of his father's secret pact with the Devil. One day he would have his father's power for himself, Marco told the others. How they had laughed at him. "Devil baiter!" they had jeered, and looked behind him for his tail. Put their hands on his ass. Yes, poked and pried. Looking for the Devil, they said.

One day he'd had enough of his tormentors. He had taken on five boys, one at a time, knocking them into bloody heaps, straight into the infirmary. He'd come close to killing one of them.

"Crazy Devil!" the kid had yelled, and Marco couldn't hold himself from pounding, pounding the boy's head, shutting him up at last. But not before the police had taken a hand. He had the temper of a killer, the cops warned him, he must control himself or he'd end up dead, or in prison. "We'll see you locked up for good," they had threatened, not releasing Marco until he'd spent a night in a square stone box of a holding cell.

The university had come close to sending him home. "You've got the Devil's luck," they said, "that kid survived." Their eyes judged Marco different than themselves: Rebel, Indian, yes, Latino, and cursed with a killer temper. "Keep hold of yourself, kid," they'd warned him.

"I never told Papi," Marco said. "He emptied his pockets to send me to college, I know that. I would have finished, but he died. Papi lived life too hard. It's his temper I've inherited."

Too much of his father in him, Marco knew that. He was hard on himself, starving out hungers, tamping down desires a lesser man would have satisfied.

Marco was on his feet, pacing the room, remembering Papi's girls. Love is the Devil's trap, Papi had warned, in love a man forgets himself. A Devil Man must not take risks, Papi said. Five women, he said, never one alone.

He would rub his scarred arm, and sometimes he let Marco touch his Devil's Mark. It was with Papi's good humored blessing that Marco, when he was old enough, enjoyed whichever girl caught his eye.

Marco wanted fine words, now, to explain his father. But words could not capture the essence of that man. Too, Papi's enormous presence had crowded, frightened the boy, Marco. Sometimes, even now, when the rain rattled on the roof, or when he sat alone, one drink too many, Marco heard again the laugh-sprung gusty breathing of that huge clown he had called Papi.

"I knew he was proud of me," Marco said. "I read him stories from books I'd bring home. Quixote was one of his favorites. He'd call Jesu and the two of them would sit and listen, beg like kids for more."

Elizabeth spoke softly, "It was a different world, wasn't it?"

Yes, a different world. If Papi was alive now what would he do? He'd bloody more than the General's nose. "He'd have started a war," Marco said.

"He'd be dead," Elizabeth said, flatly. "Your General doesn't fool around."

Dierdre was adamant. "Your Papi would have won his war!"

"No," Marco said. "Papi would be dead, his soul in hell. Which is why I won't make trouble here."

Eric was curious. "When it was time, did you want the Stone?"

Marco did not hesitate. "Of course," Marco said. "This Stone," and he folded his hand across his scar, "belongs to us Rodriguez men."

He would not confess his fears, the confusion of his younger years. He'd outgrown all that, or so he insisted. More than twenty years now and the Stone firmly nested in his flesh.

Eric persisted: "I want to know how you got it," he said.

Marco smiled. "I was nineteen, back from New Orleans with a new mustache—jeans, cowboy boots, and a silver buckled belt. Carnival there, and here, too. Papi didn't expect me, I wanted to surprise him. I waited here, in this room.

"Papi and his girl, they came late from dancing. I heard them giggling in the kitchen. She was dressed up like an angel—white wings and silver spangles.

"I watched from behind the door. They were drinking from a bottle, fooling around. Papi took the angel on his lap. Their voices were so loud they woke Jesu, and he watched with me, mouthing his everlasting prayers.

"All of a sudden Papi picked up that girl, swung her about, making her wings flap. He spread her right there on the kitchen table. Laughing to split his sides, he pushed up her angel dress…"

Marco had forgotten his listeners. His eyes glowed, seeing his father clear. Devil take the man—what a way to go! Straight to Heaven astride an angel! Now that he was older Marco could appreciate that scene. Then, he had been shocked to the pit of his belly.

He saw Elizabeth's face pale, he sensed her distaste.

"Go on," Dierdre urged. Eric nodded. Elizabeth was silent.

"I will finish soon," Marco told her.

"It will never finish," she answered him.

"One helluva story," Eric said, his eyes glowing.

"It is truth," Marco said. "Papi's heart gave out. The girl screamed. A scream that lifted my hair. I jumped and knocked her off the table. Jesu cut the Stone from Papi's arm. One swipe of the knife. Papi passed quickly. He was smiling."

Yes, one big glorious come—Marco remembered his father's sperm spewed, the old legs twitching. That angel girl screeched like a witch when the gold cross slid from Jesu's bloodied fingers, fell to the floor. Jesu had scooped it up, said a prayer over it.

"Yours?" he had asked, and Marco could taste now that fear he had swallowed then. Just nineteen, New Orleans dust still on his heels, his tongue trained to a language he had learned to love. He'd planned to invite Jesu and Papi for his graduation, just months away.

Jesu had said the right thing: "I know you are scared, boy." Softly, in Spanish: "You have fear."

"The hell I have!" Marco had snatched the cross from the old man. "I'm a Rodriguez, born to this Stone. It is mine!" The cross had been set in Marco's arm that night.

"Holy shit!" Eric's mouth hung open. Dierdre lay with her face buried in his lap.

"Yes, that same night," Marco said now, his eyes on his scar. He'd given up a dream for this. The loss of finishing his education lay silent in him still. Which is why he'd started his English school. Just one room—he'd built it himself. Learning was available, no charge, if the kids wanted it. Some of them did.

Marco spoke rapidly now, wanting to finish. "I put the girl out of the house. A fishing boat took her back to the city. I buried my father in the Spanish cemetery, near the other old pirates. And that's about it."

Elizabeth squirmed, feeling acute embarrassment, and ashamed somehow of that embarrassment. She knew herself inadequate, an outsider. Marco had become a stranger, his crudities exposed now in his heavy jaw line, the brute thrust of his neck as he leaned forward.

He did not tell them all of the story—how scared he'd been, and the pain. His arm had swollen to bursting. He'd taken the weight of the Devil full on him. The taste of evil soured his stomach. He'd jammed his knuckles in his mouth, so that he wouldn't vomit, or cry out.

Near forty now, he had lived hard, outrunning the Devil. Too hard, perhaps. Only Jesu knew about the dizziness that unsteadied Marco sometimes, his shortness of breath. Jesu, and the city doctor who had warned Marco to take life easier.

What did a doctor know? Life was supposed to be easy for a Devil Man. But it wasn't—not the inside gut level part of living. Marco's temper smoldered deep in him. He rode it hard, aware it could slide out of control.

Looking at Elizabeth now, Marco saw her shocked face.

"If all this is true," she said, "you are a lonely man."

"A war inside you," Eric guessed. He shrugged. "But each of us has that."

"One thing sure," Dierdre said, "you can't take a step on this island without running into the Devil Man. The Rodriguez name is on the clinic door. And," she smiled at Marco, "I saw where you teach English, a kid told me. And I bought a papaya today, and the man said it was good because it was grown the Devil Man's way."

Marco corrected her. "Nature's way,"

Yes, it was in his power to stop the villagers from harming themselves. They feared the Devil Man's anger. Only once they'd seen it loose, heard the growl in Marco's throat when, with his own two hands, he'd smashed the boat of a Colombian smuggler come ashore to steal girl children. He'd had two little ones on board when Marco found him. Marco's roar of rage, still it echoed in hearts and ears. And the foreign sounding words of his Devil's curse. No, a man didn't want that in his life. Do it Marco's way, that was best.

"The General," Elizabeth said now, "there's your Devil, Marco."

"Yes," he agreed. Because any fool could read the trouble coming. Marco had schooled himself to ignore those things against which he was helpless. The General's open dislike of him, Noel's increasing involvement in the drug trade, these threats endangered the island, and Marco was aware of this. Still, he did nothing. It was not death he feared, it was dying with the Stone still in him. It was Hell terrified Marco.

Placing his hand over his scar, he said, "I have told you. I will not place my soul at risk."

Elizabeth spoke into the silence: "Who is Marco Rodriguez without his Stone?"

It was Marco who replied. "Nobody."

Eric scowled. "Who are any of us without our props?"

"Enough of this now," Marco said. Suddenly, he wanted these people gone. All of their kind. Yes, off his island, out of his life. They would take his story, repeat it to others like themselves, tell it again and again. Until it wasn't real. Until he, Marco Rodriguez wasn't real. Until God wasn't real.

It was these people, their kind, who wanted to incarcerate him. They would if they could. Yes, even she, the pale one sitting there, blue eyes staring. Marco knew she wanted out.

Past lunchtime and she was starved, Elizabeth thought. About as far from Gauguin's world as she could get. And what was she doing here anyway? Listening to a Halloween story. Because that's all it was, a story right out of that ignorant campo. Scary enough if you believed that sort of thing. Ugly, certainly. Take Marco's Indian mother. Throw in heavy duty Catholicism and a Jesus freak and look what you get. He is a mixed bag, this guy is. Miami, New Orleans—it was comic, really. A Devil Man wandering about, buying New Age paperbacks at Walden's. Had Marco studied medieval history? She remembered reading something about the nuns and monks of that time; how, in order to protect themselves from evil, they had inserted the fingers and toes of dead saints into their flesh. A shuddering thought, and she turned.

"Marco, stop torturing yourself!"

Dierdre was adamant: "I think you're the bravest man I know."

Eric nodded. "What you've been dealt, you gotta play hard ball!"

"No," Marco replied, slowly, "I do what is expected of me. I am a Rodriguez. I inherited my Stone."

Yes, Elizabeth realized, and felt a great sadness. He could not behave otherwise.

Jesu stood in the doorway. "La comida," he announced.

*T*hank God, Elizabeth thought, welcoming the interruption. She followed the others into the dining room.

"I welcome all of you," Marco said, gesturing at his table set with a bright blue and yellow pottery, crowded with platters of fried plantain, corn on the cob, and steak frizzled brown in tomato sauce.

Jesu set a fresh loaf of bread on the table. When he was gone, Eric guffawed. "Jesus and you—it blows my mind!"

"Tell me someone better for the job," Marco retorted. Elizabeth saw his face relaxed; he was a generous host and she wondered at the handwoven linens, the old fashioned heavily embossed silverware, its monograms blurred.

Marco answered her unspoken question. "Papi set our table with silver bought in the pawnshops in Panama City. Antiques were a passion of his."

"Now this is civilized," Dierdre said. "We've been gypsies too long, I don't even know which fork."

Marco put his hand over her small one. "Not to worry, little one."

The girl's half in love with him, Elizabeth guessed. She was hoping they had left the Devil behind them, in the living room. A new subject was what they needed. She addressed Marco: "Tell us about your island."

Marco promised he would show them everything. He told Eric he would not charge him anchorage fees; they could stay as long as necessary. "And it is I," Marco said, "not Noel, who decides these things. A word of warning: Noel is no good. Stay clear of him."

"Taboga is yours as long as you behave yourself," Marco told Dierdre, giving her a look that melted her bones. "I like you," she replied, "I really like you."

"And I like you," Marco replied. The girl's candor delighted him. He pointed at Eric. "That one there with his mouth full of corn—what's he to you?"

"My life," Dierdre replied simply.

The more fool you are, Elizabeth thought. Grass and sex—that merry-go-round, and when Eric's had enough he'll move on. She wasn't hungry anymore, all she really wanted was iced tea. No sooner had she wished than Jesu was at her elbow, setting down a tall glass of tea. He was polite, but Elizabeth felt the old man did not like her. What should she call him? It was beyond her—asking Jesus for a slice of lemon!

She sipped her tea, thinking to herself that Marco had designed a stage setting—the present cast of characters, this marvelous house.

"All this is hard to believe," she said. Under the table, Santo curled himself at her feet. From across the table Marco was smiling at her.

"It's you is hard to believe," Eric said. "Tell us about you, lady, you're just too beautiful to be all by yourself on an island."

"Oh, I'm real enough," Elizabeth said.

Dierdre waggled buttery fingers. "Not fair," she said, "I eat compliments—give 'em to me, I'm starved!"

After the meal Marco told the young people they could explore his house. "But you won't find black magic or voodoo," he warned, "not even in the herb cellar. I'll have Jesu show you around. Maybe he will give you his love potion."

"Love potion?" Dierdre clapped her hands.

"You won't like it," Marco told her. "It is pressed humming birds preserved in their own juice." He grinned at Dierdre's shudder. "Yes, killing birds is against my principles too. I've told Jesu so, that he must concoct another kind of love recipe."

"That's easy," Dierdre said. "Take this man, and this woman"—she pointed at Marco and Elizabeth— "and shake well."

Marco chuckled. "On your way, young lady…"

Dierdre slid her arm around Eric's waist. "We'll see you all later."

"**W**hen it is cooler," Marco told Elizabeth, "I will walk you down the hill."

He gestured towards two chairs close together, near the large window. "Let's not make conversation," he said. "Tell me who you are."

"Not much to tell," Elizabeth said. "And I don't like talking about myself. But you, Marco? That was quite a story you told us. It wasn't pretty." She was thinking how sure of himself he was—*macho*, like that father of his. She could not erase that kitchen scene from her mind.

He pulled his chair closer. "I said too much. You don't like me now."

"Because I can't accept you—not your story, Marco." He was insisting on an intimacy she did not want.

"What I really came for..." she began. "Well, I need ice cream."

He laughed. "Why didn't you say so? I'll tell Jesu, he'll bring you some."

"Not for me," she said, "it's for a woman in town. Friends asked me to look her up. Her name is Mrs. Amado. I met her yesterday. Do you know her?"

"Here we all know each other." Marco was puzzled. "I don't get the connection."

Elizabeth shifted in her chair. "I promised her ice cream."

"Indeed," he said, "we eat it together at least once a week."

Elizabeth laughed. "That's what I get for playing Lady Bountiful!"

"I bet you bought Pizarro's sword?"

"Almost." Elizabeth hid her face in her hands. She peered at Marco through her fingers. "Does she sell them by the dozen?"

He did not laugh. Leaning forward, he pulled her hands from her face. "It was the paintings you wanted to see. That's why you went there."

Elizabeth kept her voice level. "Yes," Elizabeth said. "I told you, I'd like to see them."

"She didn't show them, did she? She's not allowed to, she knows that. The house and everything in it belongs to her grandson. He's a merchant sailor; he left her in my care. Believe me, Elizabeth, she owns nothing of any value. Gauguin is an old story, that's all it is, a story. You, and others, will kill that old woman with your questions. There was someone, about a year ago——he broke into that house, frightened her almost to death."

Elizabeth wasn't listening. "Gauguin right here, top of your hill," she said, "painting that marvelous tree out there. Hard to believe, I agree. But possible, yes." She rose to her feet. "I think it's time I went home."

"If you insist," Marco said.

They walked out into an afternoon where sky and ocean blues were just beginning to shift to purple. Shadows sifted through the tall grass.

Elizabeth spread her arms, drew a deep breath. "It is lovely up here. The grass hums, doesn't it?" She was determined to make peace with this man who, obviously, knew more about those paintings than he would say.

"That tree above your house?" Elizabeth persisted, "What kind is it?"

"A Guayacan. It has dropped its leaves, and is ready to bloom— yellow gold for Easter." Marco tucked her hand in his arm.

"You talk like an artist, Elizabeth. Is that what you are?"

She shook her head. "I'd like to be that, but I'm not. I've got to earn a living." She hoped he wouldn't ask how.

"Yes," he said, "you've got to mess with the world out there. I'm the lucky one, I know that. Here is a bit of paradise. Careful now, this field has potholes."

Elizabeth chuckled. "Potholes in Paradise."

Suddenly something hot and heavy shoved between her legs, unbalancing her.

Marco cursed. "That damned cur—he haunts me lately."

Elizabeth glimpsed the black dog, a shadow circling. Marco found a stone and threw it, and the animal yelped and turned tail.

"Out of here, damn you!" Marco shouted.

"Whose dog is he?" Elizabeth asked. "He doesn't like me. I saw him wandering around the church."

"Nobody's animal," Marco said. "Lately he's adopted me."

The dog spooked Marco. No one he'd asked knew where it came from. Juana said it was a phantom. An omen, she said, a creature born of an evil wish. Marco respected Juana; she could see and feel things not even he was aware of. "That dog's starved," he'd told her.

"Evil is always hungry," she'd answered.

Now, dropping Elizabeth's arm, Marco brushed at the sweat stinging his eyes. This damned heat was getting to him. No relief from it. Other years, Easter so near, rain clouds were banked on the horizon. This year the bleached sky plunged straight into a paler sea.

The villagers wanted a miracle, and Marco had run out of miracles. I can't make rain! If he told them the truth, they would not believe him. Because he was their Devil Man. The power with which they invested him—sometimes it appalled him. One real disaster now, and he would be stripped bare, ordinary as the next man.

Marco frowned. It was that black dog gave him these ugly thoughts. He glanced at Elizabeth. "Forgive me if I wandered."

They had reached the path. It was shadowed now, and steeper than she remembered. "Why not make an easier way down?" she asked.

"I do not wish to invite the world up here."

"But people will come, Marco. You are a legend around here."

They sat down, their backs against a tree. "Full of questions, aren't you?" he asked.

"So are you," she said. "One thing I know, you're scared."

He picked up a stick, snapped it in two. "Aren't we all?"

She shrugged. "Maybe. But you, Marco, you're running."

He did not answer her immediately. Then he said, "Lately, I have wondered—can a man outrun the Devil?"

She stared at him. "You are serious, aren't you?"

He did not reply.

She hesitated, then she asked, "How do you know for sure you've got a soul?"

Her words hung between them, and he allowed them there, until he felt them drop wherever questions fall, unanswered, like stones to the bottom of a well.

Her shoulder rested near his own and, for a moment, she allowed herself to feel the real comfort his presence gave her. Or was it the quiet here lent her peace, the green above her head, the broad tree trunk supporting her?

"I think I like it here," she murmured.

He laid a finger on her lips. "Don't speak," he said. "Whatever is soul, ours touch now."

She straightened, slid beyond his reach. "Marco," she said, "that is an old line and I won't fall for it. Listen, this power you boast of—and you do boast—it's nothing out there in the real world. I bet that's what scares you?"

She saw his face darken and knew she pushed too hard.

"Where you come from, Elizabeth, they would not believe me. Which is why I live here."

"Marco, the world is such—even islands must be shared."

It was then he exploded. "This rotten dictatorship! Not long ago, a priest in the campo, one of those rare, real men of God—he was tortured, dropped from a helicopter." Marco lifted his face to the sunlight, and Elizabeth saw the glitter of tears in his eyes.

"Man's right is freedom to think and be what he wishes. It was that way here, once." His voice broke. "Not anymore.

"No choice now, Elizabeth. We are not allowed choice. The old gods have been put to death, we must kneel to soldiers. The icon of power is a gun. Oh, yes, Elizabeth, your world intrudes on me!"

"Marco," she appealed, her hands closing on his, "you cannot stand alone. If the General decides to move in, you don't have a chance. Stop pretending! Face up to what's real."

Marco was adamant. "That butcher sets himself above God and the Devil."

"You have met him?" Elizabeth asked.

Marco nodded. "He sent someone, a whore's son of a lieutenant, to inform me his General needs this island for a private airport. He wants a drug drop, I know that. Contraband is his business. I refused of course."

"What happened then?" Elizabeth was remembering her own interview with that man, her fear.

"That prick in gold braid laughed at me. Señor Brujo, he called me, and he spoke of reparation, but his General will use my island as he wishes."

Marco's voice was harsh. "I lifted him by his dirty neck, and gave him and his boys my Devil's curse—they, and their General too. I showed my Mark, and they turned tail. *Cobardes!*." Cowards.

"But they will come back, Marco. They won't forget."

"He wrote me an order. I'm to take my curse off him, he said, or he will have me arrested, placed in the mad house." Marco nodded. "He can do that."

Elizabeth nodded. "I've met your General. He's the kind does what he wants."

"I wrote him back. I said I'd leave my curse where it fell, between us. And I sent him the Devil's own offering—a woman, greedy as himself." Marco smiled, "Veronica made him forget my island."

"Veronica? Noel's wife?"

It was all coming together now: Noel's misery, his hatred of Marco.

"No wonder Noel despises you," she said. "You used his wife, then gave her away—a sort of bribe. That's horrible!"

"Noel is a pimp and a pusher," Marco retorted. "If his wife left him, that's his fault."

"Did she leave him for you, Marco? And you tired of her? You are your father's son!"

Marco caught her hands. "Listen to me. Veronica came to me of her own free will. She was looking for an out, she told me. I pointed the way to what she really wanted: high living, easy money. She chose her own path."

Elizabeth dropped her head in her hands. "Marco, I'm tired, I want to go home. We could sit here all night, arguing sex and souls. I'm not sure I want to do that."

He was on his feet, offering her a hand. She refused him. Marco leaned above her. "We'll get through this, we must!"

"Why must we? What is there to get through? No, Marco." She shook her head.

"But it is you confuse us, Elizabeth. Looking at me you see a dozen others who have failed you."

He grasped her hands. "I should tell you," he said, "love is forbidden me. Love makes a man careless. The moment my guard is down, the Devil will have me. So I have been taught."

She stared at him. "That is life, not love, Marco. Turn your back, and things happen."

He smiled. "There is the real Elizabeth. You are afraid."

"Not for a long time, I'm not."

"Afraid of love," Marco said. He spread his arms wide. "I dare you."

She would take his dare. Smiling, she linked her arms about his waist, entered his embrace. "There," she whispered, her head on his chest, hearing the thump of his heart, "I'm not afraid of you."

Lightly, he touched that shining hair. "I am afraid you are not real."

She smiled against his shoulder. "Of course I'm not. None of this is real, Marco. That's the fun of it, we can pretend. For as long as we like we can make this whatever we want it to be."

Her arms linked about him, she stayed where she was until her need of him threatened to burst inside her. She stepped backwards. "I'm going now, before this spoils."

He nodded. "You will return."

"No promises," Elizabeth said, walking away, knowing he stood there, watching her. He'd stand there forever, waiting, somehow she knew that. She turned. "Marco, don't!"

Don't wait for me, is what she meant. She was playing. Returning him some of his own medicine.

But there he stood, his eyes full of her.

"Flirt," she accused.

"Tonight," he said, "in the plaza."

*L*ater that afternoon, floating on her back, her body rocked in the blue hammock of the sea, Elizabeth smiled up at the sky.

Seductive, this great blueness, the constancy of its embrace.

Elizabeth rolled to her stomach. Opening her eyes under water, she saw minute fish, fluttering schools of them, just beneath her. She played, touching the sandy bottom with her fingers, stirring up small terrors in that undersea garden. After her swim, reluctant to leave, Elizabeth wandered the beach, turning over shells with her toes, bending to examine bottle fragments, smoky with age. She found a clay beer bottle, 1800s maybe. She wondered what other treasures lay buried in this sand. Marco had mentioned buried treasure.

Lifting her head, she saw the roof of his house. How did he fill his hours in this place where nobody seemed to have anything to do but watch and wait for something to happen? Here, imaginations worked overtime. A pink conch caught her eye and she dredged it from the sand. It had the rosy sheen of living flesh and she set it back in the sand, its lips turned to receive the rising tide.

Oblivious to everything but sand and sea, she had strayed far along the beach. Sunset now, the village lights coming on. A solitary light in Marco's house, and Elizabeth imagined Jesu laying the table and Marco sitting down to his solitary supper. Did they talk much together, the old religious man and the Devil Man? What a pair, and Elizabeth smiled, what an incongruous pair! She remembered she was to meet Marco later in the plaza. If she wanted to, he had said. She did want to. They must talk. The Gauguins of course.

Turning back to her house, Elizabeth did not hear the soft sucking plod of footsteps behind her. Loco was trailing her, stumbling like an old man with too much whiskey in him. He was near his Lady; he yearned to touch her.

"*Señ-o-rah?*" he burbled. "*Señ-o-rah?*"

Elizabeth wheeled, saw him, froze where she stood and Loco tumbled. They collided, head on. He clutched at her, his nails raking her thighs. She screamed. He reached, his calloused hands grasping at her. His smell was graveyard and fish.

"*Señ-o-rah* . . ."

"Get out!" Her scream tore from her throat. She raised the clay bottle and brought it down, missing Loco's head but scraping his cheek, bruising his shoulder.

"Ugh!" He scrambled up the beach, fled into the bushes.

Shaking with terror, Elizabeth collapsed where she stood. Her thigh had a long bloody gash and she touched it, and stared at the blood then, on her fingers. It stained the sand under her.

Something moved behind her, and Elizabeth turned to see the black dog squatting near. She dared not move. The dog and she sat looking at each other. He came no closer, but she knew he smelled her fear. Low in his throat, he growled. Elizabeth clutched the clay bottle and threw it hard. Her aim was bad, but the dog wheeled, and was gone.

The sun was low on the horizon. Elizabeth limped up the beach, reached her back door steps and climbed slowly. Stepping inside her house, she slammed the door shut, and locked it. Seeking a safe corner, she waited, wide eyed, her back to the wall. That humped shadow there, or there—near the bedroom door. She moved then, on tiptoe, turning on lights. Stripping off her wet suit, leaving it where it fell, she showered, rinsing her body clean, again and again.

Wrapped tightly in a robe, she went into the kitchen and made coffee. The kitchen window was open and she peered from it, her ears straining for a sound beyond those of the rising tide, the clatter of village radios. She heard the cry of a girl child, a shout of anger. She heard a slap, and a small cry. The kitchen curtain trembled. In the sink a dish rattled.

Alone at the table, Elizabeth lowered her head into her hands. Loco's image insisted. The stink of him clung to her and she retched. She went into her bedroom to search the drawers for her sleeping pills. Back in the kitchen, she found orange juice in the frig and swallowed two tablets. She went to bed, leaving all her lights burning.

*M*arco's loud knock wakened her.

She woke to his shout. "Elizabeth, what happened?"

She heard him enter the house and move from room to room, turning off lights. Stumbling from bed, she joined him in the kitchen. "What time is it?" Her mouth was cotton wool, her hair sticky on her shoulders.

"I waited for you," Marco said. "In the plaza, remember?"

She nodded. "I've been asleep. Something's happened."

He poured her a glass of water and she drank it all. "Thanks." She remembered her loose robe and started up, spreading her hands over her breasts. "I must look a fright."

He smiled. "How can you not know how lovely you are?"

She huddled in her chair. "Marco, I was attacked. Right on the beach. Something—it grabbed me, it had long nails that scratched, and one awful tooth. I hurt him, I hit him on the head with an old bottle I found. There was blood everywhere. He ran into the bushes. And that black dog—oh, Marco, it was awful! I can't stand blood, hands grabbing..."

"One tooth?" Marco chuckled. "It must have been Loco. But he never hurt anyone. I've seen him weep over a dead fly."

"Loco? Yes, The crazy one. It was him. Rape, Marco, that's what he wanted. How can you permit such a creature to wander about? He could have hurt me, he wanted to..."

"He means no harm, Elizabeth. I bet you scared him. You say you hit him with a bottle? I'd like to have seen that. Loco has the mind of a child. He's part of this village. We love him."

"Then you're all crazy as he is," Elizabeth said. "He's always hanging around here. I don't need this, Marco."

Because he sat placid, amused—not jumping to her rescue, Elizabeth was angry. "Yes, I've had enough, I'm out of here tomorrow!" She wanted to shake him. "Listen to me, Marco. It's too weird here. The people stare at me, they don't like me. Noel sneaks around like some third-rate movie character. And those stoned kids, I don't trust them either. Flore—I don't know why you employ her, she's so damn jealous..."

"And you now, Marco"—she was on her feet, looking down at him. "I was almost raped, and you think it's funny!"

She was flinging words at him, wanting to move him to some kind of action. "Yes, you, Marco, you sit there telling me how wonderful your Loco is, how much you love him. Well, before I leave here, I'm going to have that old man taken care of. He lives hand to mouth, nobody to watch him. He's pitiful, and dangerous."

Marco grabbed her flailing hands. "Don't mess with things you know nothing about, Elizabeth. Touch Loco, and you hurt all of us."

"You mean I hurt you, don't you, Devil Man?" Her head ached. "It is picturesque, isn't it? Having that old loony on your island? You and your ridiculous Stone, him and his Virgin. And your so-called care-taker—*Pass the lemon, please, Jesus!* It all fits your picture, doesn't it, Marco? You won't hear the truth!"

He answered her quietly. "It is not we who frighten you, Elizabeth, you do this to yourself."

She sniffed, needing to blow her nose. He pulled a handkerchief from his pocket, and gave it to her.

"I am scared," she admitted, dabbing at her eyes, sitting down again. "And that's not me. I've been a lot of places, Marco, met all kinds of people—some of them really off the wall. But I've never had lunch with a Devil Man, I've never been almost raped."

He did not smile. "Don't exaggerate, Elizabeth, Loco didn't hurt you. You are not a child. I know he frightened you, but he's harmless. No one will hurt you here. If people stare, it's because you're a stranger. And a beautiful one at that. Life is not all dirty old men, Elizabeth. Here, on this island, we grew up together, grew up liking each other."

She couldn't help herself: she was weeping. "Please understand," she appealed, "it's been some kind of peculiar day!"

Yes, he thought, a day in which he had thought only of her. He sat back in his chair, spread his arms to her. "Too much distance between us. Come closer. If you're leaving soon?"

"But I've something to do here," Elizabeth protested. "It's what I came for."

She was wanting, suddenly, to touch his dark hair. She was forgiving him now, she didn't know for what—just forgiving. Damn this confusing man!

"What you came for," Marco said. "I won't ask you what that is. If I can help..."

She avoided his reach. "I'll fix some hot coffee."

Because he must stay, she did not want to be alone, not now, spooks in her head, things not even Marco could imagine. She moved to the stove. "Yes, coffee," she said.

He spoke bluntly then, startling her. "Put something on, can't you?" Because her flanks were under his nose; her scent teased him. "Damn it, woman—don't you know better than to sit ass naked with the Devil Man?"

She wheeled on him. "I'm not ass naked as you so politely put it. If you can't control yourself, you'd better go. I am only asking for a little friendly company."

"A little friendly company?" he repeated. "Don't you know what you do to me, Elizabeth?"

She stared at him. "What do I do to you, Marco?"

Wanting the feel of him then she allowed her fingers to rest on his shoulders. "A little friendly company, yes," she whispered. She dropped her cheek to his hair. "What happens next?"

"We learn about loving," he said. He was on his feet, holding her against him.

"Not love," she whispered, "not that, Marco."

She pulled his hands to cover her breasts. "I like you," she said carefully. "That's all I can give you."

Her mouth melted to his. "Dangerous," she whispered.

"Don't talk," she told him, knowing only that she wanted him. Her fingers worked the buttons on his shirt. She slid her hands inside, spread them wide on his bare chest.

Sinking back into the chair behind him, Marco pulled Elizabeth to his lap. Burying his face in the silk of her robe, he pushed it from her shoulders. Gently he lifted her breasts to his lips and, hearing her sharp intake of breath, mistook it for submission.

"Come to bed," he said.

She stiffened, pulled her robe tight around her. "No!" She slid from his embrace, holding herself sternly beyond his reach. She wanted his mouth on hers again.

"No," she denied herself. "It's too much, too soon. Marco, you are stepping on my shadow."

He frowned, not understanding. She smiled faintly, "Just words I use when I feel invaded."

He nodded. "I can wait. Years I've been looking for you."

He took her hands, opened them and kissed her palms. "Your choice of words—invasion? You give your secrets away, *querida*."

He held her close a moment, breathed deep of her essence. "Now, you will sleep. I will see you tomorrow."

"No coffee then?" She poured the hot brew down the sink. She pulled the kitchen window closed. "So dark out there. That creature, where is he?"

"He won't bother you again, I'll see to that," Marco promised.

Elizabeth's paleness concerned him, and the coldness of her hands. "If you like, I'll stay until you are asleep."

She kissed him quickly. "Just be sure you lock my door."

Sleep came easily. She knew exactly what she must do in the morning.

*T*he police station was one cement block room with a scarred desk and a chair in which one lanky **guardia** sprawled, perusing tattered comics.

Gaping at Elizabeth, he beckoned her with his head and shambled to his black-booted feet. His pistol belt dangled, its weapon appearing to unbalance him. He shifted his wad of gum from one cheek to another. "*Si, señora?*"

Elizabeth addressed him in Spanish, telling him who she was: an American, a woman alone, here on business. He did not appear impressed. "*Que pasa?*" What's happening? He was almost insolent.

Speaking slowly and carefully then, Elizabeth described Loco's attack on her. Yesterday, on the beach, a man had hurt her, she said, she had been made ill by the episode. Something must be done to protect herself and others.

Eyeing her appreciatively, the soldier appeared to pay little heed to her words. He offered her the one chair, and eased himself down to slouch on the corner of the desk. He pulled a ragged notebook from his pocket. "Repeat, please," he said, in bad English.

Retelling her story then, Elizabeth was immediately tired of it. And guiltily aware of her small falsehoods. She was remembering Marco, what he had said about Loco.

"But the old man is mad!" she insisted, loudly, startling the policeman. "He's been following me since I arrived. And then, to put his hands on me. He is dangerous, I tell you!"

"Not that old one," the soldier said. Eyeing Elizabeth's slim blue-jeaned legs, he grinned, thinking that her story was not impossible.

Even old Loco could get fleas in his pants with *una rubia coma esta*—a blonde like this one.

"*Señor Guardia*," Elizabeth leaned forward, deliberately widening her eyes. "I appeal to you. Your General, he told me, if I needed help..."

Ah? She knew *El General?* The soldier squared his narrow shoulders. Yes, an order had come in, he remembered it now—all respect must be given this gringa. He reached for the telephone. He dialed the city office and, miraculously, got through. The bark at the other end of the line startled him into an explosive recital of what he thought had happened. The gringa's blue eyes on him now, his words sketched a crime that, knowing Loco as he did, could not have occurred. But it was a hot day, he was bored. Now, suddenly, he was a hero.

Listening to him, Elizabeth knew he dressed up her complaint considerably. After all, she had not been raped. But, yes—that could have happened. If not to her, to another, Elizabeth reasoned, that old crazy should not be allowed to wander about.

The *guardia* rattled on. The satisfied expression on his face told Elizabeth that he had the attention of those on the other end of the line. Whatever story he was enjoying, Elizabeth began to wish she had not been so hasty. Marco was not going to like this.

The soldier hung up. "Help is on the way." He appeared enormously pleased with himself.

"American *soldados* coming too," he told Elizabeth. He waved his arms. "Helicopters!"

"Helicopters? American soldiers? Why?" Then she remembered, too late now, what Noel had told her: call a policeman, you get a battalion.

"You, American lady, *amiga del General*," the soldier said.

Elizabeth watched the soldier remove his gun belt. He slid the pistol from its holster, polished it with a dirty rag and checked its ammunition. He opened a drawer and took out a heavy pair of handcuffs.

"Para el loco," he growled—for the crazy man. He dropped the apparatus on the table with a clatter that made Elizabeth jump.

"I want to explain," she began, but knew it was too late. She had set forces in motion that could not be halted. Marco, she thought, he should be told. "Do you know Señor Rodriguez?" she asked.

The soldier's face blanched. El Brujo? Was the Devil Man in on this? Perhaps he, too, had molested this lady? Ah! There was a man the General wanted!

Elizabeth heard a chopping sound. It was faint at first, over the bay, then loud above the village. Deafening then. The noise would bring the whole village out. They would land on the beach, the soldier said, that she must come with him now. He hefted the handcuffs, ushered Elizabeth outside, and around the corner to an empty lot. There was a view down the hill from there, and Elizabeth watched two helicopters land on the beach.

Cocks crowed. Sand spun in clouds, stinging the eyes of all who rushed to see what was happening. Elizabeth saw Loco first at the scene. He was dancing, clapping his hands, his mouth a wondering O.

Soldiers spewed from the helicopter doors. Some of them were Americans, and Elizabeth shrank back, seeing a young lieutenant detach himself from the crowd and climb the hill towards her. She would have turned away if the policeman with her had not detained her with a strong hand.

"Mornin', ma'am." The American officer was freckled, sunburned, his drawl Midwestern. "You havin' trouble, ma'am?"

"They didn't have to call out the entire army," Elizabeth said, but she smiled because his sunburn, his crew cut, were as familiar as home.

"Not the whole army, ma'am." He tipped Elizabeth a salute. "The name's Hank."

"Hank," she said. "They didn't have to send helicopters just because...because."

"You mean you want to change your mind, drop the charges? Now, ma'am?" He was obviously disappointed, somewhat disapproving.

She felt rebuked. "Yes," she stammered. " I mean, no..." She covered her face with her hands. "I don't know what I mean anymore..."

She drew a deep breath. "Look, Hank, this old man—he is crazy, nobody pays any attention to him, he sleeps in the graveyard, can you believe that? He has been following me. Yesterday he grabbed me. Scared me half to death. And I'm still scared. I have work here and I can't do it with that looney trailing me."

Hank wrote busily. "All we need, ma'am." He snapped his book shut, put it in his pocket. "That's your word on it now. We'll put the old coot where he belongs." He looked closely at Elizabeth. "You here by yourself, ma'am?"

She nodded. "And they will blame me," she said, pointing at the villagers who had turned from the helicopters to stare at her. "They don't like me," she said.

"Us," the lieutenant corrected her. "They don't like us Yankees." He stepped nearer, spoke in a low voice. "It's a queer country, ma'am. You've to watch your step. If you need anyone—well, I'm Liaison."

"Liaison? Thanks," she said, lamely.

He hesitated, then he said, "Truth to tell, ma'am, we've got our eyes on this here island. The General keeps trying to pin something on this guy, Rodriguez. Do you know him? He's said to be a witch. All I know is he's got one hell of a temper. He beat up the General's aide, I'm told. As I understand it, Rodriguez is the trouble maker—this government and all.

"We're in this country to protect the status quo, whatever that is. Most of the time it's the General's orders carry the day. His real business is drugs, arms too. I figure this Rodriguez is moving in on his territory, maybe. This whole country now, it beats me!"

"I don't know Rodriguez," Elizabeth lied. "Tell me, the old man now? He'll be taken care of?"

Hank shrugged. "We just hand 'em over. I hope he didn't hurt you, ma'am?"

"No," Elizabeth said, truthfully, "but that was one scary scene." She was watching Loco, the soldiers closing in on him. She saw him lifted into the waiting helicopter. Before the door closed, he turned and waved, pleased as a child off on a journey.

A fisherman shouted a protest. The crowd surged forward. Propellers churned, and the sand whirled, pushing the onlookers backwards.

"Where will they take him?" Elizabeth asked.

"Probably the nut house, where he belongs," Hank told her. "You're not to worry, ma'am. I'll just go and phone this in from the station here." He saluted her.

"I'll go with you," she said. Because the villagers were pointing at her. A man, his fists raised, ran towards her.

"Take me as far as my street," Elizabeth said. "They will blame me for this."

"Americans are always to blame," Hank said. "We want to clean things up, next thing you know they're shooting at us."

He walked close beside her, hurrying her along the street. He left her in front of her house. "Want me to come in?"

"Thanks, but I'm okay now," she said.

"Anytime, ma'am." Again he saluted.

*M*arco had let himself in, he was waiting for her.
"I watched the whole miserable business from my house, through my binoculars," he said. He had stood there with Flore who had run up the hill to tell him what was happening.

Elizabeth saw his face tight with anger. "So you watched it?" she demanded. "You stood up there like some sort of god?"

He was pacing the room. "Armed soldiers here, Elizabeth. What do you want? That I fight the whole god damn army? Two armies! Your country's, and mine!"

"But you've got the power," she taunted. "It's you who pull the strings here, Witch Man!"

"You are wrong, Elizabeth." His voice was cold. "I mind my own business. It is you set this thing in motion."

"And you decided to let it happen. Why couldn't you spread your big black wings, play Batman maybe?" Elizabeth laughed. "Village savior, isn't that you? Marco, tell the truth now. You wouldn't do anything because you were scared. You saw the police helicopters and you thought they were coming for you."

For a moment he had thought so, yes. And he had felt powerless, watching them take Loco away. Even Flore had stared accusingly.

Marco thought of Loco, and the horror of the government mental asylum. Elizabeth might as well have killed the old man. "Why did you do this?" he demanded.

"Because I can't live like this, Marco! That old man. He needs to be taken care of."

"We all cared for him. Where he's going now—I've seen that holding cage!"

MARCO'S GIFT

"Anything's better than a bed in the graveyard," Elizabeth retorted. "At least he'll be properly fed. And he won't attack anyone. You
shouldn't permit this kind of thing, Marco. Crazies running around—
there isn't a tourist will set foot on this island!"

"One innocent old man," Marco said. "You have sent him straight
to hell."

"It wasn't much fun for me, Marco, you forget that."

She turned from him, went to the window. Sullen faces stared
from the street. "Look, Marco, they're right outside!. Did you lock
the door?"

"They are angry, Elizabeth. You have stolen someone they love."

"But you refuse to understand! That man hurt me!"

"Loco has lived here, beloved by all, since before most of us can
remember."

Elizabeth heard a shout. Someone banged on the door. She stared
at Marco. "If they get in here?"

He was unrelenting. "You will have to explain."

"Marco, you could have stopped this from happening!"

He shook his head. "If I had tried to stop the soldiers…"

"They would have taken you too," Elizabeth flared, "that's what you
think. Well, that's ridiculous. People just don't get picked up, spirited
away for no reason at all."

"In this country that happens," Marco said. "If I had intervened,
I'd be in that helicopter with Loco now. On my way to prison, or the
asylum."

"So?" Elizabeth was triumphant. "You admit you have no power?"

Marco was moving towards the door. "My people, they will not
understand. Somehow I must explain."

The shouts outside were louder. Elizabeth pulled the curtains shut.
Someone threw a tin can, it rattled against the door.

"They hate me," she said. "Stay with me, Marco."

"Only because you are frightened?"

"Yes...no..." She reached for him. "It's not just Loco," she admitted.

"But why, querida?" The endearment slid easily from his lips.

A fist banged the door. Elizabeth clung to Marco. "Send them away, please!"

"Stay here." Marco went outside. Standing on the steps, he told those waiting not to bother the American *doña*. They must leave her alone, he said, if anyone hurt her, spoke ill of her, he would punish that person. None of this was her fault, he said.

His orders, Marco said, his voice harsh, foreign to his ears. He sensed the crowd's astonishment. He had never threatened them. Now, he, their own Devil Man, was defending a gringa! He knew each of them by name. Not a few had known his father. Not a one in the village had ever suffered the Devil Man's curse.

"Go home," Marco said. It was clearly an order.

So be it. They bowed their heads, ashamed of their fear of him, ashamed too, of this new Marco.

Watching their faces, he read their confusion. "Get out!" he shouted, knowing he threw away a little of their love now, some of their trust. Like trashing pieces of himself. He knew they saw a different man. He had given them reason to fear him.

He saw Elizabeth's pale face, watchful in the window. For a moment, he hated her. Retrieving a tin can from the top step, he tossed it over the heads of the astonished crowd. "Why don't you clean up this damned place?" he shouted

Shaking their heads, the people backed off.

"Cobardes!" Marco shouted. Cowards. The word stuck in his throat.

He returned to the house. "They've gone," he said, flatly.

Elizabeth's smile was radiant. "I couldn't hear what you said, but I saw their faces. They are scared of you, Marco."

"I don't like myself, either," he said. He knew he would not forget this day.

"I forgive you." She was soft, smiling.

"But will Loco forgive us?" Marco asked.

Ignoring his question, she fetched a wet towel from the bathroom and bathed his hands and face. "There," she said.

He did not respond and she had the feeling he did not see her.

His eyes stared through her, searching out his own misery.

She reached behind her head and unpinned her braid. She shook out her hair. "Look at me, please..."

She took hold of his arm and wound her hair around it, bandaging his scar. "Now," she teased, "you belong to me."

"Yes, I am yours," he said. He did not smile.

He loosed himself and, cupping her face in his hands, he said, "If you are mine, pray God keep your soul, Elizabeth."

She laughed softly. "But I haven't a soul to keep. Perhaps I can share yours, my darling?"

*T*he noon sun blazed, grasping sea and sky in its hot fist. The villagers drew their curtains and slept. Juana shuttered her store and spread herself in her hammock. Old and young, they came to her, placing the threads of this new story in her hands. She would weave a new fantasy from the old. Their choosing. She waited to see which way the wind blew.

It was the Devil, so they had decided, not Marco, who had defended the gringa. It was not Marco who had refused to help Loco; Marco was Loco's friend. It was the Devil, they said. It was the Devil had Marco's tongue now.

"Marco is bewitched," Flore said. "He is blind and deaf to all but the gringa. Marco is not the man he was!"

"He is more of a man," Juana said. "The Devil Man is in love."

"More fool, he!" Flore said. "This is the gringa's fault. No soul of her own, she has stolen Marco's."

Yes, the gringa held Marco in the palm of her hand. He paid little attention to anyone else. Easter was approaching and the church must be cleaned. It was Marco who unlocked the doors, organized the processions. It was he who provided the rum, the music for dancing. Marco loved Easter. This year, or so it appeared, he had forgotten it.

And not a sign of rain! It was the Devil who prolonged this drought. It was possible, yes—and here the story ballooned, large enough to tingle everyone's skins—yes, the gringa was another of the Devil's disguises!

And something else. Flore said it first. The gringa had made the Devil Man impotent. Flore spun that tale. Marco had turned her down flat. She had tried but she couldn't get a rise out of him.

Juana would not cooperate. "Just because he can't do it with you," she said.

Flore hung her head, picked at a callous on her dusty heel. "Nothing I didn't do," she muttered, "all he taught me, I tried to please him. He stayed small as a sardine. Yes, the gringa has stolen his manhood.

"He can't do it anymore," Flore said. "He told me so."

Juana chuckled. Marco wasn't impotent. Stone or no Stone, that man was a stallion. "He's tired of you," Juana said bluntly.

"You've no magic to help?" Flore asked.

"You can't put love in a bottle, and love is what he needs. He's run after it all his life." Yes, Juana had seen it in his eyes, that bleak look some men have, women crawling over them but never the right one.

"I love him," Flore said.

Juana hawked loudly, spit at the girl's bare feet.

"But I do," Flore said. "He'll be done with her soon."

"No." Juana shook her head. "They've a long way to go, those two, before they're done." She shot Flore a shrewd look. "I've medicine to take the child if you don't want it."

Flore clutched at her stomach. "It's his son I carry!"

"He won't live to see the creature," Juana muttered. Her words startled her, striking her dumb. She pretended a yawn, and covered her mouth,

"Is Marco ill then?" Flore asked.

Juana paid the question no heed. She was reaching for truth. "The Devil's shadow, it eats at his heels."

"I will wait," Flore said.

Juana nodded. "Always an ending." She was tired. This girl was a mosquito. She turned in her hammock, and was soon snoring.

Against the dry persistent wind, spiders spun webs, the frail jasmine shed its petals.

Past noon, and Elizabeth opened her eyes. The sheet was tangled under her; her hair was moist against her cheek. Propped on an elbow, she looked down at Marco beside her and saw his skin like copper, cool and smooth. She moved to rest her head on his chest, breathed with him then, hearing her heart beat to his rhythm.

He opened an eye. "Hello." He slid his hand across her belly.

What time was it? she wondered. Since last night, they'd made love, over and over. "Go back to sleep," she told him, wanting to curl in the nest of his body forever.

There is no forever.

He will not stay .

"Let's do something," she said, "go somewhere different."

He pulled her tight against him. "I've been somewhere. Places I've never been before." He kissed her. "Do you always run away, Elizabeth?"

"What time is it, I wonder."

Marco smiled. "Meaning you would like me to leave?"

"Yes, maybe...there are things I must do." She put her arms around him. "No, don't go, not yet."

She touched his lips with her fingers. "Have you forgiven me?"

"Forgiven you?" he was puzzled. Then he remembered. "You mean Loco? Well, that can't be undone, can it?"

He caught her hand. "With you, I forget who I am."

"Me, too," she admitted.

The auburn of his skin intrigued her. She was wanting him again, and knew her need must show in her face. She ducked her head, and sat away from him, her legs out straight like a child's. He ran his hands over her ankles, across her knees, past her thighs. She shivered. "Don't, Marco!"

His fingers were between her legs. He withdrew his hand, put it to her mouth. "Taste our love," he said. "It is our feast. We cannot leave each other now."

"But we will," she said.

"Not yet, *querida*." His lips were on hers. She fell backwards, holding to him. "Slowly, slowly," he said, "we've got all time, all there is…"

Mi estrella, mi paloma…My dove, my star…

His words, his language, and Marco exulted. He had never used such patience, professed such tenderness. Not his Devil, it was Marco himself loved now…

Later, he told her, "I will never hurt you."

She smiled. "Men—they promise the world!"

Her fingers tight in his hair, she dared him: "Marco, come away with me!"

"To Boston?" He sat back against the pillows. "No, *mi amor,* you will stay here with me."

"You forget, I'm a working girl."

"Yes. Tell me."

"It's complicated," she hedged. "Let's just say I'm very good at what I do. Call it finding paradise for others." Not such a lie, she told herself, some said the painting they wanted reflected paradise.

"Paradise," Marco said. "We have found ours, Elizabeth."

She shook her head. "But it won't last forever, Paradise is not supposed to. One day it's over, finished. Bang! The End."

Marco shook his head. "There can be no end to love." He took her hands in his that she listen. "What we learn from love, we keep. It becomes part of us."

"Tears, yes," Elizabeth said. "Maybe even death."

"Promise me something," Marco asked.

"Please," she answered. "I don't believe in promises."

"Don't make one you can't keep," Marco said. His face close above hers, he said, "It is you now has care of my soul. That is love, Elizabeth." His words cut through him, chilling as ice water.

With a nervous laugh, she protested, "Just you is all I want."

Slowly, she ran her hands the length of his torso. "You please me," she said. She leaned to lick the salt sweat on his chest. Where her lips touched him, her mouth smarted.

*T*he hours passed and the tide turned, Marco felt its tension and release within himself. Contentment filled him. There was only Elizabeth, the sun through her hair, the astonished blue of her eyes.

"Stay," he whispered, "stay…"

There was someone at the front door. "Don't answer it," Marco said. Elizabeth pulled on her robe. "Who is it?" she called.

"Me," It was Dierdre's voice.

Reluctantly Elizabeth opened the door. "Yes?"

"Lady Liz, you've been locked up here by yourself too long." Dierdre insinuated herself inside.

"I'm not by myself," Elizabeth said. "Marco is here."

"Oh?" Dierdre's laughter rippled. "I knew you two had something going. Eric said it—he felt sparks. Lady,"—her eyes were teasing, appraising—"is he a devil, is he…well, you know…?"

"I hardly think…" Elizabeth began.

"But we've got an expedition planned," Dierdre said. "Eric and me, we want to visit the caves. They're the other side of the island—we've heard there's pirate treasure there. Come with us. Marco, too."

Elizabeth hesitated. "I don't know, I've things to do…"

She was drained. Needing a cool swim. Caves? Buried treasure? The Gauguins would not walk away, there was always tomorrow.

"Spanish treasure?" she asked. "You promise?"

"Can't promise," Dierdre said. She touched Elizabeth's arm. "Who gave you that smile, lady? You're different. You could be, I knew that. The right kind of magic…" And Dierdre giggled. "We'll meet on the beach, front of the hotel."

Marco refused the invitation. "Those caves are full of bats, nothing there, Elizabeth. I don't want you to go."

He had been about to invite her for a swim in his waterfall. It was his sanctuary, deep in the jungle. He had never taken a woman there. "Come with me, by ourselves," he urged.

Elizabeth shook her head. "But we've had enough of each other now. We'll wear it out, whatever this is." She was wanting him again. If she stayed another moment, she'd be lost. "I'm going," she said.

She went into the bathroom and showered, and emerged, in a cloud of lavender mist, a towel wrapped around her.

Marco regarded her from the bed. "I can make you stay," he threatened.

"How?"

He grabbed her, pulled her down beside him. His mouth everywhere on her. She tasted herself on his lips. "Yes, oh yes," she whispered. Because she felt all powerful. She rolled on top of him. Her hands on his shoulders, she said, "But I haven't got time for this."

Marco smiled, and freed himself from under her weight. "So? We will not make love."

Her eyes darkened. "I knew it," she said. "You don't want me."

Quickly, he cradled her again, spoke gently. "Who hurt you, Elizabeth? There's a shadow on you, dark as my own."

"Shadows?" she asked. "I don't permit them, Marco."

"But yours insist."

"What is this? True confessions? I told you I haven't time." She slid from the bed. "I hate a sloppy aftermath. Let's just enjoy—okay?"

"Okay." He was gone from her. She heard him whistling in the shower and the sound annoyed her. He was letting her go, as if all this meant nothing.

She pulled on yesterday's jeans and a long-sleeved shirt. When he came out, she was brushing her hair in front of the mirror. Standing close behind her, he slid his hands under her shirt, cupping her breasts. "Look at us," he said. "Look at you!"

She was on fire, she felt so. Her hair sparked, her cheeks flamed. She was pleased with this new image of herself. Marco's darkness of skin accented the whiteness of her own. She reached a hand to touch his reflection. "Who are you?" she asked.

"I am your love," he answered, touching her lips with his fingers, in the glass.

The knowledge came to her that she would not, ever again, see herself without him there behind her. "Tonight?" she breathed.

He smiled. "You have only to ask."

He kissed the top of her head. "Take care, querida—those caves, they are used now for all the wrong purposes. If you need me, speak my name."

She could not resist. "How convenient, this power of yours."

"It's gotta rain soon," Dierdre said. "They say Easter brings the first storm."

Elizabeth, holding herself stiffly in the center of the dinghy, saw the scruffy dryness of the island's coast. She was missing Marco already; he had told her not to do this.

"It's people energy makes it rain," Eric said, rowing vigorously. "We just haven't built up enough of whatever we need yet. But it's coming. Heavy, I can feel it. Marco told me, that sky's gonna pour down!"

"Is that what you want, Eric?" Elizabeth asked. "A magic to make rain?"

"Marco's no medicine man, lady. If it rains, it rains." Eric was not feeling himself, a gathering of pain in him, dull but sharpening now. Damn! Nam was only a memory, but it had left its poison in him. He looked at Elizabeth. "Why are you always putting Marco down?"

"To protect herself," Dierdre said. She was lolling in the bow, trailing her fingers in the water. "You know what that fortune teller in the village told me? She says Elizabeth has blue eyes, which means she doesn't have a soul."

"She put that old man away. Not nice," Eric said.

"But he attacked me," Elizabeth said.

Eric hooted. "Don't tell me it was rape—not that old goat!"

"He needs care," Elizabeth said, "He slept in an empty grave—that's what's cruel."

"He liked his bed," Dierdre said. "We followed him there one night, Eric and me. He tucked himself in like a baby, said his prayers to the moon. Everyone loved Loco, I know they did."

The dinghy was moving around the point now and, looking up, Elizabeth could just see the roof of Marco's house. "Let's go back and get Marco."

Eric shook his head. "The tide's changing. There's no time."

"So now you miss him," Dierdre teased.

Elizabeth changed the subject. "Tell me about the caves."

"Pirates here once," Eric said. "They say there's treasure hidden somewhere. Look," he pointed. "We'll beach the dinghy there."

Elizabeth saw three steep cave entrances between the rocks that fringed the small beach. At high water, she knew the caves would be submerged. "The tide's coming in fast," she warned. This was the windward side of the island, cold and blowy.

Eric jumped ashore, set the anchor firmly. "I've got a flashlight," he said. "Let's try that big one first." He led the way towards the largest cave. It was rough going. Elizabeth lost her footing and would have fallen if Dierdre had not caught her.

Suddenly Eric doubled over. "Christ damn!" He sat down, his head buried in his arms. Dierdre knelt beside him. "You hurting again?" Eric nodded. His face was beaded with sweat.

"What is it? What's wrong?" Elizabeth asked.

"He was in Nam, river patrol," Dierdre said. "He picked up a poison—one of those killer chemicals they used." She was stroking Eric's hair.

"We'd better go back," Elizabeth said.

Eric shook his head. "Not if Dierdre's got what I need." His lips were white, but he managed a grin. "My kind of magic, huh?"

Dierdre was rolling a joint. Elizabeth was dismayed. "But Eric's sick, we can't stay here..." She meant it was foolish to get stoned. She hated it; marijuana was a band aid at best—it certainly wasn't healing. "The tide," she said, "we'll be trapped. You can't just sit here and smoke grass, Eric!"

"He's hurting," Dierdre said, and she lit the reefer, drew on it, and passed it to Eric. "Slow now," she crooned. "You'll feel better soon." Kneeling behind Eric, she massaged his shoulders.

Elizabeth looked from Eric to the beached dinghy. "Please, let's go."

"Let him be, he'll be okay." Dierdre stripped off her shirt, wadded it into a pillow. Eric lay flat. He inhaled, held the smoke in him, then exhaled slowly.

"Where do you get that stuff?" Elizabeth asked. "It's illegal, isn't it?"

"You going to turn us in too, like Loco?" Dierdre's voice was sharp. "Listen, lady, I'd go to the moon for this if I had to. It's the only thing gets Eric by." Gently, she stroked his eyes closed. "Yeah," she said, "grass works. And it's easy to come by."

"Where?" Elizabeth asked.

"Noel, who else? He's into all kinds of stuff. Whatever I need, Noel's got it."

"Noel?" But Elizabeth was not really surprised. The man was sleazy enough to be dealing anything and everything. "He is exploiting you," she said.

Dierdre looked blank. "Whatever you call it, lady. What I do is get Eric what he needs. Hey, you waste a lot of energy worrying about what's right for others. What about yourself?"

Eric was alert. "I'm better now. I need to take a pee. Be right back."

Elizabeth waited until he was out of sight, then she said, "But you have to pay Noel?"

Dierdre shrugged. "Someday, sure. He writes it down, what I owe him." She picked up her shirt and shook the sand out of it, and pulled it over her head. "I know what Noel really wants," and she waggled her tongue at Elizabeth, "but we'll be gone long before he tries to collect."

"Noel's no good," Elizabeth said. "He'll hurt you, Dierdre." She knew these kids had no money—like Marco said, they just floated around the world.

Dierdre shrugged. "I'm used to his kind. Lots of these dealers—well, I never tell Eric the way it is—he'd kill me, or them."

"You mean, you...?" Elizabeth was dismayed.

"Never—not me!" Dierdre said. "Noel's a spook though, he scares me. He's got like something rotten in him—even his sweat stinks!"

Suddenly Dierdre was crying. "I'm scared, lady! Eric's my life, and he's sick a lot of the time. I kid about Noel, but the old goat's after me for real. We haven't a dime, you know, not to buy dope anyway."

"Go home," Elizabeth said. "Leave Eric, Dierdre, and take care of yourself. Listen," and she leaned towards the girl, "you say I hurt people? What do you think Eric's doing to you?"

"Yeah...but I love him, and that's different. I can't leave him. Haven't you ever been in love? What kind of woman are you—telling me to leave my guy?"

Elizabeth shrugged. "Have it your way. But it's no good, Dierdre." Seeing Eric coming towards them, she put a finger to her lips. Quickly, Dierdre mopped her eyes with her shirt. "Don't tell him what I said, promise?"

Elizabeth started towards the cave entrance. "We'd better hurry if we're going to explore."

They peered into the cave. Blackness; a stink of mold and bat droppings. Dierdre wrinkled her nose. "Should we?" she asked. Eric giggled and gave her a push. She stepped inside. He followed, and Elizabeth squeezed in after them. It was dark, wet, the air was difficult to breathe.

"I can't see a thing," Elizabeth complained.

Eric switched on his flashlight. The beam wavered on the rock walls, and up toward the high ceiling. Elizabeth felt the suck of the sand beneath her feet and she walked gingerly. Slowly her eyes adjusted to the dimness, and she saw the shapes of old barrels, the curve of a rusted anchor. Something about this place—like it was not uninhabited. She wished for Marco.

Eric shouted. "Stuff stashed here!" He beckoned with his light.

Dierdre and Elizabeth joined him. They saw several wooden crates wrapped in waterproof covers, tied with wire.

"Contraband, for sure," Dierdre whispered. "I bet it's Colombian coke."

"What the hell!" The shout. An explosion.

Elizabeth ducked, blinded by the sudden flash. Dierdre shrieked. Eric's light wavered. "I'm shot," he said, his voice high, unbelieving. Noel's laughter clattered.

Light spewed from Noel's hands, flooding the cave floor. Elizabeth saw Eric sprawled, his shoulder bloody, Dierdre huddled above him.

Elizabeth stared at Noel. "We're...we were just exploring," she faltered, her ears still ringing.

Eric stumbled to his feet. "It's okay," he said, "the bullet grazed my shoulder."

"What'd you find?" Noel demanded. He did not move from the cave entrance. His light pinned them where they stood. The tide hissed at his heels.

"Nothing here," Dierdre said. She spread her hands, stepped towards Noel. "A bunch of old boxes, that's all we've seen. Come on, Noel, quit playing cowboy and let us out."

"Don't know that I can do that," Noel said. The stash had been left here for him last night, and he had walked over now to check it out. "Don't know that I can let you go," he said. He looked down at his gun as if wondering whether or not to use it again.

Elizabeth stepped towards him. "Noel, for God's sake!"

"You," he said contemptuously, "I thought you were better than this. You were the lady here, too good for us bums. That's what I thought—until I heard different. You're thick with Rodriguez, I know. If I let you go, you'll tell him."

Elizabeth shrugged. "What's to tell?" she asked. "Listen," she pleaded, "you have to let us out of here, people will be looking for us."

"Put that gun away, Noel." Eric moved slowly towards Noel. "We haven't seen anything. Nothing in here but trash, I'll swear to that."

"Your word?" Noel spit at Eric's feet. "The word of a doper? You'll have to do better than that, boy."

"Noel, be sensible," Elizabeth said. "You'll have more trouble if you don't let us out of here." Her head was aching; she was chilled clear through. She couldn't take her eyes off the gun in Noel's hand.

A shadow filled the cave entrance, blocking the light. Deirdre cried out. Noel's light flickered, and fell, struck from his hand. He cursed.

Elizabeth rubbed her eyes. "Who?" she whispered.

"Our witch man!" Dierdre said.

A lantern beamed directly on Noel's face, then swung round on Elizabeth, Eric, and Dierdre. "Damn fools, the lot of you!" Marco shouted.

He lifted Noel by his shirt collar, dragged him to the cave entrance and tumbled him out. He turned to the others. "Get moving, fast—all of you! Elizabeth, give Dierdre a hand with Eric."

Eric staggered and fell to his knees. Elizabeth stepped towards him, then recoiled. "All that blood, I can't..."

"You gotta help, lady!" Dierdre appealed.

Elizabeth shook her head. Eric's hands were bloody, his shirt too—wet, stained dark. "I can't," she repeated.

She was aware of Marco's eyes on her. "The blood," she repeated. She knew he did not understand. "Marco...I..." she began.

But Eric had his attention. "Let's get the hell out of here!"

They were outside. Marco set Eric on his feet. "You'll be all right, boy. Flesh wounds bleed heavy."

The bright sun dizzied Elizabeth and her legs crumpled. She sank to the sand. She saw Noel, backed against a rock. Saw Marco kick the man's gun into the sea. Marco towered over Noel. "If your boss knew this..."

Noel shrugged. "But its your contraband, Witch Man. the General won't like this when he hears of it."

Marco jumped, pinned Noel to the ground. Noel yelled. Marco

kneed him, stripped him of his pants, and flung the garment to the tide. Noel was on his knees.

"Stop, the two of you!" Elizabeth cried. She caught desperately at Marco's arm.

He held her to him. Drawing a ragged breath, and then another.

"Get going, the three of you, into the dinghy," he said.

When they were in, Marco pushed off and jumped aboard. The boat scraped free and Marco hefted the oars. Noel shouted.

"That bastard will find his own way," Marco said. He put his hand to her forehead. "You've got a fever, Elizabeth."

Her head was reeling. "Marco," she said, "you cannot allow..." She did not finish, but slid to the floor of the boat.

"Island fever. It's nasty but it won't kill you," Marco said. "Jesu has medicine."

Dierdre spoke from the stern where she sat, Eric between her knees. Her voice was small. "Noel shot at us."

Marco nodded. "The rat's capable of anything." He cut his oars deep. "I knew his stash was in those caves. This is my fault. I should have cleaned this up months ago."

Dierdre tied her shirt tightly around Eric's upper arm, halting the bleeding. "Witch man," she said, "you and this island—you are heading for deep trouble."

"I can handle it," Marco told her.

"Don't wait too long," she warned. She shot a derisive look at Elizabeth. "You're one person I know not to ask for help!"

"That's right," Elizabeth mumbled, hating this kitten of a girl who did everything wrong, but got it right somehow—got Marco right anyway, the way he was smiling at her now.

Marco bent to his oars. "I'll take you all up to my house. Eric will be more comfortable there."

Dierdre managed a smile. "Thanks, but we've got all we need on the boat. You can drop us off. Leave the dinghy on the beach. We'll pick it up tomorrow." She smiled at Marco. "There when we needed you," she said.

"A talent of mine," Marco replied.

Earlier, intending to order Elizabeth's ice cream, he'd met the island ferry. Talking to the captain, he had heard a cry—sudden, clear in his head. Elizabeth? He had run like a boy, a path only he knew, across the island and down the other side, to the caves. Approaching the caves, he'd seen Eric's dinghy, heard the gun shot.

"Stay away from Noel," he told Dierdre now. "What he's got, you don't need."

"You're wrong there," Elizabeth said. Nobody heard her.

Dierdre was smiling at Marco, her eyes so full of trust he had to look away. "You won't let anything happen to us," she said. "I know we're okay with you."

"Yeah, sure..." Marco gripped his oars. Dierdre was like an orphaned puppy—appealing, but he didn't want her on his conscience. Her, or anybody else. He had his own life to live. Things happening lately, people pulling at him. This damn fool rescue mission now. Nothing made sense anymore.

A wave spilled, tipping the dinghy. "Keep Eric dead center, can't you!" Marco yelled.

*S*he awakened in a place she did not at first recognize.
Only Marco's face was familiar and she clutched at him. "I've been ill. Where am I?" She struggled to lift herself from her pillow. "I haven't an ounce of strength. How long have I been this way?"

"Four days," Marco told her.

She was lying on the couch he had pulled opposite his fire, a fire he had kept burning day and night. He had bunked on the floor, close enough so that when he slept his head was near her own.

"Four whole days?" Elizabeth managed to push herself to a sitting position. She put her hand to her hair and was surprised to find it smoothly braided.

Marco smiled at her. "You are better. Here..." He lifted a glass to her lips. "Drink this—it is wild sage, Jesu's recipe."

She drained the glass, and wiped her lips with the back of her hand. "I must look dreadful," she said, impossibly glad to see him, feeling she had returned from a long journey. But four days? "Marco, I've wasted so much time!"

He sat down next to her, held her close. "Patience, *querida*..." His words and look were so tender they brought her near tears. "I'm weepy," she apologized, "so tired. What happened to me?"

"Island fever," he said. "You had a wet trip to the caves. And what happened there shocked you. This heat, a sudden chill—you're not used to it."

"That cave, yes..." Elizabeth lay back and shut her eyes. "Noel had a gun," she said, slowly. "He would have killed us. He hurt Eric. Those kids are playing with fire, Marco. Drugs, guns—God knows what else. Noel is big time, he's got to be stopped."

"Noel will destroy himself," Marco said.

"And take others with him." Elizabeth shivered, remembering Noel's face, and the things Dierdre had said about him. Marco pressed a cool towel to her forehead. "You rescued us," she remembered. "How did you know we needed you?"

"You called," he said. "Don't talk now, you need rest. And don't worry, I got the kids a tow through the Canal. They'll be in the Caribbean until Noel cools down."

"I need to go back to my place," Elizabeth said, "I've things I must do." She pushed up from the couch, tried to stand but her knees buckled. "Damn!"

Marco shook his head. "Whether you like it or not, you're staying awhile."

She could have wept with frustration. The old lady was waiting, the promised tea party, the Gauguins...

Two days more of headache and languor. Elizabeth forced herself to eat and drink. Marco never left her side. It was he who, against her protests, bathed her and brushed her hair. He sponged her constantly with a sharp-scented lotion. "Herbs?" Elizabeth asked, feeling her skin come alive under the sponge.

"Papaya," Marco said. He slipped a clean nightgown over her head. "Flore brought these for you," he said. Elizabeth giggled. "I'm surprised she didn't stick pins in them. That girl doesn't like me, Marco."

"She's jealous," he said.

Elizabeth sniffed at her fingers. "What do I smell of?"

"My mother's mixture, she left it to my father. It's written down somewhere. "A song goes with it. Do you want to hear it?"

"Um-mm..." She snuggled into the soft blanket. "Sing to me, Marco."

"I rub you with leaves of elder bark," he began, reaching far back in years for the words: "I wrap you in the skin of a civet cat. A girdle of emeralds against lust, and one topaz against excesses." He stroked Elizabeth's cheeks and forehead, dragging his fingers up across her scalp.

She smiled drowsily. "More than one topaz needed," she said. "Tell me more, witch man."

"Bind the toe of a frog in the flesh of a nightingale. Take the tongue of a lizard, the tail of a mouse, the right eye of a serpent, and swallow all in one ounce of oil."

"Ugh!"

Marco kissed her. "I have forgotten most of the words. Something about oil of mace and rose salve, and grapevines too. It was Jesu who taught me, too many years ago."

"Marco, tell me..." Elizabeth sat up against his arm. "I want to know—how do you summon your Devil?"

"No need to call him, he is never far away."

"He can't frighten me because I don't believe in him," she said. "I've enough of horror with what's real. Blood sickens me. And death. I won't go near accidents."

"Or love, Elizabeth."

"I've seen what love can do. I don't want it."

What she wanted, but she wouldn't tell him, was the sound of his voice near her ear, his breath against her eyelids—then she could sleep without nightmares. "I have bad dreams," she confessed, "Eric bleeding like that—it reminded me..."

Marco kneeled beside her. "Turn your dreams around, Elizabeth. Explore your darkness. There is light behind it."

"Nonsense," she murmured, her eyes closed. "What is your Devil's name, Marco?"

He went to the fireplace and rubbed his fingers on a charred log.

"Lucifer is the oldest name," he whispered, tracing a black cross between her breasts. "Selah, All Powerful," he said, and pressed his lips against the mark.

Elizabeth pushed him from her. Spitting on her fingers, she rubbed at the black stain.

Marco put his hand on hers. "My kiss protects you, leave it there."

"It is you protect me," Elizabeth said. "You saved my life."

He was sitting cross legged on the floor beside the couch She saw the fire reflected in his eyes. She would not be deterred. "We will speak of your Devil, Marco. He stands between us."

"Yes, between me and what I want."

"Only because you insist on his being!" Elizabeth said. The fire leapt high at her words, and died as quickly. Shadows stretched themselves, a black pool reaching, touching the very edge of the firelit circle where they sat.

Elizabeth tossed her covers aside, swung her feet to the floor. If she could have she would have kicked the shadows back to wherever they belonged.

"I can 't help it, you spook me, Marco!"

"You spook yourself," he said. He stood, and threw another log on the fire.

"Tomorrow I'm going back to my place."

"If you must run away, Elizabeth."

Abruptly, she changed the subject. "You're not going to do anything about Noel, are you? You won't lift a finger, even now."

Marco's eyes narrowed. "I'll take care of Noel my way. You stay out of this, Elizabeth."

She was angry. "If you weren't afraid for yourself, you could have Noel arrested now. He will ruin this island. Turn him in, Marco."

"Yes, Elizabeth, one phone call will bring the police here. Just the excuse the General is waiting for. I'll be the one taken away. Without me here, the pirates will have a field day. There'll be nothing left of my Taboga."

She wanted to shake him. "You say you love this place, Marco. But you won't even try to save it."

"Save it?" he asked. "But I've spent my life saving this island."

"How? Tell me. Rum and carnival? Magic tricks? Iguanas? That's all very fine, but…"

"My school, I haven't told you because teaching English is against the law," Marco said quietly. "The bright kids, those with promise— I help them off the island, free of this damn country. They won't be caught here, as I was."

Elizabeth stared at him. "You've got a school? Marco, that's wonderful." She put her arms around him. "Forgive me. I was thinking you bummed around, scared of your own shadow. And now I find out what you really do. You're a teacher. It's beautiful! I should have known."

"Perhaps you'll help?" he asked. "You're a woman in business. I've got girls in my class. They need to know they've got a chance."

"Me? Teach?" Elizabeth laughed. "Anyway, I'm going to be busy here. I've got less than a month left."

"To do what? Map out a hotel complex? Which reminds me, I want to show you this island. Once you learn its secrets, you'll understand why tourism mustn't happen here."

"That's not my decision," Elizabeth said.

He took her hands in his. "Look at me," he said. "When will you say you love me?"

She answered without thinking. "Never." And was immediately sorry for the harshness of her denial. "You ask too much of me, Marco. You—you love so easily that I must envy you. Yes, believe me or not, I envy you your simplicity. And your soul. I would like to believe in Heaven, angels, too. I cannot."

He heard the pain in her words, and drew her close. Oblivious of the dying fire, the darkening room, they held each other. Somewhere in the house a door creaked, opened, and the black hound crept inside. His claws ticked on the tiled floor.

Marco lifted his head. "Who the hell let that one in?"

"Open up there!" A fist against the door, an American voice.

Elizabeth freed herself from Marco's embrace. "That's Hank," she said.

"Damn!" Marco was on his feet. "I told Jesu no visitors. And who in hell is Hank?"

"An American soldier. You'd better let him in."

"Yes," Marco was heading for the hallway, "his kind breaks down doors."

*H*ank and his uniform filled the room.
Pulling the blanket up under her chin, Elizabeth stared at him.
"What on earth?" she asked.

"Orders," Hank said. "That hotel keeper, Mr. Noel—he called headquarters. Said he was worried, he didn't know where you were, ma'am." He glanced at Marco. "Nice house," he said.

"My house," Marco replied. "Your business here?"

"Just checking. I see you're okay," and Hank winked at Elizabeth. "There's a story you'd been kidnapped. Lots of rumors lately. Some time last week a ship dropped off a load of coke here." Hank paused. Marco's gaze discomfited him. And the lady was pale as a ghost. "You really okay, ma'am?"

"I had a fever," Elizabeth said. She wished Marco would stop prowling the room. "Island fever, I guess. And Marco—Señor Rodriguez—decided to take care of me. No, I'm not kidnapped."

Hank looked at Marco. "You hear anything about that shipment from Colombia? It was dumped in the ocean yesterday, from the beach in front of the hotel. Real official. All the top brass there, playing Boy Scout."

Marco did not smile. "I live up here, and what goes on at the bottom of the hill is no concern of mine."

"It should be," Hank said. "From what I hear, this island belongs to you."

"Then you are trespassing," Marco said.

Hank reddened. He had no official permission from his office for this visit. Just a nudge from the Panamanian High Command, they were always eager when the talk concerned Rodriguez. Noel had called them, and they'd passed it on: the gringa was missing, *El Brujo* had kidnapped her.

The coke had been a front-page story, all the local papers. A photo of Noel and the General on the beach, caves behind them, overseeing the dumping of the stuff. Hank was not surprised. The colonels, the General too, gave themselves medals for finding their own stashes, when it behooved them to do so. Lots more where this came from, Hank knew that. Shit! The stink of this isthmus spread worldwide.

Hank was taking his time now, looking around. He'd heard this place was something else. Where did Rodriguez get the money to live like this? Was he in on the General's racket? Or crashing the General's territory? The latter would be why *El General* used any excuse to go after him. This kidnap story now—it was hogwash, Hank knew it, the lady looked right at home. Hank hid his grin. The two of them here, like his mom said it: snug as clams.

You're dead, Rodriguez, Hank wanted to say, what the General wants he gets. Hank had seen a victim or two, headless one of them, the other minus his privates. It wasn't nice, and Hank looked at Marco now. Should he warn him? But the guy lived here—surely he knew things were coming down?

"The General wanted a search party," Hank said. "I told Liaison this lady here," and he grinned at Elizabeth, "she can take care of herself."

Marco clenched his fists. "You know your way out."

"Marco!" Elizabeth struggled to her feet. "There's no need to be rude."

"It's okay, ma'am." Hank turned on his heels. "Sorry, sir, but I had my orders."

When the door had closed behind Hank, Marco wheeled on Elizabeth. "How does he know you?"

She sank back on the couch. "Calm down. Hank's nice. He meant no harm, he's only doing his job. Your government and mine—they're keeping an eye on me."

"On me, you mean," Marco said. "I don't like uninvited visitors. The Butcher's at the bottom of this."

"No, Noel is, Hank said so. Marco, why didn't you tell him we saw that stuff in the cave, that Noel threatened us with a gun? This was your chance to get Noel."

"Why didn't you tell him?" Marco asked. He smiled. "Were you protecting me?"

Elizabeth knew her cheeks reddened. She seized his hands. "Listen, Noel knows we found him out. He was scared we'd report him. So he played Mr. Innocent and dumped it. And gave the General a share of the applause. He won't forgive us for knowing his secret."

"Marco," Elizabeth begged, "If you love this place. And I know you do, report Noel to the General. Before it's too late."

Too late? He buried his face in the fragrance of her hair. Weeks ago it had been too late. When he'd first met this woman, then was too late.

"Tell them he used a gun. That should be enough."

"Guns are not outlawed, Elizabeth. And Noel is not the only pig at the feeding trough."

"You're scared," she said. "It's this devil thing gets in your way."

"He is part of me."

"It is you allow that." Tears started from her eyes.

She reached for her clothes. She wanted out of here. She pulled her nightgown over her head, and stood a moment, knowing her body all revealed. Firelight played on all her secret places. She heard Marco's sharp intake of breath. She was beautiful, feeling a new power spark through her and she squared her shoulders, offering her full breasts to the man there in his darkness.

Neither Marco nor Elizabeth saw the black dog slide into the room and fold himself down, licking his jowls, his eyes the color of flame.

The trade winds had stripped the crepe myrtles of their blue blossoms. Ylang-ylang flowers fell, drenching the island air with perfume.

Marco and Elizabeth were in the kitchen of her house. "The Guayacan will soon shower its gold," Marco said. "You must see that, Elizabeth."

"Maybe…" She had called her Boston office and told them she needed more time. No, she had not seen the paintings yet, she had told Janice, the owner was being difficult. Now she asked Marco: "If I need to stay longer, may I keep this house?"

"You don't have to ask, *querida*. But I want you to live with me."

"No, I've things to do. This island's giving me ideas. There's lots can be done to bring tourists here. A Caribbean cruise perhaps, painters and their islands—stuff like that."

"You mean, Gauguin and Taboga?"

Marco's direct question startled her. He gave her a hard look. "Your tea parties will get you nowhere, Elizabeth. Nothing in this village goes unremarked."

"Just two so far," she said. "And they've gotten Señora Amado somewhere. I've paid for half a dozen old bottles. She thinks I'm about to buy those chairs we sit on."

Marco smiled. "And the canvas remains rolled up on that shelf."

"Yes," Elizabeth admitted.

"She won't sell them, I won't permit it," Marco said.

"Can't I just look at them? Not even touch, just look?" Frustrated, Elizabeth hunched above her cold coffee. If Marco loved her as he said he did, he would get her what she wanted.

"Marco." she began.

He pushed back from the table. "Come on, we need to get out. I'm going to take you somewhere special. You like antiques? I'm going to show you a real one, our Spanish convent."

The building was up the hill, a short walk out of the village. A ruin, it had no roof, but the grace of its high brick garden wall was still evident.

Elizabeth stood speechless, delighted, in the inner courtyard overgrown with orange and lime trees. Arches, Spanish tiles, fragments of statues still in their niches. Elizabeth discovered the remains of a mosaic floor in what had once been the downstairs hall. "Marco, this is fabulous!" She was on her knees.

He smiled. "Come upstairs now."

The broken stairway without a railing climbed to the second story. Arched windows showed the green hills and the sea.

Elizabeth entered a small room and sat gingerly on a rusted brass bed. "No roof, just the sky above us," she said, and spread her arms to Marco. "Come..." They lay together on worn rags, oblivious to the squawking springs.

Elizabeth wrinkled her nose. "This is not early Spanish," she said, "it is Late Squatter!"

"Shh," Marco hushed her. "I want you to hear the ghosts of nuns singing."

"Oh, but I do, I do," Elizabeth whispered. "Lately, my whole world sings."

Then they stood together on the second floor balcony, feeling the tipsy slant of it under their feet. "Marco," Elizabeth said, "you must fix this place up, make a museum of it."

"Somebody else was here first," he said. "There's rum stashed in the cellar, and a still in the garden. This is anybody's place now." He did not tell Elizabeth, but partying too hard, unable to climb the hill to his house, he had crashed here himself.

"I'll show you a secret," he said. "Come down to the cellar."

"A magic show?" she teased, and could have bitten her tongue because, lately, they'd kept to an unspoken truce: they never mentioned his Devil.

Ignoring her jibe, he said, "Come, I'll show you how the nuns talked with their lovers."

She laughed. "You are irreverent."

He led her down the steep wooden steps into a vaulted cellar. "Stand over there in that corner." He pointed across the room. "Turn your face to the wall. I will stand here, my back to you."

She did as he told her. "Now what?" she asked, her face near the dusty wall. "Lean close," he instructed, "and whisper that you love me."

Looking at the wall in front of her, she found it quite ordinary. "I feel like a fool," she said.

"Be quiet and listen to me." Marco set his lips against the wall and barely breathed his words: "I love you. I love you…"

His voice was as clear to her as if he stood beside her. "But how?" she asked. "I don't understand."

"A kind of magic," he told her, "for lovers only, Elizabeth. Speak the words now, whisper love to me."

She leaned, opened her mouth to speak, but could not say the words he wanted. "I can't," she whispered.

"Tell me, Elizabeth…" His voiced called to her, as if he were sealed inside, buried there, and she felt an immense sadness. She closed her eyes, pressed her fingertips to the wall. "There is grief here, Marco."

"What grieves you, Elizabeth?"

He would not turn to look at her. He knew her despair. Maybe here, he hoped, her back to him and her face concealed, here she could confess to that weight in her. Her stone, Marco thought, he knew how it pressed, suffocating the life out of her.

Elizabeth bit down against the words, threatening. They crowded now, words that wanted out. Marco could not see her face. This place, she thought, it has heard a thousand wretched confessions.

"Yes?" Marco whispered. He would not go to her. She must do this alone.

He heard her indrawn breath. "Okay," she said, her voice low, but reaching him clearly through the wall, "in here's as good as anywhere, I guess. There was this little girl…"

"You," Marco said.

"For God's sake, let me tell it my way!" Elizabeth was weeping, her face to the corner. "That little girl was—she is not anymore."

"But she is," Marco insisted, "she is there, in you. What does she say, Elizabeth?"

"That I killed her, yes—I killed her."

"Killed who, Elizabeth?"

"Mother!" Elizabeth's whisper was an anguished cry.

Her mouth near the wall, the stench of centuries in her nostrils, Elizabeth continued. And it was not so painful, once she had begun. As she spoke, what had happened lost substance. It might have been another's history, told centuries ago. Speaking of her stepfather, the memory of him faded, was difficult to describe. Elizabeth had never told anyone of the seduction. Now, trying to recapture both her aversion and her fascination, she heard herself becoming almost clinical.

She told it straight through, unhurried, clipping her words, straight to the end—the blood-spattered bathroom, the body on the floor…

"The hot water was full on," she finished. "Steam, and I couldn't reach the faucet, I almost fell in, on top of her. That's why I can't stand blood, Marco. Not the sight or the smell of it. Mother had cut her wrists."

"Oh!" Elizabeth's cry echoed through the stone vaults. "Marco, that wretched child!"

"You," he said. He was standing behind her now, and he took her in his arms. "Elizabeth, you have told me and it is gone from you."

She wept, an abandoned sound. "He left without a word," she sobbed. "And Mother loved him, she wouldn't hear a thing against him. I never told, I think she knew—I couldn't tell her, could I? He left because of me, the guilt he felt. I could have stopped it all, stopped it from happening. I didn't. Her death was my fault. I killed her!"

Marco held Elizabeth until her sobbing subsided. Her face was drawn, her eyes clouded. "Do you still want me?" she asked.

He told her then what she needed to know. "I will not leave you, Elizabeth."

She managed a faint smile. "I did what you said, didn't I? I went straight into that darkness. It is not as terrible as I have imagined it."

"Nothing is as we imagine it will be."

"But it will come back," she said, "I know it will."

"Only if you invite it, Elizabeth."

She shook her head. Her smile was too bright then, and he knew she was closing herself away from him. For a moment, he had felt her break free. Now, again, she looked behind her, hesitating.

He seized her hands. "Why do you insist on punishing yourself?"

"Mother," she said, her voice low, breaking, "I hated her, Marco, for loving him, not me. She left me, she didn't care."

The old shame was returning. Elizabeth felt its unrelenting grip. She tried to shrug it off, could not, and pretended to smile, touching her hair, straightening her skirt. "Such theatrics! I am sorry, I should be ashamed. What you must think of me, Marco?"

"It is your courage I admire," he said. "Despite what happened, you have made a life. And allowed me inside. You will not shut me out again, Elizabeth."

"A bit late for that, isn't it?" she said, sharply. "I mean, there's nothing you don't know about me now. I could hate you for that."

She pulled free of him. "Enough of this now."

"Wait—first you must know the magic of these walls, how they carry sound. It is a forgotten art. The mortar was mixed with the blood of bulls, honey, and the whites of eggs."

Elizabeth's laughter then was genuine. "I do not believe you!"

"But you laugh," he said. "And one thing more, before we leave. Secrets told here, Elizabeth, are not repeated." He knew she needed this assurance.

She shrugged. "Who's to tell?"

Outside, the sun was hot on their heads. "I must see this garden," Elizabeth said. "I wonder who is buried here." Gnarled trees, ragged rose bushes, a struggling jasmine vine. Marco showed Elizabeth the broken still. He picked two limes from a tree and they sat in the shade, sucking the bitter fruit. Elizabeth had found a sharp fragment of old china. Absently, she scratched the ground next to her. "The earth is loose," she said. Then, "Look, Marco, something's buried here."

It was a box, its wooden sides half rotted, rust marks where a latch had been. Elizabeth opened the lid. "Look! A gold crucifix, and a chain. Oh, Marco, who did these belong to?" She held the ornaments close. " May I have them?"

He took the articles from her, weighed them in his palm. "It belongs to whoever was buried here."

"She won't miss it now," Elizabeth said. She strung the cross to the chain. "I wonder," she said, "it's been a special day—for me anyway. If I gave these to St. Peter, would he bless us?"

Marco smiled. "Do we need a blessing?"

Elizabeth laughed. "If anyone does, you do, Marco."

She pocketed the jewelry. "I won't forget being here," she said. She stretched her hands to Marco. "I should thank you."

"No, it is I should thank you, *querida*. You have shared yourself. I know you better now."

She knew she blushed. "Perhaps too well," she said.

A bright green leaf had fallen on his black hair and she reached to touch it. And left her hand there. "All I've told you," she asked, "how can you want me now?"

"*Doña*...lady!" Placing his hands on Elizabeth's shoulders, Marco rocked her gently. "If I could," he said, "I'd shake your stone from you."

"I can't get at yours either," she said. "Maybe stones are that way?"

"No, love melts all the hard places," Marco insisted.

*M*arco and Elizabeth wandered up through the village.
Everyone watching saw their Devil Man hand in hand with the gringa. He was changing before their eyes. He never stopped anymore, to ask about anyone; he had no time for teaching class or, more importantly, to plan the Holy Friday procession. Because it was Marco who must open the church, choose the young men who would stand guard as Roman Soldiers. And who would play the Devil this year? Marco was the one who decided that.

But he had eyes now for the gringa only. She walked as proudly as ever, perhaps more so. And what was she doing, visiting Señora Amado almost every day? They had asked the old woman, but she just smiled, and showed them the dollar bills she kept, wadded in her pocket.

"He is bewitched," Juana whispered, watching the Devil Man pass, seeing Elizabeth's hand in his. Try as she might, Juana could not spin a future for anyone lately. The dry season wind spoke in indecipherable whispers, the dust spun wild in unreadable patterns. All Juana knew, and this most surely, was that Marco must take care, look behind him. His shadow fattened, the black cur dogged his footsteps.

"Why do they stare?" Elizabeth asked. "Tell me, how many women have you paraded through town?"

"One after another," Marco teased.

"When will it rain?" Elizabeth asked.

"When you tell me you love me, the earth will be green again. Not until then, Elizabeth."

"I want to see your Easter," she said. "You will open the church?"

"I celebrate the story," Marco said. "It is one of great courage. You must be part of it. We make a garden in the church. The procession is staged in the Spanish tradition—centuries old. It is I choose who will play the Devil. He tries to steal the Christ figure from a glass coffin."

Elizabeth laughed. "But why isn't that Devil you?"

Marco grinned. "I have always wanted to play that part."

"Who better than you?" Elizabeth was wishing she could see this charade.

"Because it is only theater. The Devil is real. I cannot play him as a fool."

"Perhaps, if you did...?" she wondered.

They had reached the plaza, and they climbed the steps of the church. Almost reverently, Elizabeth touched the blue carved doors.

"Marco, you don't realize the history you have here. But you can't come in." She was half teasing. "The color blue keeps the Devil out."

Ignoring her, he unlocked the doors, and they went inside. He held her back a moment. "Whatever it is you want from Taboga, what if you must leave without it?"

"I must leave without you, Marco."

She was looking down at their joined hands. His skin was so much darker than hers. Suddenly, she was dizzy with desire. He intuited her feeling, and grinned at her.

She frowned. What was it, this wanting him that came on her so hard? She couldn't help herself. This was not like her. "You're not good for me," she said.

"You would not say that if you could see your face now." He shut the doors behind them. "We are alone. Shall we make love?"

He took her in his arms, buried his face in her hair. He felt her body stiffen. "What's wrong?"

"Look," she pointed. "Look who came in with us. He's like a statue there."

The black dog lay on top of the altar. His ears were pricked, and he whined, eyeing Elizabeth and Marco. It was she who moved towards the animal first, her hands stretched, palms down. He growled at her, his scruffy hair prickling.

Marco stepped forward. "No, Elizabeth. Let me get rid of him."

He approached the dog, and it cowered. Marco seized it by the scruff of its neck, carried it down the aisle, opened the doors and pitched it outside. It howled as he threw it. He dusted off his hands.

"Damned filth!" he said, slamming the doors shut.

Marco saw Elizabeth as he had that first day, standing by the altar, her hair washed in the sunlight that fell from the high window. He went to stand beside her. "Do you remember us?" he asked.

She nodded. "St. Peter there." Elizabeth spoke softly. "I will like you always, because of those shoes you gave him, that key to the wine cellar."

"You laughed at me," Marco said, "and I was angry. I wanted to shock you. Even then I thought of making love to you." He was standing behind her, and he placed his hands on her hips.

She swayed, let her head fell back against his shoulder. "You frightened me, that first time—I remember that." The force she had felt in him then drew her now.

"You were a very proper lady," Marco said, sliding his hands under her blouse. "Tell me, would you let me love you here, in this place?"

"Of course not," she whispered, her mouth dry with longing. "We must not make love in a church."

"Why not?" He swung her up, seated her on the altar. "We are not religious, you and I. There has been no priest here for years. What are you afraid of, Elizabeth?"

"You," and she leaned to kiss his lips.

"No," he said, "it is this church, its God who frightens you. There is a corner of you that does believe!"

She pulled him between her knees. "I only know that to make love here is wrong. I don't know why, but it is."

His hands were under her shirt, massaging her back.

"No," she begged, but leaned to kiss him again.

With one swift movement he was up on the altar beside her. "You want me," he said, and he chuckled because this was a moment worthy of a Devil Man. "I dare you, Elizabeth, love me here!"

"We must not," she said, but she did not refuse him when he lay her down, and stretched himself above her, his legs urging her thighs open. His face close to hers, he said, "We could call this a marriage, perhaps?"

"Why not?" she challenged. "Our kind of ceremony, Marco." He must not guess her unease. Her body trembled. "We won't forget this," she whispered, her lips against his throat.

Marco stripped off his shirt, bundled it to make a pillow for her head. She reached for him, sank her teeth into his shoulder, shutting her eyes against her guilt. Who could be watching?

Marco saw her eyes washed pale. Light from the window above them flooded her hair and throat. "You are not afraid?" he asked. Because the hair on the back of his own neck prickled. He glanced over his shoulder at the Christ figure on the tall cross. He thought it moved.

Elizabeth saw it too. "No!" she cried.

Christ's forearm had dropped. His hand swung empty at His side.

Elizabeth buried her head in Marco's chest. "I do not believe this!"

Marco was chuckling. "I'd forgotten...last Easter, that nail wouldn't hold. His arm fell loose. I thought the whole village would take off."

"It's not funny," Elizabeth said. "I thought it was real...that He was real. That's the most macabre thing I've ever seen, Marco. You've got to fix it!"

"Now?" he asked. He was smiling, stroking her breasts.

"Later," she said, softly.

He spoke in Spanish: "It is here, *querida,* that you will say you love me."

"I admit to nothing, not even here," she said, wishing again she had not confessed everything to him. "Words, Marco, they aren't good for us."

"They are good, when truth is spoken." But desire had died in him. He lifted himself from her. "You are right. This is not the right place."

"Where is our right place?" Elizabeth asked. She sat up, and felt in her pocket for the cross and chain. "We must make a prayer with these."

He jumped from the altar, and lifted her down. "Shall we give them to St. Peter? But that's one hell of a climb!"

Elizabeth tucked in her shirt, ran her fingers through her loosened hair. "I'm glad we didn't make love."

"I'm not," he replied, denying his own sense of relief.

"Wait for me," she said. "I will give this cross to the Virgin."

She walked down the aisle towards the statue, Marco close behind her. Looking up at the Virgin, Elizabeth said, "She is a real treasure, Marco—all the way from Spain." She bent to pick up the tarpaulin fallen at the statue's feet. "Why isn't she covered, like the others?"

He took the cloth from her, folded it, and set it on a bench. "This was Loco's Lady. He brought her flowers. If I cover her now, they will know he is not coming back."

Elizabeth picked up a candle stub. "If you have a match, I'll light this. For Loco, if you like? And for those we disturbed in the convent garden."

He found a packet of matches in his pocket. Kneeling, Elizabeth lit the candle. Its light fell across her face, transfiguring her. Marco watched her.

"Elizabeth?" His voice broke on her name. He did not understand her, not at all. A moment ago, she had lain, fearless, on the top of the altar, wanting him to love her. Now, she kneeled and lit a candle to the Virgin.

He watched as she took the cross and chain and, reaching around the statue's waist, pulled herself up on to the pedestal. She tied the chain to the Virgin's wrist, and set the cross in her open palm.

"There," she said, and climbed down again.

Wordless, Marco pulled her tightly against him. "Who are you?" he asked.

"Whatever you believe, I am that to you."

"You have my soul," he said.

"But that means nothing. It is you I want."

"**G**od damn!" *The curse echoed, startling them.*
They peered through the gloom, and saw Eric in the door-way. "That cur bit me!" he exclaimed, rubbing his leg.

"Look!" Dierdre walked towards them. She had what appeared to be a broken skull in her hands. "We were exploring the Spanish grave-yard, and we found this. I guess someone forgot to bury someone."

"Let me have it," Marco said. "It could be recent. The government cemetery charges too much and the villagers find a space somewhere else."

"You can't have this one," Dierdre said. "I'm mailing it to the General!"

Elizabeth laughed. "I thought of that."

"Or perhaps," and Dierdre giggled, "we should put it in Noel's bed?"

"It belongs where you found it." Marco was firm and he relieved Dierdre of her burden. He set the skull on the floor. It gleamed white-ly, and Eric kneeled to examine it. Elizabeth crouched beside him. "Marco is right," Eric said. "This must be returned."

"You can give it to me," someone said, in Spanish.

They turned. Dierdre's mouth fell open. "A real life cop!"

Eric hooted. "He's come to say his prayers."

Marco approached the soldier. "This church is closed. I don't allow visitors here."

"This is God's church, not yours," replied the soldier. He pushed at the skull with his booted foot. "I must report this."

Marco picked up the skull and, with a bow, presented it to the soldier.

"Brujo!" The man spit the word, and turned too quickly and the skull spilled from his hands, cracking and rolling across the floor to lie at the Virgin's feet.

"*Diablo!*" The soldier fled.

"Wow!" Dierdre sank to the floor near the skull. She picked it up. "I guess he thought we were mixing up a snatch of black magic."

Elizabeth was doubled over in giggles. "We'll be the talk of the island! If he'd come earlier, Marco, the altar and all," she gasped, "imagine if..."

Marco was not amused. "We're lucky," he said. Eric looked from Marco to Elizabeth. "What the hell have you two been up to?"

"Oh," Elizabeth said, "we talk to walls, expect them to answer back. We bowl skulls down church aisles, we——" and she looked at Marco, "the things we do, you wouldn't believe us," she said. Again giggles spilled from her.

Eric shook his head. "Lady Liz, I thought I knew you. I don't!"

"You are not alone, Eric." Marco picked up the skull. "I'll leave this safe with our Virgin."

"I wish we could mail it to the General," Elizabeth said.

"Imagine it," Dierdre said.

Elizabeth nodded. "Wrapped in pink tissue paper, ribbons."

Both women laughed.

"It is not so funny," Marco said. But he knew they wouldn't understand. Lost skulls did not happen in their country.

Carefully, he settled the skull at the Virgin's feet. He would leave it there until things settled.

*I*t was Dierdre who suggested it: *"Let's have our fortunes told."* It was another day and Marco had planned to take Elizabeth to the Spanish well. Dierdre took his hand. "Come on, you look like you can use a cold beer."

"I haven't time," Elizabeth said. Marco put an arm about her shoulders. "Just a little while more won't hurt," he said.

Lately it was always a little while more.

The four of them surprised Juana. She rolled from her hammock and, at Marco's request, pushed a six pack across her counter. "Anything else?"

Marco gave her a grin that turned her to jelly. "How much?" he asked. Juana could not resist a broad wink. "For you, señor, everything free."

Eric hooted. "So the beer's on the house too? Marco, you've got it made!"

"But we should give her something," Elizabeth said, in English.

Juana gave her a dark look, spoke rapidly in Spanish: "I want for nothing, señora, it is you who are in need. And our Loco, where he is—that is *la pobreza.*"

"Enough!" Marco said. Elizabeth put a hand on his arm. "It's okay."

Dierdre came to the rescue. She spread her palm. "My fortune?" she asked.

Juana hesitated, then took the small calloused hand in her own and studied it. She waited, just long enough to stir Dierdre's curiosity. "One dollar?" she asked. Dierdre nodded.

"A pretty hand," Juana crooned. "A giving hand, much loving." She paused again, knowing that fortunes, to be believed, must take a long time in the telling. "Take care," she warned, reading danger, certain grief. Noel's face was clear, and Juana looked sternly at Dierdre. "Best you leave this island."

Dierdre pointed at Eric. "I won't leave here without him."

"Danger," Juana insisted, releasing Dierdre's hand. She reached for Eric's and traced its deeply etched lines. "Sickness," she said immediately, and paused, confused by Eric's seeming strength and health.

"A choice," Juana said slowly. "Money will be offered."

Dierdre pulled Eric's hand from Juana's grasp. "No more, please!"

Juana shrugged. What was needed would come to pass, one way or another. It was Elizabeth's hand she wanted to see. "You, *doña?*" she asked.

Elizabeth hung back. "It's too hot," she said. There had been revelations enough for one day.

"A free fortune," Juana insisted, "No dollar." Again Elizabeth shook her head.

Eric pointed at Marco. "What about him?"

"He knows his future," Juana said. She saw Marco's hand reach for Elizabeth. "Don't hold too tight," she warned.

Dierdre attempted to slip an arm around Elizabeth's waist, but was rebuffed. "Let's go," she said.

The sky was blue above their heads. The purple of the jacaranda painted shadows on the brown hills. "Come on," Marco said, "I'll show you the Spanish graveyard. It's cool up there."

The four of them walked out of the village. Dierdre dropped back to walk with Elizabeth. "Spooky, that fortune," she said.

"You didn't believe it?" Elizabeth asked.

"Of course not," Dierdre scoffed. "So where's the trouble in my life—except for that one there." She pointed at Eric who was walking ahead with Marco.

"Could be he's it," Elizabeth said.

Dierdre skipped a crack in the sidewalk. "Then trouble's what I want. Hey, how about that scene in the church? We looked like a bunch of Satan worshipers—that skull and all. I bet the cop reports it that way."

"Sure he will," Elizabeth said. "Anything to make Marco look bad. The General will love it."

Dierdre kicked a stone. "Why can't people just leave Marco alone?"

"They won't be satisfied until they've run him off. Until they have this place to themselves. Noel, the General—they have no tolerance for a man like Marco."

"Jealousy, maybe," Dierdre said.

They had reached the Spanish graveyard. It stood high above the sea. The sun was bright on the old stones, on the stained marble. Elizabeth pitied the fallen angels, their stone eyes turned blindly to the blue sky. She wondered if Gauguin had walked here.

Marco was calling her. Stepping across a broken stone, she leaned to read its inscription. "Esmeralda somebody," she said. "Sounds like a woman pirate. How old are these graves?"

"Early sixteen hundreds, maybe earlier. Don't fall in a hole," he warned. "You'll drop through to Spain."

He was spread-eagled on the grass beside Eric. Elizabeth kneeled beside him. "Take care," she whispered, for no reason she knew, and kissed him with a tenderness that surprised her. "I'll be right back." She wandered off with Dierdre.

Marco and Eric lay quiet for a moment. Then Eric said, without raising his head, "Do you believe in fortunes?"

"You make your own," Marco answered.

"Maybe," Eric replied irritably. "Me—I don't know where I'm headed."

"Follow your girl, she loves you." Marco stretched, wanting to feel the earth fit every contour of his body. Papi was nearby, buried deep. Marco wanted, some day, this same earth around him.

Eric was off on a track of his own. "If I had your Stone, Marco, then maybe I'd know what I want."

The older man smiled into the sun. "It's not that simple, Eric."

"But you've got everything perfect. I mean, nothing can hurt you, can it?"

"I'm human, like you. I've got to be careful. Suppose the Devil catches me off guard, nobody there to take my stone..." But Marco was tired of explaining. These kids, they needed miracles in Technicolor.

"You know who you are," Eric insisted, "and that's real power. Me? I'm a wanderer, always running. The pain never lets me be. Like your stone, maybe. My memories of that shitty war won't let me be. Grass helps, but the highs don't last."

Marco sat up. "You've fought a war, Eric. You're one hell of a sailor. You've brought that boat of yours halfway around the world. That's who you are. And Dierdre—the girl loves you. She's your way to go."

Eric closed his eyes. "Dierdre should cut loose of me."

"But she won't." Marco got to his feet. "Come on, let me show you this place."

Eric stumbled to his feet. "It isn't right. I use Dierdre's love, but give her nothing in exchange. She keeps me alive. I owe her."

"You need her, that's enough for her." Marco flung an arm around Eric's shoulders. "It is good, isn't it, this need of another? Listen to me, kid, we've all got scars, marks that won't fade. There's all kinds of wars out there, inside us too. What's important is you've got a girl who loves you—there's your magic.

"And don't tell me you can't face up to things. You've been all kinds of places, gotten yourself there and back, the weather not always with you..."

Eric was smiling. "Thanks. You're one hell of a guy, you know that? But talk about war, Noel's got it in for you. He's over his ass in dirty business. Between him and that General, they could blow you away. I wouldn't like to see that happen."

"Noel will drown in his own shit. And the General's sort—they don't last." Marco said. He closed his hand over his scar. "I take care of myself. Come on, let's find our women."

*S*tone roses and faceless cherubs littered the ground. Holes where graves had been, graves where bodies had rested.

"Where's your old man?" Eric asked.

"Right on the edge, near the sea." Marco was picking his way carefully, remembering his boyhood and his explorations here, his spills into pits that seemed to go to the bottom of the earth. Papi had had to rescue him more than once.

"It's an ant hill," Eric said. "One grave on top of another. Is that allowed?"

"Burial is free here," Marco said. "The new graveyard, up the path a bit, the government charges plenty for a space. It was my father opened this to everyone. The villagers fixed those gates" He pointed at the heavy wrought iron portals. "Papi said everyone is entitled to a royal burial."

As a boy, Marco had searched here for his mother. It was Jesu told him, after Papi died. His mother was up at the house, under the Guayacan. The grave was unmarked.

"Don't lose your girl," Marco told Eric now. "Papi's gone, my mother too. We never got to speak the words we should have."

Marco looked around him. "I used to come here, a kid wanting his mom. She died, birthing me. I always thought that was my fault."

Elizabeth's words came back to him: *I killed her...I never told her I loved her...*

Marco returned a bouquet of plastic flowers to an angel's empty hands. He looked at Eric. "Maybe we all think we killed someone who loved us?"

*F*lore could not guess how long she had sat here, on the hotel porch, waiting for Noel.

She had passed the time, first by pretending to be a *turista*. But that only made her more conscious of her bare feet, the ripped hem of her skirt. She counted up her one pair of gold sandals, two new handmade dresses, and an almost empty bottle of cologne that boasted, in gilt letters, the scents of a tropical island. Flore must laugh at that one because all she smelled here on her island was pee and fish guts.

Noel owed her money, and Flore had time to wait. She seldom brooded; somewhere, she believed, a kindly God recognized her need for shoes, lipstick, and Marco. The concept of sin didn't bother Flore because there was pleasure to be had from men's bodies. Hadn't Marco himself told her that what felt good could not be sin? Suffering is a sin against life, Marco said. Why not take Heaven now, he argued. Flore must agree with him.

Except right now she hated Marco. Gingerly she explored her belly. She was larger every day; soon she'd be the joke of the village. Where was Marco when she needed him? He had sent for Elizabeth's clothes and Flore had had to carry the bundle up the hill. Jesu had met her at the door, taken the bag from her and sent her on her way again. *Como una esclava!* Like a slave. Not long ago that fine house had been almost hers. Now the gringa was queen, parading herself as if she owned the whole island.

Noel's voice interrupted Flore's musings. "What do you want?"

"You owe me money, señor. I've worked three nights straight now and you haven't paid me. I won't do it again."

"You won't do it again?" Noel laughed harshly. "Flore, you are not the only whore on the island. There's more than a dozen girls here can take your place."

She shook her head. "They are not like me. You forget—the Devil Man taught me. You will not find another like myself."

Noel edged closer, his eyes appraising. Sweat darkened his armpits; his boredom lay heavy as wet towels on him. "What does he teach, this Devil Man? I'll pay you double what I owe you, girl, if you'll show me."

Double what he owed her? Flore did some fast calculations in her head and realized a sum she had never seen altogether. "*Seguro?*" she asked, Are you sure?

Noel nodded. "Come on, my room." He was excited. Perhaps Flore could fix what was wrong? He'd learn Marco's secret and have a woman like Elizabeth at his feet. At the very least, he could give Veronica what she needed.

Veronica. She must know by now how he'd played hero, dumping coke in the sea. That had had to be: Marco had found him out so he'd had to move fast, play innocent. He had claimed to have discovered the coke hidden in the cave. He'd asked the General to participate in the dumping and the man had been only too willing. An anti-narcotics stance kept U.S. dollars coming.

After the hoopla, over drinks at the hotel, Noel had directed the General's attention to Rodriguez, saying the brujo had abducted Elizabeth.

"She's missing," Noel had said. "She was last seen with the *brujo*." The General had ordered his men to look around, and told the American liaison officer to search Rodriguez's house.

The gringo lieutenant had returned with the information that the American lady was all right.

"It appears she's been ill; Rodriguez is taking care of her," Hank had said.

That news had made the General snicker; it had sizzled Noel's guts. Noel could not understand why Rodriguez hadn't turned him in.

Elizabeth, too, why hadn't she told the American Embassy about the cave, the stash, and the gun he'd fired, wounding the kid? She'd been quick enough to accuse Loco.

Noel's head ached. That cave episode had scared him. And the General was on him again today. Some rumor about Devil worship in the church. Satanism, the General called it, saying Noel must get the key to the church, board it up if he had to. If an American hotel was going to be built here, the General said, things had to be cleaned up. "Get rid of Rodriguez!" he had shouted.

"How?" Noel had asked.

"Burn him out if you must," the General said. "He's got a school. There's a law now, no English taught in this country. Take care of Rodriguez."

Noel understood. It was an order. As if he had nothing to do but chase witches! Guests coming in tonight. More Americans, probably on Easter holiday.

Now, in Noel's shabby room, the air conditioner humming, Flore undressed. She sat down naked on the edge of the bed, the swell of her belly spreading her legs. "So take your clothes off," she said.

"You do it," Noel muttered. He wanted to be undressed, nursed like a baby until his smallness engorged to manhood. "Little mama," he said, sighing, lying down beside her.

She removed his shoes and socks, his shirt. Her hands moved to his belt. "Hurry!" he gasped, his tongue thick with anticipation.

But Flore took her own sweet time, undoing the belt, moving the trouser zipper down, freeing the pale hairy legs. Noel was not pretty; he was old, and Flore did not conceal her distaste. Wrinkling her nose, she licked and tickled his wrists and ankles, his chest and belly, and his small unresponsive penis. Noel kept his eyes shut, willing his earthquake.

"Now?" he asked.

"Now," Flore said, aroused despite herself, straddling Noel. She lowered her hips and choked back a cry of surprise. *"Dios,* you can't—you really can't!"

"No," Noel whimpered. "But you'll teach me. You're the Devil Man's whore, you'll show me."

She tried. With every trick she knew, driven by her own frustration. Noel was slack as dough without yeast. At last, slippery with sweat, Flore collapsed in helpless giggles.

Noel lay inert, hating the girl there pulling on her cheap panties and smirking. Hating himself too. Flore would talk, the whole village would know. Veronica had laughed just this way—she had laughed, and left him.

Flore was standing above him, her hand out. "Pay me," she demanded.

"For what?" Noel asked. He pulled up the sheet to hide his shame. "You're no good," he said.

Flore reached her hand under the cover and flicked his penis. "Not even the Devil Man's woman can get a rise out of that," she sneered. "I was sorry for your wife, for what Marco did to her. But it wasn't him, was it? It was your fault. Pay me," Flore insisted.

Noel was staring at her belly, feeling a heat in his groin, an idea stirring. "Want to get your man back?" he asked.

Flore blinked. "How?"

Noel sat up, pulled on his underpants. "I'm going to tell you how to send that *gringa* witch running from this island."

Flore edged closer. "You, too—you think she is a witch?"

"She's a woman, isn't she?" Noel's remark amused him. It passed straight by Flore. "Listen," he said, "get the gringa alone somewhere. Tell her you're pregnant with Marco's child." He snapped his fingers under Flore's nose. "Simple as that."

Flore's mouth rounded. She had never considered so easy a solution. She imagined the scene: Elizabeth's face gone white, then the hurt bruising, turning it ugly. And Elizabeth's anger then, yes—at Marco of course.

"It might work," Flore said slowly, "if she believes me."

"You've that lump in your stomach," and Noel poked it crudely. "She's in love with the man—that's why she'll believe you."

Flore frowned. "And if Marco finds out?"

"He won't hear it from me," Noel said.

The ferry whistle sounded. "Guests coming, Americans." Noel pulled on his clothes. "If you do as I say, Flore, and the gringa leaves the island, which she will—you'll consider yourself paid."

Flore stared at Noel. If the Devil was anywhere he was here, in this man's eyes. "You want the truth of this?" Flore asked. "I wish the gringa dead!"

Juana's voice in her head: *Want it badly enough, it comes to you.*

*T**hat next evening Dierdre rowed Marco and Elizabeth out to*
the boat.

Eric was busy in the stern. "Welcome aboard!" he shouted. Elizabeth smelled fish frying, garlic, onions, and marijuana. Eric handed her an open bottle of wine, telling her to drink it straight, he and Dierdre had forgotten paper cups. "Real glasses we have two of, only," Dierdre said.

Elizabeth knew immediately that she had dressed wrong. She was in her long white caftan, Dierdre wore shorts. No matter, Elizabeth had resolved she was not going to spoil things.

She had spent last night alone, her own choice—and gone early this morning to see Señora Amado. Still the old lady refused to show the pictures. She had intimated, more strongly than ever, that others had visited her, wanting the same thing. "Are the pictures worth so much?" she had asked Elizabeth, who had taken the plunge then: "I'll give you one thousand."

The woman was obviously shaken. *"Un mil?"* Too quickly, she had pushed Elizabeth from the house. She was tempted, Elizabeth was certain. Next time she would bring that offer, in one dollar bills—a stack of them. Señora Amado would not be able to refuse.

Elizabeth knew she was close to the prize. Tomorrow night the paintings would be hers. And then? She felt a twinge, an ache stronger than regret. She reached for Marco's hand.

"What will I do without you?" she asked, more of herself than of him. He gave her a startled look. She raised the wine bottle: "To us!" she said, and she drank deeply. If she had to, she'd get blind drunk, past pain, past love.

Eric grinned. "It's gonna be a wild one!" He toasted Elizabeth. "Lady, you are one beautiful woman—when you want to be!"

She wanted to be just that: beautiful. Not a thought in her head but those stars now, this sea. "I want a moon burn," she said, envying Dierdre's tan, her thick unruly curls.

"And I want to look like you," Dierdre said wistfully. "I've been sailing so long I've forgotten how to dress up. Eric wouldn't notice anyway."

"I notice you," Marco told her.

His shirt glistened white as the small waves slapping the boat. His arms were dark as the night sky. Looking at Marco, Elizabeth realized how little she knew this man. Just as well, she told herself.

"Because you don't know me either," she challenged. "I mean even if this were our last night forever, we'd still be strangers."

"Strangers?" Marco cocked an eyebrow and grinned. "If we are strangers, what's it like to be friends?"

Dierdre interrupted. "How are you, Devil Man?" She wriggled herself between him and Elizabeth and slid her hand under his shirt. "Take this off—relax now."

Marco shrugged off his shirt, drained the last of the wine and tossed the bottle to Eric. He disliked drinking parties, but for Dierdre's sake he would try to enjoy himself. He sensed Elizabeth's restlessness. An aura about her tonight: she glittered. What did she mean—their last night forever? Marco shivered, and Dierdre noticed and slid her arm around him. "Don't be sad," she whispered. He managed a smile.

"We'll skinny dip later," Eric said. He was standing in the bow, and Elizabeth thought he might as well be naked—those scarlet briefs. These were not her kind of people; this wasn't her world at all. Be decent, she reminded herself, when this is finished, I won't remember their names.

"Elizabeth does not belong on a boat," Dierdre said. "We'll have to unwind her." She giggled. "Noel's spying on us from the beach. He thinks we throw orgies out here."

Elizabeth leaned close to Marco. "They're smoking grass, do you mind?"

"I'm higher than they are, just looking at you."

Eric took the fish from the grill and divided it on four paper plates. He ate with his fingers, munching noisily. "Girl," he told Dierdre, "this is super. And where'd you get the wine?"

"Noel—on credit," Dierdre said lightly.

"I wouldn't owe him," Marco said. "Noel will collect your soul if he can."

Dierdre grinned. "Like your Devil maybe?"

"There's our moon," Elizabeth said quickly.

A white balloon swung above the horizon. The boat swayed, dead center of the moon's path.

Don't talk, Elizabeth wished. She wouldn't mind if this were the last night of the world. "Let's pretend," she said, "it's the last time we'll see that moon, the last of those stars, the end of everything. Dierdre, make a wish."

The girl raised her arms, threw back her head. "But there never will be an ending to me and Eric. I won't allow it."

"Nor I," Marco agreed. "I command this night to last forever."

"It won't," Elizabeth said. She knew she lied: his face was engraved on every part of her.

"Me, I like the sun," Eric said. He collected their plates and slid them into a plastic bag. "You know," he said, "I sailed the Med once, under a moon like now—that sea was slick with garbage bags. It's people will make the end of all this."

"No doom and gloom," Dierdre said. "That is a wishing moon. We've got to make us some magic."

She fumbled in a wooden box and pulled out an oilcloth pouch. She rolled four joints, took one herself and gave one to Eric. She offered the others to Elizabeth and Marco. The latter shook his head. "I don't need it," he said.

"Yeah—you've got your own trip," Dierdre teased.

"My own," he agreed. He did not like marijuana. He had tried it but it brought him down hard, down into depths that wrung the life from him. He had come out of it spooked.

Dierdre drew on her reefer. "It helps you dream," she said. She was feeling tender, this was her third joint in as many hours and she she was soft, sexy, melted butter inside. She inched nearer Marco, pulled his hand to her cheek. "Ever tried sex and grass together?"

"Loving is magic enough," Marco said. This girl was a kitten; he wanted to stroke her. He drew the cork from a bottle, put the bottle to his lips and drank deeply.

Dierdre inhaled and blew the sweet smelling smoke into Marco's face. "You're too good," she said, not knowing quite what she meant, but loving Marco, wanting him to love her. "Not sex," she said, "just you. Can I count on you, Devil Man?"

"I'm here," Marco said.

"I'll have some of that grass," Elizabeth decided.

"You won't like it," Marco warned.

Dierdre helped Elizabeth light up. "The lady's going to know what it's like to feel—first time maybe."

"Keep the smoke in your lungs," she told Elizabeth, "and let it out slow."

Elizabeth did as she was told. She was scared, uncertain of how she should feel. Nothing happened. She shut her eyes, inhaled again, held the smoke in, then exhaled and opened her eyes. "Nothing at all," she said, her tone so disappointed that Marco laughed. She sat down next to him. "I can handle this," she said.

Eric stood, stretched his arms wide. "I'm going to make us some music." He took up his guitar. "Celebrate that old moon," he said. "Dierdre girl, dance for us."

Dierdre went forward to the bow. She hummed, turning slowly. She was sketched slim against the starred sky, the moon caught on her fingertips.

"Lovely," Elizabeth whispered. She felt nicely dizzy, and she leaned against Marco. "Look at me," she said. Because he had turned away, was looking at the island. "Do you smell smoke?" he asked.

Elizabeth giggled. "I guess so." She slid on to his lap, set her hands across his eyes. "Kiss me," she said.

So many lights. Marco wondered. He saw his own house dark, Jesu gone from it, he guessed, the old man must be in the village. Elizabeth's hair was in his eyes, blurring the island. "I love you," she murmured, running her fingers up and down his ribs, marveling at the smoothness of his skin, the play of his muscles as he breathed.

Eric's voice was deep. " 'Are you going to Scarborough Fair ...' "

Elizabeth turned her head. " 'Parsley, sage, rosemary and thyme...' " She knew this song. Eric was Pan. "Down in the reeds by the river," Elizabeth quoted. "Not a guitar," she said, "you must have a flute." She let her head fall to Marco's shoulder. "I love you," she whispered, talking to the moon because her mind was up there somewhere, she was ready to fly.

"I love you," she told the moon.

"That's the grass talking," Marco said gruffly. He waited, wanting to hear Elizabeth speak those words again.

Dierdre interrupted. "Lady, it's time you danced."

"I don't know how," Elizabeth said. And she giggled because Dierdre was holding the moon like a ball, she was going to bring it down.

Eric moved into a Latin rhythm. Dierdre swayed, clapping her hands. Elizabeth felt the music's pulse; the waves against the boat kept time with the beat of Eric's music.

"Come on," Dierdre urged, and Elizabeth rose unsteadily to her feet. "I want to dance," she said. She took one more drag on her reefer and threw it overboard, and heard it sizzle. Tentatively then, she put one foot forward. Eric slapped the side of his guitar, and cheered.

"Playtime," Dierdre said. "Come on, lady, take off that dress."

"Maybe," Elizabeth murmured. She reached for the wine bottle, tipped it to her lips. "There isn't any left," she said. The deck tilted under her. Above her, the stars swung in lazy arcs.

"Easy now," Dierdre crooned. She helped Elizabeth on to the bow, turned her around to pull down her zipper. "Step on out now, lady, let's have a whirl."

Barefooted, in her bra and panties, Elizabeth felt the wind embrace her. "Make believe," she said, up on her toes, looking at Marco, her hands cupping her breasts. Marco stumbled to his feet, reached for her. Elizabeth eluded his grasp. Eric hooted. He bent low over his guitar. Elizabeth raised her arms to the moon. "Music!" she commanded.

Elizabeth and Dierdre embraced, revolved. Their bodies blurred, blended. "Awesome," Eric whispered, and set down his guitar because the girls were singing softly, words and a tune of their own making.

Marco sat back, watching the magic unfold.

*M*oonlight over Elizabeth, *it melted her bones.*
She released Dierdre, wanting to stand alone, to feel the the night absorb her. Clinging with one hand to the bow stay, she swung far out over the water. Shadows were fishes, dancing. Marco stepped towards her. "My own darling," he whispered.

She evaded his eager hands. Immersed in her own wonder, she would not be disturbed. "Go away," she told everybody, and leaned to trail her fingers in the water.

"Elizabeth!" Marco spoke sharply "Don't fall."

"Leave me be!" Elizabeth swung out above the water, her toes clinging to the bow, her hands gripping the stay.

"Hey, lady," Eric called, "come back and join the party."

Clutching the stay, Elizabeth crouched, reached down, trailed a foot in the water. "Lovely," she whispered, swinging low.

Marco stepped up, stood close to her. His broad hands reached, almost caught her. She smelled wine on his breath. His voice was dark: another's voice out of long ago. Hands grasped her. *Child... oh, child...*

"No!" Elizabeth cried.

Marco lunged. Elizabeth let go of the stay, and tumbled backwards into the water. She went straight down, struggling, and came up again—to Marco's face, his reaching hands. Panicked, she turned, and struck out for the shore. She swam strongly, escaping the nightmare. Salt stung her eyes, blurred the silver crescent of beach ahead of her. She heard a shout and a splash, and knew Marco followed her. She paused, breathless, treading water, aware suddenly of her near nakedness, and a figure on the beach, waiting at the water's edge. Her feet touched bottom and she crouched, cowering in the shallows, all the lovely feelings draining from her.

"Need a towel?" It was Noel's voice. She grabbed at what he offered. "Come out," he said. "You'll catch your death, Elizabeth."

Shivering in the night air, she stood, turned her back, and wrapped the towel around her. "A party," she said, lamely, feeling like child caught red-handed.

"Big-time parties on that boat," Noel said. "But you, Elizabeth?"

His question stung her. "Why not me?" she asked.

And suddenly then, it was all so funny—herself and this soppy towel, Noel's scolding, Marco splashing around somewhere, shouting for her. She started to laugh, and couldn't stop. Weepy laughter that left her drained, but clear-headed.

"I can smell that weed all the way to here," Noel snapped.

"Would you like some?" Elizabeth asked.

Marco stumbled from the water, Elizabeth's dress in his hands. She stared at him, seeking in his comfortable bulk that monster she had imagined. "I'm sorry," she said. "Perhaps we should go home?"

Noel thrust close to Marco. "Goddamn it, man!" His voice was ugly. "What in hell have you done to her? Look at yourself! You're out there partying, and we've had a fire. Your schoolroom burned. I've called the Guardia. Grass on that boat, it stinks to hell and back. I can't have this, I've got guests, this is my property. You're outside the law."

"My school burned?" Marco seized Noel's arm. "How?"

Noel shrugged. "Some drunk, they told me."

"My school?" Marco growled. With his free hand he gripped Noel's shoulder. "You'll tell me what happened, or..."

Noel yelped, shook himself loose. "I've got guests waiting. All I know is—it was an accident."

"My school," Marco said, and lunged at Noel. "You did this...damn you!"

Noel's knees buckled. Marco held him erect. "I'll break your neck, you bastard—"

"Don't!" Elizabeth cried. She flung herself between the two men.

"What in hell?" A stranger's voice, and Elizabeth turned. Two men stood behind her. They stepped towards Marco. Elizabeth intervened. "Don't touch him!"

And quietly then, because Marco was a hair's breadth from a rage that threatened to explode; she herself could feel it, Elizabeth spoke directly to Marco: "The island needs you," she reminded him.

His eyes were black, unreadable. She put a hand to his shoulder. He shuddered. "Don't touch me."

She insisted. "Marco, it's me—Elizabeth."

He stared at her, his breathing ragged. Slowly, his hands dropped to his sides. "My school burned," he mumbled.

Noel backed out of reach. "Careful," he warned. He turned to the two men behind him. "Give me a hand up the beach, will you? I need a drink."

"Sure." One of them offered Noel an arm.

"What the hell's going on?" the other one asked. He was staring at Elizabeth's near nudity.

"You'll excuse us?" she asked. She took Marco's hand. "Let's go home now. Hush." She spoke gently, as if talking to a child. "Quiet, quiet now," she murmured. She and Marco turned their backs, started up the beach.

Watching, Noel saw Marco's shadow then, a separate entity fingering Marco's heels. He shuddered, certain he was seeing the Devil plain. "Damn near killed me...," he muttered.

"It's late-night TV," one of the strangers said, and giggled.

"No, it's for real," Noel said. He rubbed his aching throat. "You won't believe this," he began, and stopped because these two newcomers, Americans both of them, New Yorkers, would not believe this story. "Someone set the guy's schoolroom on fire," he said. "The name's Rodriguez—stay clear of him."

"Don't worry," said one of the men.

"Whatever the guy is, he's bigger than both of us," said the other. "We're not here to tangle with anyone—we hope," and he shot his friend a wink.

Why are you here? Noel had been wanting to ask that all evening. No time though, it had been one hell of a night. The General had wanted a burning. Noel had given it to him. That drunk he'd found, he'd asked twenty dollars to do it, plus the can of kerosene.

"Shall we go in?" Noel suggested now. Perhaps, over a brandy or two, he'd learn his guests' intent. A couple of fags, he'd guessed that already.

Dierdre's voice floated from the water. "Better find them…"

Seeing the dinghy, Noel shouted, "You can't beach here. Not until you've paid what you owe."

"Aw—go to hell," Eric yelled. "Marco says we can stay for free." But he turned the boat around, leaned to his oars again. "Dierdre girl, let's cut out of here."

"Elizabeth?" she said, "It was a good party 'til she jumped ship."

Eric wasn't listening. "Look at that out there," he said, pointing at their sailboat. "Isn't she beautiful? I mean she's all we want, isn't she?"

Dierdre didn't answer. She was coming down fast, thinking about Noel, what they owed him for wine, grass, other stuff…

"I hate Noel's guts," she said, kicking out with her bare feet, bruising her toes on a coil of rope.

Eric lifted an oar towards the village. "Hey, there's smoke there."

Dierdre moved to lie on the floorboards, her head between Eric's knees. "I'm coming down," she said, "real time, Eric, and I'm scared. Noel just about owns us."

"The moon's in your eyes," Eric said.

Dierdre grinned. She loved Eric this way; he wasn't thinking back or forward, just living the moment now.

"Make a wish," she said, "I hope Marco and his lady will be okay."

ANITA MCANDREWS

Eric chuckled. "Somebody sure spooked somebody. She jumped like a harpooned fish!"

"Do you think Marco's a witch, really?"

"Naw, he's just a guy living his life the way it is. One thing sure, he's under that lady's skin, itching at her."

Dierdre giggled. "She's scratching."

Eric shipped his oars, bent to Dierdre. "How about me getting under your skin right now?"

"**Y**es, I could tell you sea stories," Noel said, leaning back in his chair, eyeing his two guests.

"You—Ralph, isn't it? And?" he raised his eyebrows at his other guest. "Sorry, but that fracas earlier has addled my brains. And this damned heat. It's winter where you're from, isn't it?"

"Coming from New York this sun is a miracle," said Ralph. "We're antique dealers on a businessman's holiday. Avery's my last name, and he's Tom." He pointed to his partner. "Tom Close."

"Antiques?" Noel smiled. "You could call this whole island exactly that."

"Your church is pure Spanish colonial," Ralph said. "We wanted a look-in, but the place is locked."

"Yes," Noel said, "that crazy you met tonight, he keeps the keys. I heard he's working some kind of voodoo in there. The police are watching him."

"Kind of rough, isn't he?" Tom said. "But tell us, who was that mermaid you introduced us to? Where did she float in from?"

"You mean Elizabeth?" Noel asked. "You won't believe it but she's a Bostonian, into some kind of overseas investment—that's why she's here."

Tom chuckled. "We caught her with more than her pants down, didn't we? Tropical islands will do that, even to Boston bluestockings. Is she alone?"

"It didn't appear so," Ralph said. "That voodoo guy, he followed her out of the water. He's a real primitive, isn't he?"

"*Puro indigena,*" Noel said contemptuously—pure Indian.

"And that boat out there?" Ralph said, "I could smell their dope. Lots of that stuff around, I imagine?"

Noel gave him a sharp look. "Whatever you like," he said, easily, and drained his brandy and called the waiter for another round.

Ralph shook his head and got to his feet. "I'm going to call it a night."

Both men wished Noel a good evening. As they left the verandah Noel saw Tom slide his arm about Ralph's waist. Noel grinned. Antique dealers, were they? They were something else too. They'd asked for a double room facing the ocean. Enjoy, Noel thought now, but wondering how two men got sucked into loving each other. Just that way, Noel thought, and he chuckled at his own humor.

He was alone again: empty glasses, the vacant moon. He could see the sailboat, light as a moth on the silvered water. Those two kids, Noel thought bitterly, fucking themselves stupid like it was their last night on earth. It was that kind of night, heavy on a man. Noel felt a darkness in himself.

He stood, and scratched his belly. Too damned quiet. Except the frogs drove him crazy—chirp chirp, fucking their heads off too, this whole damned world doing it! Except himself. He'd like to be a fly on that sailboat, see how the dopeheads did it...

Noel gazed up at the night sky. Not a breath of air. He sniffed. That schoolroom fire still stank to high heaven. Why the whole village hadn't gone up in flames he didn't know. Nicely done though. Tidy. When Rodriguez saw those ashes, all hell would break loose.

Noel's phone rang as he entered his room. "Yes?"

"Darling, so nice..." Veronica's husky unmistakable voice. "What's wrong? You sound muddled."

"Surprised, that's all. You don't call that often."

"Listen, I'm through here, Noel. We need an out and I've found one." She giggled. "Whatever you've got, there's a pretty lieutenant will buy it all. I think he's fronting for you-know-who. So get your stuff to the mainland—now, darling. We'll be paid on delivery. We'll leave together, go far away."

Noel jammed the receiver tight against his ear. "Veronica, you mean this?"

"Just get it over here soon as tomorrow. Can you do that?"

Noel nodded. "I've got the man for it. A sailor boy here on his boat. He owes me a favor."

"Tomorrow evening," she said. "This sailor you have in mind—is his the kind of yacht we might want, darling?"

"A pigsty," Noel said, "trash it."

"And its captain too, we will," she said. "Call me back, let me know what time."

"Soon," Noel breathed.

He waited until she hung up before setting down the receiver. He stared at the phone, thinking hard. What he needed now was Dierdre; only she could talk Eric into sailing the stuff over. First though, he had to pack it. Noel switched off all but one small light, and pulled the shades down, the curtains tight. He locked and bolted the door.

Veronica. She'd have the cash in hand, she'd said. The minute Eric docked he'd be picked up; they'd throw the book at him, lock him up until hell froze. The boy deserved it, living loose as he did, having it all his way. Kids like this, they had it coming.

Noel sank into a chair, reached under his shirt, stroked his belly, let his fingers wander. *A fool to believe Veronica!*

Hell! No time now, for questions. Noel heaved to his feet. He had two hundred leather camera cases packed flat in a suitcase under his bed. He pulled this out, then opened his safe, emptied it of the bags of precious powder stashed there. It would take the rest of the night to fill the cases.

Excitement fumbled Noel's fingers. His turn now. Not only would he have Veronica back, he would leave Rodriguez hurting. His school burned and, if Flore spoke her part right, Elizabeth gone on the next boat. Ah, it was too good, too good! What had he done to deserve this? Noel dusted his hands, cut the coke, and treated himself to a line.

A couple of hours more, and the camera cases were full. Noel hauled a steel crate from the closet and pushed it into the center of the room. By three in the morning the crate with its contraband was secured. He was tired, but he wouldn't sleep. He'd wait until sunup and send for Dierdre.

He pulled a bundle of porno slush from under his bed and lay down to leaf through the tired pages.

*I*t was five in the morning when Noel sent for Dierdre.
"What's wrong?" she asked. Someone from the hotel had rowed out to the boat to get her. Eric had not wanted her to go, but she'd known she had to.

She wrinkled her nose against the odor of Noel's room. She left the door open, and stood next to it, her hand on the jamb. "I'm not coming in," she said.

Noel eyed her tight jeans, her turtleneck sweater. Wrapped up against me, he guessed, and he grinned. "Keep your clothes on," he said, and patted the edge of the bed next to him.

Like he calls a dog, Dierdre thought. She had resolved that if Noel got nasty she'd tell Marco. Then, with no other goodbyes, she and Eric would cut out.

This five o'clock summons now—she was puzzled. She had believed Noel would jump her. But he was all grin, belly hanging out, playing friends. She did not move from the doorway. "I haven't got all day," she told him. "What is it you want?"

Noel got off the bed, pointed at the crate. He slapped its side. "I need someone to take this to the city today. If you tell him to, Eric will do it. He'll be paid on arrival, the fish market dock. A couple of hours sail to the mainland, he can do it. When he brings me the cash, I'll cancel your debt."

Dierdre eyed the crate. "I don't trust you," she said. "Whatever's in that box, Noel, if it's yours, it's no good."

She approached the crate cautiously, circled it. Big enough for a corpse, she thought. Eric's not going to like this. "I don't know..." she murmured. "Why not send it on the ferry?"

"None of your business," Noel snapped. "And you'll do this, girl, or," and he shot her a lewd look, "you'll pay me other ways."

Dierdre hugged herself. This man scared her. There'd been others wanting what Noel wanted, and she'd managed them okay. But this one, he was evil for real. "I'll ask Eric," she said, "but that doesn't mean he'll do it."

Noel stood so close to her she could smell last night's brandy on his breath. He wasn't touching her but she felt him all over her. Eric was hurting too much lately, using painkillers now, prescription drugs. When he hurt, she couldn't think straight. A sail to the mainland? He could do that and be back before she missed him. She swallowed hard. "Okay," she said, "maybe."

"Certain as shit in the morning," Noel said.

"And you won't bother us again, not ever?"

"Never," Noel said.

Still Dierdre hesitated. She didn't like committing Eric and his boat to something as uncertain as this. "If he won't go?" she asked.

"If your man refuses, I'll tell him about you and me—how you pay your debts, what a little whore you are."

"Not true...not with you, or anyone else, ever!"

"But Eric will believe me," Noel said

"He won't!" Dierdre cried.

"He'll look at you different," Noel said. "Put a worm in the apple, nobody wants the apple. How have you paid your debts? Eric will ask that."

"He trusts me," Dierdre said, her voice small.

Noel grinned. "Sure he does—until he hears different."

Yes, Eric was that way—wouldn't think twice. Like stepping on a roach, he'd smash Noel. And ever after, if there was an after, Noel was right, Eric would see her differently.

"Okay," Dierdre decided. "Eric will do this for me."

Noel nodded. "He will. Pick up the crate when you're ready." He gestured Dierdre from the room and waited until he was sure she was gone. Then, pursing his lips in a whistle, he dialed a number. It rang several times before Veronica answered. "Who?"

"Me," Noel crowed. "It's as good as done. Late afternoon. Have your man on the dock. It's a crate of cameras, a big one. Tell your goon to slap the boy in solitary, pronto. He's on drugs, rabid if his boat's in jeopardy."

"Of course, I understand." Her soft laughter tickled Noel's ear. He heard the click of the receiver as she put it down. Something gave him pause: the laziness in her voice, her quick hang-up. A set-up? he wondered—the bitch! If she did him in now…

It's okay, Noel told himself, just a matter of time. Time and patience. Perhaps his New York guests would have breakfast with him? Noel pulled a clean shirt from a drawer. He draped a blanket over the crate. Leaving his room, he hung a "*Do Not Disturb*" sign on his doorknob.

Down the hall, he knocked on the Americans' door. His hand raised, he heard voices, soft laughter, and he hesitated, listening.

Grunts. A word or two. A sigh, "Jee-suz…"

Girls in there? It sounded like…? Noel grinned. No women needed here. Holding his breath, he leaned against the door—a man could get a hard-on just listening…

"Gauguin…" Noel held his breath, pressed an ear to the door.

"We're not the first, we know that." A mumbled answer, then the same voice: "Got to get our hands on those paintings now, get them out of here fast…"

The other spoke: "Amado, isn't that the name?"

Gauguin? Noel knew the story. He'd heard about the old lady and some paintings. Elizabeth visited Mrs. Amado, and he'd wondered why. And before her, and these New Yorkers now, others had been here—Americans, arty types. So the Gauguins were real? Noel's breath caught. Genuine Gauguins?

He heard the word "Millions..." and, "the art market now, it's through the roof..." The voices faded.

Noel returned to his room. He couldn't sit for excitement. Round and around the crate he paced. What he didn't know about Gauguin would fill a book, but he had a couple of friends who made these deals. Talk about money! Hell, he'd bring Veronica a gift not even she could dream of. They'd be set for life, he'd buy her a palace on the Riviera.

How to get his hands on those paintings? Everyone knew that old woman was ready to drop dead. A heart attack maybe? He could frighten her bad, rumple her up—that'd finish her, and no questions asked. Snatch the canvases, and get the hell out.

Then what? Noel flung himself on his bed. He didn't know a fuck about dealing art. He'd be better off dealing with those queers. Let them buy the paintings from him. Noel jumped to his feet.

In minutes Noel was knocking on his guests' door. "Breakfast on the house," he called.

Seated on the verandah, he called for a double gin. It was not long before the men joined him. He told them to order whatever they wanted. "I'd like to show you around, but I've an errand in the village. If you can wait, I'll be back in an hour."

"We've got something we must do," Ralph said. "We've been told to look up a woman, a Mrs. Amado. There's...uh...a cousin of hers, works for us in New York."

Yeah, Noel thought, Elizabeth had used almost the same excuse. "Amado?" he asked, pretending ignorance.

"Do you know her?" Ralph asked.

"I know who she is. She's senile. Lives alone, the last of an old French family here. I'll take you there later."

"We'll find it," Tom said quickly. "We'll walk there after breakfast."

"Okay." Noel's brain was racing. So let them go first, check out the pictures; the old lady wasn't about to give them away.

Meanwhile he'd see his crate on to the boat, send Eric on his way.

He'd wait until evening, take a stroll into the village, visit the old lady. It was a done deal. Noel drained his drink.

Glancing at the harbor, he saw the sailboat sleeping like the gull she was named for. Sleep your last, kiddies! Noel grinned. Everything his way now. Come tomorrow, this damned island would be no more than the memory of a bad dream.

*E*ric was pacing the deck when Dierdre returned from seeing Noel. "What took you so long?" he asked.

"Things..." Dierdre replied vaguely. To avoid saying more, she cooked breakfast: fried fish and the last of the plantain. Eric made a face over his coffee. "This is slop, girl!"

"Yesterday's brew—it's all we've got left," she said. "Eric, we've got to get our act together, pay up, and get out."

"How we gonna do that?" Eric laughed. "Baby, we're planted here for good."

Dierdre did not smile. "Noel said if we do him one favor, he'll cancel our debt."

Eric raised his eyebrows. "A favor? Already it smells."

"It's a crate—he wants it in the city today. Someone will meet you at the fish market dock. He'll pay. You're to bring Noel the money."

"That's it?" Eric poured his coffee over the side. He didn't feel like sailing, not today anyway. Rain coming on, you could taste it. Heavy, the air now, it made him jumpy—like waiting for something about to happen.

"We won't get out of here any other way," Dierdre said. "There's so much we need, Eric."

He pulled her across his knees, tangled his fingers in her hair. "What do we need? We've got each other. I missed you when I woke up. What the hell kept you?" He studied her face. "I've never seen you scared. It's Noel, isn't it? What'd he do?"

"Nothing." Dierdre hated lies. "He talked mean though."

Eric was on his feet. "What did he want? Hell, I know what he wants!" He pulled her up next to him. "Did he try anything? Tell the truth!" His eyes burned into her.

Dierdre hesitated. "He…well, sure he wanted it, they all do. If we don't pay, you know…they get nasty." Dierdre shrugged, turned her face away.

"Damn right I know!"

"Oh God," she begged, "you don't think…you can't think that I…"

He wheeled on her. "I don't know what to think! Except you were a long time gone. What happened, girl? If he touched you, I'll…"

Dierdre drew herself up. "What's happened," she said coldly, "is Noel's right. He said you wouldn't believe me!"

She flung herself at Eric, clutched him tightly. "If you think I'd ever…"

He held her hard against him. "No, I won't believe that. I won't even think that. It's me I'm angry at. What kind of guy would send his girl to a shit like Noel? The way he looks at you…hell, lots of times I feel like nothing," he said.

"You? What about me—how I feel?" Because Noel's words had cut deep, she almost didn't trust herself now. "You've got to be wondering, Eric."

"Not about you, never," he said. "It's that slime—he frightens you—that's what gets to me. That, and it's me who lets this happen." He drew a deep breath. "It's me should take care of money owed, stuff like that. Yeah—when I'm out of dope, it's me who should get it. Hey, maybe if I've got to go look for it I won't want it that bad?"

"I'd like that," Dierdre said, quietly. "I've been thinking, Eric, smoking grass is a downer. Both of us get mixed up, we could lose each other."

Eric had made a decision. "I want out of here. I'll take that crate across the bay."

"You will? Just like that? It's not dangerous?"

ANITA

Eric shrugged. "I'll check it out. Deals like this, a guy can't be too careful."

"You won't fight him, will you?"

"I'll pay my debt, and get the hell out." He took Dierdre in his arms. "Wherever we go from now on, its cash on the line."

She laughed. "Us? How?"

"I've got a plan."

Dierdre sniffed the air. She could smell the rain now. She imagined a black sea, thunder. "You'll hurry back?"

"Maybe a jib or two, depending on the wind." Eric ruffled her hair. "Love these curls! I'll be back. You wait."

She went into his arms. "Tell me you trust me…?"

Eric spoke softly into her ear. "Girl, if I don't, I've lost my compass. Like the Devil Man said, you're my way to go. These past days I've done some heavy thinking. Been wanting to tell you. What do you say we transit the Canal, sail up the East Coast—somewhere warm, Florida maybe? We could set up shop, boat maintenance or something—you and I."

"You mean it?" Almost reverently she touched his hair.

"I'm not one for words, you know that." He took her small hands in his, rubbed her roughened palms. "You told Elizabeth you've forgotten what dressing up is all about. I don't want my lady in dirty jeans."

"But are you ready?" Dierdre asked. "Are you ready to live ashore? I mean, the way you feel—that war and all. Taxes, Eric, all that government stuff you don't like."

"I don't want to run anymore. Marco—he made me think, made me feel good about myself, what I can do—all that. I'm not that shadow wimp I drag around, he's not me."

Eric hesitated. Then he said, "Maybe even a kid of our own?"

"Oh…" Dierdre was crying. "You do love me!"

Bewildered, Eric shook his head. "Women!"

He held her at arms length, studied that face he knew by heart. "No, girl, you wouldn't cheat."

She kissed him fiercely. "You won't even think it!"

"Other things on my mind," Eric said. "We've got to get *Gull* ship-shape for sailing."

"You'll be back this evening," Dierdre said. "I'll wait on the beach."

"I won't promise when," Eric said. "This wind now—it'll be against me all the way home."

He studied the horizon. "That's one hell of a storm coming." He turned to go below. "I want to check a chart."

"Eric!" She was alarmed. "Since when did you need a chart for this bay? We know it blind."

"Anchorages," he said. "I may have to check in somewhere."

He wasn't telling her but he'd run stuff before he knew her, he'd done what was asked, taken his money and sailed. This time though, this girl the prize, he was going to be extra careful.

"Hey," he said, crossing the deck to her, "I've done deals like this, blindfolded. Your problem is you don't trust no one."

"Anyone," she corrected him. "Except you of course."

He chuckled. "That's a given." And he kissed her.

Dierdre cupped his face in her hands. "Tell me again—no matter what you hear, what anyone says—about me, I mean—you won't believe them?"

Eric shook his head. "What I want to believe—that's it. I don't go no further."

Dierdre laughed. "Any further!"

*L*ater that morning, Eric loaded his boat with Noel's crate and set sail for the mainland.

Dierdre stood on the dock, waving until he was out of sight. Behind her, Noel, surprisingly good-humored, whispered, "Red sky in the morning, sailors take warning."

"Not to worry. My Eric's the best sailor around."

"Coffee?" Noel suggested. "I've some interesting guests you should meet. Too bad you missed that fire last night."

"Fire?"

"Rodriguez's school. Some drunk did it. The whole place burned, the books too."

Dierdre was aghast. "Where's Marco now?"

"With the gringa, where else?"

Dierdre stared at him. "You did it, didn't you? You won't rest, will you, until everything's down!"

"I'm gone, then," Noel said, with such assurance Dierdre felt a distinct unease.

Curious, she trailed him to the hotel verandah where Noel introduced her to Ralph and Tom who were finishing their breakfast. "New Yorkers," Noel said, seating himself too close to Dierdre. She slid her chair sideways, away from him, and turned to the strangers. "What are you doing here?" she asked. "It's the beginning of our rainy season and it can get wet."

A couple of gays, she guessed; too sophisticated for this place though. She wondered what they wanted.

"We're island hopping," Tom said. Dierdre thought the two looked exactly alike: city men—blow-dried, sugar-coated, talcum and after shave.

"Do you know a Mrs. Amado?" Ralph asked.

"Sure, that's the old woman Elizabeth visits," Dierdre replied.

"Elizabeth? You mean the lady from Boston?"

"Yes," Dierdre said, "she goes to see Mrs. Amado all the time."

"Interesting," Tom said. He looked at his companion. "Ready?"

Ralph pushed back his chair. "We'll see you later?"

Dierdre nodded. "Maybe."

Dierdre headed for the beach, thinking she'd walk that way to Elizabeth's house. Maybe Marco was there. Noel had set this fire, Dierdre would swear it. Things were building up bad. And Eric gone now.

Ralph and Tom took the path towards the village. They looked out of place, and knew it—their thongs, their look-alike Gucci jeans.

"Do we know the way?" Ralph asked.

"We take a right, up the hill, and past the church," Tom said. "Noel told me it's a yellow house."

Ralph wrinkled his nose. "What's that smell? Fire, somewhere. Let's hope it's not our Gauguins!"

Tom grinned. "It'll be the find of the year. What do you think of the Bostonian? She's after what we want, obviously."

"I don't doubt it. And Noel told me there've been others here, rooting around. A rumor like this one, it can't be kept quiet." Tom glanced at the sky. "So where's this rain they talk about?"

"We're going to get wet," Ralph said. "Let's speed things up. We'll offer the woman a sum she can't resist, get those paintings off the island tonight."

"How much cash have you got on you?" Tom asked.

Ralph touched his pocket. "A couple of hundreds. But we won't have to go that high."

"A steal," Tom said, remembering Spain, that slum in Seville; he and Ralph had unearthed a Murillo study from under a pile of fish bones. They'd paid beggar pennies for it. Tom always let Ralph do the bargaining; the man had a hunk of ice for a heart.

Ralph stopped in front of a yellow house. "I guess this is it."

The two climbed the steps, and Tom knocked on the door. The old woman answered, opening her door just a crack. *"Si?"* she asked.

Tom gave her his 100-watt smile. He bowed like a Spanish don, and had himself and Ralph inside the house, the door shut behind them, before Mrs. Amado knew what had happened. *"Si?"* she asked again.

"Elegante, su casa!" Tom exclaimed. He lied in his teeth. He had seldom seen such bare-ass poverty.

Just about as elegant as an outhouse, Ralph thought. He looked around and, glancing up at a high shelf, he saw the rolled canvas. That's it, he guessed, that's them! He nudged Tom. "Up there..."

Tom hushed him. He turned to the old woman. "We are collectors," he explained, in Spanish. "We've been told you have antiques?"

The old woman grinned. "Oh, yes, I have many things—from French time, Spanish time. I sold Pizarro's sword the other day." She shrugged, spread her gnarled hands. "I have to eat."

"It's paintings we're interested in, any kind as long as they're old. Books too, of course," Tom added. There wasn't a book in the place, but he didn't want the the old bag to get suspicious.

"A bible perhaps?" Tom asked. He smiled boyishly. "I adore old bibles."

Mrs. Amado shook her head. She knew what these two wanted; they couldn't keep their eyes off that canvas on the shelf. Just like the gringa, but that one was kind. These two—the smell of them made her sneeze. She did just that, and wiped her nose with the back of her hand.

"Up there," Tom said, pointing. "It looks like canvas. Pictures maybe?"

Mrs. Amado nodded. "Paintings, very old. A man from France did them, gave them to my family." She shook her head. "Not for sale."

"Just a look?" Tom asked.

"No, señores." Mrs. Amado was adamant.

"Supposing we buy that canvas without seeing it?" Ralph suggested. "I'm willing to take a chance." He pulled a wad of bills from his pocket, counted off fifty in ones, and held them out in plain view.

Señora Amado licked her lips. "You spend that much without seeing first?" But she was not really surprised. "Many come here, do same as you. They pay anything for those paintings."

"Many come here? Who?" Ralph asked.

"Gringos—and the new señora now, the pretty one. She's always wanting to see the pictures. But I won't take them down. My grandson forbids it."

"And where is he?" Tom asked. "Perhaps...?"

"He is gone, on a ship. Many months away. He will beat me if I touch that canvas." Mrs. Amado opened her door. *"Buenos Dias, señores."*

Ralph and Tom could do little more than exit. On the street again, disconcerted, they looked at each other. "I'll be damned!" Tom said. Ralph nodded. "Stubborn old bitch, isn't she?"

"Maybe Noel can help?" Tom suggested. "We don't have to tell him why, just that we're interested in French paintings."

"Gauguin within reach, I could have touched him—shit!" Ralph slapped Tom's shoulder. "That woman, the Bostonian—she's on to it. We've got to move fast."

"Sweetheart, those paintings are ours! Let's get a swim, cool down a bit. Noel knows the old woman, we'll talk to him."

The two men rounded the corner into the plaza, almost colliding with Marco and Elizabeth.

"Good morning," Elizabeth said. She forced an embarrassed smile.

"Once more you'll forgive me. I'm not at my best. This time it's a fire; we've put it out now, I hope." Her cheek and hands were smudged with charcoal.

Marco's eyes were red-rimmed. "I would wish you good day, but it isn't."

Tom smiled. "We won't bother you. We're nosing about. It's a pretty village."

"The church is closed," Marco said.

Ralph was looking at Elizabeth. "Our mysterious Boston mermaid…"

She laughed. "And you are the mysterious New Yorkers."

Tom did not duck her gaze. "You are perhaps a collector? Like ourselves."

Elizabeth shook her head. "Art is a hobby of mine, but I work in tourism. You'll agree, I'm sure, that this is a corner of paradise."

Ralph grinned. "Throw in antiperspirant and bug spray—it could be."

Definitely gallery creatures, Elizabeth thought, and they've obviously been visiting Señora Amado. From their faces, she was willing to bet they'd had no better luck than she.

"This is my friend, Marco Rodriguez," Elizabeth said.

"I'm Tom, this is Ralph. We're traveling together."

From the same Madison Avenue gallery, Elizabeth guessed, two pretty boys; they stink of old masters, gilt frames, money—and secrets. How would they react, she wondered, if she mentioned Gauguin?

She dared, "You are aware that Gauguin was here?"

"Yes," Ralph replied easily, "I read his diary. He was hospitalized on this island—malaria, I believe."

Elizabeth nodded. "I like to think he painted here."

"Now that would be a find!" Ralph said.

"Wouldn't it though?" Elizabeth agreed. She looked at Marco.

Tom couldn't figure it. Because they didn't match, this Bostonian and her Indian. What was she in truth? A closet beach bum, an MBA on vacation? One thing sure, under all that hair, behind those incredible eyes, ticked a brain. Real estate—hell! She was after the same thing he was. But the guy with the ugly scowl, where did he fit in? School teacher? Tom guessed there was more here than met the eye. If this woman collected, this Indian could be a titillating find. Definitely not a take-home though, and Tom grinned.

Elizabeth slid her arm through Marco's. "Perhaps we'll see you two later? Maybe a drink at the hotel?"

Ralph grinned. "Sure, we'd be glad to. If you'll come out of the ocean again, looking as you did. It was charming, really—Venus on the half shell."

"Botticelli? Not quite," Elizabeth replied, "I won't promise anything. But perhaps you've a story or two to tell? Collections and such?"

"Collections, and such," Ralph echoed, with a broad wink.

Elizabeth laughed, and turned to Marco. She sensed his weariness. That fire had defeated him, somehow. The fire itself, and the questioning by the police early this morning.

All night she'd stayed close to him. She'd worked until her shoulders ached, passing buckets of water. Nothing but ashes left.

"You can build another schoolroom," Elizabeth had said.

Marco had looked at her, his face gray in the dawn light. "Why?" he'd asked. "Teaching English is against the law. I told you. They'll arrest me."

Now he stepped forward, between Tom and Ralph. "If you'll excuse us?"

"Of course," Ralph said. "We're heading for a swim."

Ignoring Marco, he addressed Elizabeth directly: "Just a minute more of your time. We'd love to know what's collectible in Señora Amado's house. She said you visit her often."

"Perhaps I should invite you to our tea parties?" Elizabeth parried. "Paper plates and plastic cups. Ice cream, too," and she smiled at Marco.

"Pizzaro's sword?" Ralph asked.

"Correction: somebody's machete," Elizabeth said. Her eyes met Ralph's, and she knew he had read her secret. Grateful for Marco's presence then—it offered an escape—she said, "We must be on our way."

"Good luck in whatever," Tom said. Both men raised their hands in a salute.

Elizabeth walked slowly. Her secret was out. It was her fault. She should have cut and run days ago.

He turned to her. "Elizabeth? Come with me. A place I know where there is quiet." He took her hand in his. She felt the coldness of his flesh and rubbed his skin. "Marco, you should go home."

"Come, share a last secret with me."

But she was too tired to go another step. "Is it far?" she asked.

"Far enough from all this," he answered. "Those two cupcakes just now—what do they want? This was to be our day, remember?"

"It still is," she said. She wanted to change her mind, to excuse herself from this expedition. But Marco—he was an avalanche poised, a thunderhead building. She could feel his urgency.

"Those two, they've got mean eyes."

"I know their kind. They're part of my world, Marco."

He wheeled on her. "You are going soon, aren't you?"

"I don't know," she answered, truthfully, and moved, so that the sun shone full on him, the way she had seen him that first time.

"Tell me," she said. "Noel did this, didn't he?"

"Sure he did. He knows that school was my main project here. But it's my fault the fire happened. That damn fool party, too much cheap wine, I should have been in town, I smelled that smoke, I ignored it. My school, yes. Noel knew I'd blow when I saw it gone. He had the police ready. Those questions this morning? Satan worship in the church, they said—skull and bones, they said. Enough to drive any man over the edge."

Marco gripped Elizabeth's hands. "It is you who kept me sane. And there is something else, something I didn't tell you. They've taken my boys, my students, put them in the army."

"But they're too young," Elizabeth protested. "And you can't just put people in the army."

"Here, they do that. At night, in the city, they scoop the drunks off the streets. Kids, mostly—they wake up with guns in their hands, the General's toy soldiers."

"They have no right!" she exclaimed.

"When will you learn, Elizabeth? We have no rights."

Which was why he had stood there, front of the cops, this morning, played dull as a schoolboy. His hands deliberately loose at his sides, he had answered all their questions. A skull? Not his, he'd said, he'd found it in the convent garden and carried it to the church, wanting only a decent burial place for it. What should be done, he said, is clean up the convent, the garden there.

The soldiers had fingered their pistols, shuffled their boots, closed in around him, curious, as if he were some sort of animal. He had stood there, holding tight to himself, swallowing his rage.

Marco drew a deep breath now, gripped Elizabeth's hand. So little left of this day now, he would not spoil it. "Plenty of time later," he said, "to figure all this out."

She took his hand. "Yes, let's pretend we've all the time in the world."

"Brujo!" Two kids—out of nowhere, hanging on Marco's arms.

"Brujo, no more school?"

"No mas." Marco said. He swept them off him like a couple of flies. Angrily, one of the boys spit at Marco's feet. The other gestured with clenched fists. *"Cobarde!* Coward. They call you that. A do nothing brujo! Scared to fight back."

"No!" Marco roared. "Get the hell out!" His hand went to his scar. The boys saw the gesture and turned tail.

Marco turned, looking for Elizabeth. Finding her, he swept her roughly off her feet, held her high against him, letting her slide down slowly in his arms. His tears fell on her cheeks, her lips.

"Please," she crooned, "Marco...Marco..."

"Let it finish," he muttered. "Let him have what he wants."

"Who? What?"

"The Butcher. Let him have it, and eat it. Until there's nothing left and he must devour himself."

*T**he cool swept her skin like the breath of whirring fans.*
Elizabeth paused, wondering, on the edge of Marco's sanctuary. No dryness here, only the myriad colors of shade. The flutter of parakeets broke the silence, and the rush of black water falling. Elizabeth smelled lime, banana, frangipani.

"But it is enchantment!" she whispered.

They had come up a narrow path and entered a clearing floored with smooth rocks, carpeted with ferns and moss. A perpetual twilight—sea colors misted earth and trees. Elizabeth touched a ginger lily. And a crimson Bird of Paradise. Above her head bloomed those small orchids, Ladies of the Evening. High trees leaned, and climbing lianas proffered leaves broad as table tops, smooth, cream-veined.

A jade-colored moon lay at Elizabeth's feet. Across the pool, a cataract spilled from the sky; its fine spray powdering Elizabeth's cheeks.

"Marco, it is extraordinary!"

"Yes." He was pleased with her delight. "When I was young I climbed to the lip of the falls there, and dived straight down into this pool. I haven't done that in years."

"I hope not." The water sang in her ears. "Where is your cave?"

"Almost at the top, the lip of the falls."

Marco stripped. Naked, his skin borrowed the colors of the surrounding jungle. Elizabeth watched as he stepped to the pool's edge and dived, cutting the still water neatly. She held her breath, waiting for him to surface. Then she saw his shadow; it was black, skimming the water, riding the paler shape of Marco beneath. Elizabeth cried out, and the shadow dissolved.

A moment later Marco was standing on a rock, on the other side of the pool. "Come on," he shouted.

He waited for her, spray cooling his face; the pull of the falls behind him massaging his legs and back. He was amused, watching her make up her mind. She turned her back at last, and disrobed, folded her clothes, and placed them on a rock.

She approached the pool like an anxious long-legged bird. Her arms and shoulders gleamed as she released her hair, let it fall free. In this weighted green space, she was ethereal, her paleness flickering frail as a candle flame. Marco shouted her name. She waved, and dived, disappearing for too long and Marco went in after her.

Eyes closed, they found each other with their hands. She surfaced, pulling him up with her. They played like children, ducking and racing, meeting to kiss, rising to ride each other's shoulders.

He took her on his back. "Hold on!" he shouted. And they were in, through, and behind the falls. Water pounded, stealing Elizabeth's breath. Marco lifted her to a ledge and, together, they climbed then, to the cave entrance. It was deep, hidden from view, cut into the rocky face of the cliff.

The floor was white sand and Elizabeth sank down, exhausted. She was exhausted by the climb. The din of the falls filled her head; every sense was numbed, all feelings absorbed by the unceasing rush and hiss of water beyond the cave entrance. She reached to touch it, this live thing, dragging at her.

"The world is shut outside," Marco exulted. He flung himself to the sandy floor, pulled Elizabeth down beside him. Always this place dizzied him; its secrecy gave him a sense of kingship. "Nobody can see us," he said, stroking the wet hair from Elizabeth's cheeks, licking the spray from her eyelids and lips. "No one to see us," he repeated.

She climbed on top of him, fitting herself against his body. "I saw your shadow, Marco. It swam above you. Did I imagine it?"

"Evil cannot touch us here." He spoke urgently, wanting her to feel this place as he did. "We are near Heaven," he said.

Yes! Here she must know me. Here I will give her the care of my soul.

"Paradise," he whispered, meaning the blue of her eyes.

His intensity puzzled Elizabeth. The darkness of him frightened her.

"Love me," Marco said. And deliberately then, slow as a ceremony, he made love to her. Slowly, carefully, he touched her, leaving no part of her wanting.

"My heart…my dove…my soul…" He spoke in Spanish. Because it was more beautiful, she had told him so.

He explored, caressed, and entered her then, gently insisting until all her secrets softened, melted, opened wide. And she was fierce then, with hands and tongue. She took the lead, until Marco cried out, "Wait!" and held himself still, his mouth hard on her own.

He held her so, quiet, until she felt him deep in her. And felt herself submit then: every part of her reaching, aching to give.

Never before, never like this. Elizabeth gave herself, like the water to the falls. Lost in her own passion, she cried aloud. Her body arched, lifted to his weight. "Please, Marco, now, please…"

"No, not yet."

He held himself, and her—carefully, back from the edge. "Be still," he told her. "Listen. Hear the water music."

Her fingers wound tight in his hair. "Now, Marco!"

He could hold her here forever. Hold her like this until she broke in his hands, streamed through him, over him…

Thunder—heard it then, behind the water's music. A new fresh smell, green in his lungs. He lifted his head, saw lightning flash, and leaned to her lips again.

If he doesn't take me now, I will die of wanting.

"Come with me," he whispered, "yes…yes…"

They moved as one, breath and breath, one being. His lips against her ear, he called her name: "Elizabeth!"

"Yes, Marco." She sought his mouth, plunged her tongue deep, all parts of her wanting release.

"*Te amo, querida*...I love you..."

"Tell me, Marco..."

Thunder, somewhere. Lightning behind her eyelids.

"Promise me...Promise me..." Marco's voice.

"Yes, yes..." Because anything now in the world she would promise. She could not wait another second. "Yes, Marco!"

"You will take my Stone from me when it is time. Swear this, Elizabeth." He spoke against her open mouth, pressing his words slow and hard. She must hear him. "Swear this, my love..."

"Yes, yes, I promise. Anything, everything, Marco, I promise..."

She cared for nothing and no one. Her body ached to be gone, to float free. "I promise," she said, "yes, Marco..."

And he released her. Only the beat of their hearts now, the water's tumult, and the rain outside filling every dry crevice down to the center of the earth's being.

High above, the river roiled, swollen with rain. The pool below moved in dark uneasy ripples. Marco dreamed he fell from a great height, fell down through a sky blue as Elizabeth's eyes. She slept deeply as a child, without dreaming.

When she wakened, she was cold. "Marco, wake up! Look, it's raining out there. I'm half frozen."

He smiled. "Not I. I will never be cold again."

He stood, and helped her to her feet. He turned her to face the falling water. "Remember this," he said. "We have made a ceremony."

Elizabeth was shivering. "Yes. Yes. But please, let's hurry."

She wondered why he stood there, staring at her as if seeing her for the first time. "Come," she said sharply, "it will be dark soon."

He didn't move. "Tell me you will not forget this place and what has happened here, between us."

She frowned. "What has happened?" Then she smiled. "But of course. How can I forget how you have loved me here?"

"And you are not cold, you couldn't be."

She had no words for what she felt—an absolute weariness, tinged with a foreboding that chilled her. She wanted nothing more than to be dry and warm. "Can we go?"

Marco took her hand. "Follow me."

The rain had stopped, the storm receded. Slowly they descended. "Now, dive with me," Marco said. Holding her hand he pulled her with him, deep into the darkening green of the pool.

When they were out, "Let's stay," he said. "We have the afternoon."

Elizabeth shook her head. She was drained. "There's nothing left of me," she confessed.

"Your house or mine?" Marco asked, rubbing her dry with his shirt.

She turned to him. "Will you understand that I need to be alone? It's been quite a day." She gestured at the pool, the waterfall. "I'm overwhelmed."

"A moment more." He led her to the pool's edge and pointed at her image there, in the water. "Look at yourself, Elizabeth. See the woman you have become."

The water wavered like old mirror glass. She peered at the shadow of herself, and at him, dark beside her. "Those two—they look so," and she hesitated. "So lost, Marco."

They are there forever, those two—they have no other place to go but here...

"Two lost souls?" she wondered. "But I don't believe in souls."

"I have given you the care of mine," he told her. "And you have given me your promise."

Elizabeth picked up a pebble and threw it into the water. "Look," she said, "how one small stone disturbs the whole."

And one small word. I said yes, yes to all he asked.

She touched his cheek. "Marco," she said, "don't expect too much of me."

He took her hand in his and pressed her palm tightly against his Mark. "You will give me Paradise." He spoke in Spanish: *Paraiso.*

"Marco," she protested, "I am not strong enough!"

Never had she been so cold! The rain had begun again. She knew the river was filling fast. The falls drummed, rapid as the sound of feet, running.

"Will the river overflow?" she asked. Because the village was plywood and wicker, it could wash away, everything gone.

"The river will rise," Marco said, "and this pool will overflow. Nothing here but swamp then, and sea birds fishing shrimp. Look," he pointed, "the mango trees flower. Soon the parakeets will be gone."

I will miss them.

She turned from him that he not see her tears.

*D*ierdre was waiting outside Elizabeth's house. She was distraught, her cheeks stained with tears.

"Marco," she cried, "you'll help me! Elizabeth, please—Eric's been arrested! Noel just told me. They picked him up at the fish market dock. For smuggling coke—it was in that crate Noel gave Eric this morning. I don't believe it...I won't believe it! But Noel swears it's true."

"If Noel told you, I don't believe it either," Marco said.

"I do," Elizabeth said. "It makes sense. Noel set it up. Eric's hands aren't clean, Dierdre. I told you something would happen."

Dierdre glared at her. "Spoiler! You've no faith in anyone. My Eric—he's not stupid, he wouldn't walk into a trap like that."

"Hold it," Marco said. "Let's talk about this inside." He led the way into the house. Flore was in the kitchen. "Not now, Flore," he said.

Flore nodded. She'd been waiting all morning, a little more time didn't matter. She had her speech all planned. That glow now, on the gringa's face—it wasn't going to last.

Marco closed the door behind her and turned to Dierdre. "Stay here with Elizabeth," he said. "I'm going up to check with the police. Give me half an hour and I'll get to the bottom of this."

"Okay," Dierdre said, "but I'm going to the dock. I promised Eric I'd be there. He said he'd be back before dark. I don't believe Noel. He hates the world. He wants everyone miserable as he is. He can't stand to see anyone happy."

"But why would he pick on you and Eric?"

"Because we're happy, that's why!" Dierdre drew a deep breath, swallowed hard. "If it's true, if Eric is in jail—you'll get him out, won't you, Marco?"

Marco hesitated. "If I can——"

"Don't ask him this," Elizabeth said. "He'd be putting his life on the line."

"And he will," Dierdre said. "Marco's that way."

"I'll do what I can," Marco said.

Dierdre followed him out to the front steps. "I'll wait on the dock," she said. She gave him a quick hug. "Eric will be back, you'll see."

Watching her run down the street, Marco thought how very young she was. He would not, could not fail this child.

Flore spoke from the shadows. "A stupid girl."

Marco turned on her. "Why don't you go home? The señora is tired."

Flore smiled. "Yes, she will be—very tired."

Something in her voice caught Marco's attention. He stepped close to her. "If you harm her, Flore, you will answer to me."

"It is you must answer to her now," Flore replied.

Marco had no time for riddles. "I'm going to the police station. Tell the señora I'll be back."

Rain spattered, he could smell the island greening, the earth softening. He ducked the black dog crossing his path. The animal did not throw Marco a glance.

Rain again, harder now. It pelted the street; a branch fell. Water scrubbed the gutters.

"Don Marco!" a boy's voice: "Hey, *brujo*, welcome! Come inside."

Next door to the Amado house: a fisherman's house. Papi used to fish with the old man here; it was his grandson who called now. Marco smelled garlic and cilantro, scallops steaming in a cast iron pot. He saw pink shells spilled on the table; he would bring them to Elizabeth later. He was hungry, tired, wanting, just for a moment, the warmth of a familiar world.

"*Si, gracias,*" he said.

*E*lizabeth heard the rain on the roof. A draft licked her ankles and she remembered she had left her bedroom window open. She hurried to close it. Catching a glimpse of herself in the mirror, she saw shadows beneath her eyes, her lips pale. She would shower, get rid of these wet clothes. And she stripped, stood naked. Moving her hands slowly down over her body, she remembered. Marco had said she was like new.

I wanted to give and give…

She shivered. *I'll catch my death…*

The hot water then, it soothed. Marco would be back. Such a fool, thinking he could help Eric. You did drugs, you got caught. Simple as that.

Stepping from the shower, Elizabeth toweled herself dry. She picked up her comb.

"Señora, I must speak with you." It was Flore, close behind her.

"Yes? What is it?"

Flore turned Elizabeth to the mirror. "See me there, señora?" She folded her hands proudly on her protruding stomach. "Look carefully, señora. I am with child."

Elizabeth stared into the glass. "But what has that to do with me?" The girl wanted money of course.

"You must know," Flore said, all in one breath, "this is Marco's baby."

The comb slid from Elizabeth's hand.

"No," she said. She could not take her eyes off the mirror—the two women there: one so grave and pale; the other round-bellied, brown, her painted smile.

"You lie," Elizabeth said.

"No, señora," Flore replied, her voice smooth as cream. She leaned closer to the glass. "I carry Marco's child."

Elizabeth raised her hand. "Get out!" she screamed. She slapped Flore's face.

Flore smiled. She had never in her life been so sure of herself. Noel was right: this gringa believed anything, everything. And her face—it was that of an old woman. Quietly as she had come, Flore turned, and departed.

*T*he silent house. Even the rain fell quietly, tears sliding the windows. Elizabeth retrieved her comb. Moved it jerkily through the tangles of her hair. She picked up her brush. It was not long before the regular lift and fall of her arm and the pull of the brush through her drying hair was comforting, the gesture numbing in its familiarity.

Unthinking—not to think—Elizabeth bowed her head, brought her hair over her shoulder and braided it tightly. Now she must look at herself in the mirror. She saw, not her own, but Flore's face. It was Flore's voice she heard, Flore's words: *I carry Marco's child.*

And another face then, her mother's. *Love is death, Elizabeth...*

She lifted her brush and hurled it, shattering the glass, splintering the ghosts there.

Standing very straight, she addressed her broken image: "You must leave here." Her voice was loud. Her words shocked her, wakened her. Quickly she pulled on the damp jeans and shirt dropped just moments ago, or so it seemed, on the floor.

Suitcases. She pulled them from the closet. Not tonight, but to-morrow, early, she would take the ferry. This time tomorrow, she'd have forgotten this island. She was good at that—forgetting what she did not want to remember.

But first, first she must get the paintings.

Think, Elizabeth Rogers—think only from the top of your head.

She pulled on a sweater and twisted her hair up under a scarf. She took some neatly folded bills, one thousand in twenties, from a pile of handkerchiefs at the back of her dresser drawer. Careless of her to leave them there, anyone could have stolen them. Foolish to believe she could trust people here.

She glanced at her clock and saw it was past five. The rain was fierce now, it spit at her windows, sneaked under the door. Elizabeth could not remember where she had put her umbrella. Marco was out there somewhere. He'd said he would be back...

Elizabeth froze. But he can't come here—I won't let him in! *I'll never, ever, let him in again!*

She opened her front door and peered out. All so ordinary, except for the rain. The street, the closed houses—their quiet denied her shattered world. Lights in a few windows only. Laughter, somewhere. The smell of food cooking. Loneliness engulfed Elizabeth, and she took it to her, knowing she must relearn the ritual of herself, by herself.

Now, only the Gauguins mattered. What else *had* mattered?

Finding the umbrella just outside the door, she opened it, and walked the wet street towards the village. What if she met Marco? She would pretend she didn't know him. No need to pretend that because she never had known him, not really. An Indian, a Latino for God's sake—how far could she get from her world?

Elizabeth splashed through puddles. She had invented Marco, that was it. Invented what she'd needed, what she'd needed most in this damned beautiful place. Women did that—Mother had. And look what had happened to Mother.

Elizabeth paused for breath. She'd known from the start what a brute Marco was. That story he'd told about his father—that should have warned her. Rain slid down Elizabeth's neck.

Marco and his crazy Devil talk. Seductive, of course, erotic in its very strangeness. That scene behind the waterfall, I would have promised him the moon. And he knew it, the bastard!

Arriving at the Amado house, Elizabeth raised her hand to knock. A man's voice inside gave her pause. What was Noel doing here?

Elizabeth pushed the door and it opened. The feeble light of the overhead bulb revealed one overturned chair, the old lady slumped on the floor. Noel was kneeling above her, his hands on her throat.

Elizabeth stepped forward. "Noel!"

He wheeled. "You? What are you doing here?"

"Better ask what you are doing," Elizabeth said.

"I surprised the old one. She's had an attack—heart maybe. I'm trying to help her."

"You mean kill her," Elizabeth said, slipping to her knees beside the woman. She took one of the frail hands in her own. "Señora?"

Mrs. Amado croaked, could not speak. Her eyes strained wide, fixed on Noel. She clung to Elizabeth's hand. There was dried blood on her cheek.

"You hurt her," Elizabeth said. She glanced up at the shelf and saw the canvas gone. "Where is it?"

She saw it had fallen to the floor, and she uncurled Mrs. Amado's fingers from her own and moved to pick up the roll. Cradling it in her arms, she turned to Noel. "Is this what you wanted?"

"Aren't you after the same thing?"

He reached under his shirt and pulled out a pistol. "Give me that canvas, Elizabeth. And leave. Not a word of this, or that kid you're so fond of—Eric—he won't live to see tomorrow."

"Eric?" Elizabeth was confused. "What has he to do with this?"

"He's in the city jail," Noel said. "If you make trouble for me now, I'll make it worse for him. Just get out of here!"

He'd struck a deal an hour ago with Ralph and Tom. He would bring them the canvases. They'd have a look and if this was Gauguin for real, they were ready to buy the paintings from him. One hundred thousand, that's what they'd offered: a bank check plus cash. Noel knew he should hold out for more, but with other things on his mind, he hadn't argued. No word from Veronica. As far as Noel knew things had gone according to plan. But where in hell was Veronica? He'd rung her private number a hundred times. No answer. The bitch! Here he had everything sewed up tight and she'd vanished. She wouldn't cut out alone. Would she? Damned right she would, Noel knew that.

The old woman had given him a hard time. He'd lost his temper, shaken her up a bit. Damn! She'd be nicely dead by now if Elizabeth hadn't walked in.

Noel lifted his gun, pointed it at Elizabeth. "Get the hell out of here if you know what's good for you!"

The front door crashed wide. Elizabeth turned. "Marco!" She stepped towards him, then stopped herself, remembering...

"I was next door," Marco said, "I heard Noel's voice."

His eyes moved from Elizabeth to the canvas she clutched, to Noel, to the slumped woman. He understood immediately. Understood all except Elizabeth's presence. "You?" he asked. "Are you in on this, too?"

She shook her head. She stared at Marco—he had saved her once again. She stepped towards him. "Marco? I..."

He pointed to the canvas in her arms. "It's those paintings, isn't it? That's all you want."

Anger choked her. "Yes," she said. Because he didn't ask, he accused her. He believed the worst. And he was right—the Gauguins were all she wanted. She spoke through stiff lips. "They are what I came for, and why I have stayed."

Noel laughed. "Sure, that's why she's here, brujo. She never wanted you. You're just the icing on her cake."

Marco paled. "Is that true?" he asked Elizabeth.

"If you choose to believe so."

He pointed to the canvas. "What else can I believe?"

A movement from Mrs. Amada brought Marco to his knees beside her. He took her hands in his, chafed them gently. "What happened, nina?" He saw the blood, and the bruises on her neck. "Who did this?"

A movement, and Marco glanced up, caught Noel inching towards the door. Moving fast, he grabbed him. "What's going on?" He stared over Noel's head at Elizabeth.

"You can't believe that I...?" she said. Looking at his face, she saw he did. "No," she said.

MARCO'S GIFT

Marco didn't hear her. He was looking down Noel's drawn gun barrel. He swung at the weapon.

Noel's gun exploded. The bullet shattered the ceiling light above. In the dark, Elizabeth screamed.

Marco raised his fist and struck at the shape in front of him. It was a bone-crunching blow and Noel groaned, crashed to the floor.

"On your feet," Marco ordered him. "Start running. If I see you in the village, anywhere around here, I swear I'll kill you!"

Noel staggered to his feet. Swiping at his bloody mouth, he stumbled towards the door. Marco grabbed him again, pulled Noel's face near his own. "One thing more—I curse you—you and yours."

Noel squealed like a branded calf. Elizabeth cowered, dropped the canvas.

Noel stumbled to the door and out into the rain. Marco moved to the old woman. Lifting her gently, he carried her to her cot. Aware of Elizabeth standing there, he said, without looking at her, "I ask you to leave. I'll take care of this now. Don't bother this woman again."

Elizabeth was numb. She saw, not Marco but a stranger, his face drawn, raked with pain, his bare feet muddied, blood smeared on his knuckles. And his shadow—Elizabeth saw it huge across the floor. She stepped from its long reach.

Marco knelt near the old woman. Speaking over his shoulder, he told Elizabeth, "For God's sake, go!"

Still, she hesitated. She looked down at the roll of canvas, fallen on the floor. "Marco," she began. But Señora Amado had all his attention.

"Look at me!" Elizabeth begged.

"Go, will you!"

The break in his voice, his refusal to look at her—something inside her cracked, opened like an unhealed wound. Carefully, she hefted the roll of canvas, held it out to Marco. "Take this," she said. "These paintings are yours."

She waited. He did not turn around. "I am giving you the Gauguins," she repeated, loudly.

217

He turned, got to his feet, facing her squarely. "They are not yours to give."

"That's true," she admitted.

"What were you going to pay her for these? A thousand, maybe two? That is stealing, Elizabeth."

She stared at him. "That you could believe this of me. Are you so perfect, Marco?" Just speaking his name wrung her heart. "All you ever wanted from me was a good lay. More proof of your power, wasn't it—to bed the gringa? Another notch in your Devil's tail!"

She blinked back her tears and turned from him so quickly she did not see him reach for her. She left the house, slamming the door behind her. She stepped into a crowd.

"*La gringa!*" The sound of Noel's gun had drawn the villagers here. They pushed forward, their faces half moons in the mist and drizzle.

"*Doña?*" Jesu stood in front of her. "He is all right?"

Elizabeth nodded. "The old woman. Noel hurt her."

A man shouldered forward. "*El brujo?*" he asked.

"Your witch?" Elizabeth laughed. "Nothing can happen to him. That's what he says anyway." She spoke in English, knowing he did not understand her. Nobody here understood her. She made a move to push through the crowd but dark shapes circled, threatening, moving closer. Cops, soldiers. Elizabeth saw the glint of gun barrels. Light from nearby houses shivered on black boots and leather straps.

"Give us the *brujo*," someone shouted.

"Marco's not here," Elizabeth said.

Pressed behind the soldiers, the villagers waited. They stood, mouths agape, enthralled in their own imaginings of what would happen next. Jesu slipped from sight, went round to a back window and knocked. He told Marco to look for Elizabeth at her house; he himself was going up the hill. He would wait for Marco there. Take care, he warned.

*M*arco made Mrs. Amado comfortable. When she slept, he slipped out the back door. He had slung the rough bundle of paintings over his shoulder. He headed for Elizabeth's house. He must speak with her.

Her lights were on, but she refused to answer his knock. Marco slumped against the door, trying to summon that energy in himself he knew would move her.

He knew she stood, listening, just the other side of the door.

"Por Dios, mi amor..." For God's sake, my love...

"No." Her voice was faint.

"Damn! Listen to me." Marco kneeled, his forehead against her door. "Open to me," he demanded. He shouted her name: "Elizabeth!"

"No," she repeated, and he sensed she moved out of hearing. He waited in silence, his body shaking in the wet and cold. Suddenly, like a blow across his face, her house was dark.

"I have the paintings," he said, loudly. She heard him, she must! "You will find them at my house." Did she answer? He thought so and, knowing he must hurry, he shouldered his burden and headed down the street towards the village.

The rain had stopped. Doors were closed and curtains pulled shut. The quiet was palpable, but Marco knew the people were not sleeping. Soldiers abroad. Evil patrolled corners and crossings: the people played safe, erasing themselves.

Only Juana had left an oil lamp burning. "Brujo," she whispered, lifting Marco's burden from his shoulders, beckoning him into her shop. An open bottle of rum stood on the counter and, without a word, she poured him a full glass. She watched him drink it.

"Ah..." he said, and gestured for another.

She shook her head. "No, go now."

"A moment," he said, and leaned on her counter, resting his head on his arms. She put her hands to his wet hair. "*Niño...niño...*" Because he wept like a boy—great gulping sobs.

"*Calmate, hijo...*" Quiet now, son, Juana crooned, stroking that strong black hair. If the counter had not been between them, she would have taken him in her arms.

When he could get his breath, Marco lifted his head. "Is this the end?" he asked.

"Not yet," Juana said. Lightning flickered, illuminating her face. "This storm," she said. "We have wished for such a one. What an Easter we will have—all the island in bloom!"

Marco nodded. He reached for the rum. Juana did not deny him. She put her finger to her lips. "I have news. Men at your house. Two gringos, and Señor Noel. They wait for you." She looked at the bundle she had taken from Marco. "Is that what they want?"

Marco nudged the plastic cover with his foot. "Many want this. The old woman is near dead because of it."

Juana spit on her thumb and made the sign of the cross on Marco's forehead. "Go with God, brujo."

"That way has always been mine."

Another drink of rum and Marco set out on the path up the hill to his house. The climb soon caught at his heart. He longed to toss the roll of canvas to the rain and wind, but it was not his to lose. He would place it in Elizabeth's hands, that was what she wished. He'd be done with all this then. Except for the pain. Grief was set in him now, he would learn to accept it, let it settle, part of him, like his Stone.

Marco hefted his burden. The Devil's own load, he thought. Hell loose on the island now: Eric in jail and Dierdre waiting for his, Marco's, promised help. He had failed her. He had failed them all. Elizabeth's door closed to him now, locked against his love.

Reaching the top of the hill, Marco paused. He lifted his face to the dripping sky, drank in the rain. Down there, in the village, lights moved, snaking their way through shadows, exploding secrets. Marco knew he must hide himself.

Thunder rumbled above his head. Lightning flashed and Marco ducked. No cover up here. He'd seen a man struck down once. He'd never forgotten the look of astonishment in those seared eyes.

He walked clumsily, the roll of canvas dragging frayed ropes. Tomorrow Elizabeth would have this burden. Take it, and go, he would tell her. Perhaps he would forget her? Marco stumbled in the high grass, almost fell.

He could see his house now. Why had Jesu turned the lights on? Where were his dogs? Coming home, it was they who first greeted him. He must tie them safe, the soldiers would be here soon. Marco walked faster. Grass tangled his feet. The rain now, even it stood against him. Once, not long ago, he had wanted it. The villagers had prayed for it. Again, Marco halted. They believe I can make it rain...

"I can't!" he shouted.

He saw Dierdre's face, the trust in her eyes. Was she sitting on the dock now, waiting for him, knowing he would help her?

Again, Marco shouted, "I can't!"

Elizabeth's face. "Give up your Devil," she said.

"I can't!"

Marco strode through the tall grass. *Who the hell do they think I am?*

*H*e approached his house with caution.

The rain had stopped. His house blazed with light. Marco saw Noel, and behind him the two hotel guests. The three were circling Jesu. Marco came nearer. He saw Noel raise his hand, strike at Jesu. Tom intervened. Then the larger man, Ralph, Marco remembered, pushed Tom aside and set his hands on Jesu's shoulders. A dog growled, hurled itself at Ralph. A gun exploded.

Marco thrust forward. Dropping his bundle, he kicked it behind a clump of bushes. He heard another shot, and Jesu's cry.

"What the hell?" Marco shouted. Noel's pistol smoked. Santo whimpered at Jesu's feet. Marco grabbed Noel's gun, tossed it into the dark. He whirled on Ralph, doubled him over with a kick in the groin. He reached for Tom.

"Señor," Jesu's voice wavered, "let them be. Give them what they want." He knelt to the bleeding dog. "Santo," he said.

Tom spoke, his voice hard. "Just give us the paintings and we'll go."

Noel spoke: "Hand them over, brujo."

Marco had Santo in his arms. Gently, he closed the dog's eyes, lay the animal on the ground. "That was a dog!" he murmured, his voice breaking.

"The paintings," Noel insisted.

Ralph sneered. "Unless you've given them to your woman?"

His woman? The words bludgeoned Marco. He jumped Ralph, threw him to the ground, pinioned him there. Rain sluiced the back of his neck, blinded Ralph's eyes.

Tom's hands clamped Marco's shoulders. "Cool it," Tom said. He hauled Marco and Ralph to their feet. "One dead dog," he said, "isn't that enough?"

"Noel did it," Ralph panted. "Can't say I'm sorry though," and he toed the corpse. "He wasn't friendly."

Marco clenched his fists. "My other two—where are they?"

Jesu pointed to the house. "I had time to lock them up." He wiped his bloody mouth with the back of his hand.

Shrugging off his wet shirt, Marco wiped Jesu's face clean. "Who hurt you?"

"Just a bit of foreplay," Ralph snickered. "The paintings now, Superman. Give them to us and we'll leave, quiet as we came."

Black clouds muttered, rolled, releasing a final cannon of thunderbolts that shook the earth. Jesu fell to his knees. Marco spread his arms to the sky. *"Por Dios,"* he whispered.

Ralph grinned. "Yeah—start praying, witch man."

Marco wheeled on him. "You and your friend, get the hell out of here!"

"Not without what we came for," Ralph said. He stepped nearer Marco. "You can't scare me. You're cock of the walk here, in your world—this one shit plop of an island. Where I come from—what we do with crazies like you, we lock 'em up." Ralph snapped his fingers under Marco's nose. "You don't want that now, do you, Mr. Rodriguez?"

Marco raised his fists. The men were too close. Their scent sickened him. Their snide laughter prickled. Only Jesu's restraining hand kept him from striking out.

Across the field then, shouts, and pinpoints of light. Ralph raised his hands in a gesture of victory. "Guess who's coming for dinner!"

"Guardia," Jesu whispered. Police.

Ralph thrust his face into Marco's. "What you gonna do now, witch man?"

Tom intervened. "Come on, brujo," he wheedled, "give us what we want and we'll end it here. Nobody's going to know."

Noel closed in. "He gives us the Gauguins—the woman will know."

Ralph blinked, was silent a moment. Then he brightened. "No, he won't tell her that. He'll say he dropped them, helluva chase, the cops and all." Ralph shrugged. "She'll forgive him. We'll be gone before she's out of his bed."

Voices nearer now, across the field. Tom nudged Marco. "Scared? What do they do with Indians around here, huh?"

"Scared of that jail cell, I bet," Ralph said, his face in Marco's again. "Dark in there, it stinks too—other crazies been there before you. You can smell their piss."

Marco's throat swelled. He exploded a roar, an inhuman sound, stunning those who heard it. Lifting Ralph, Marco shook him until the man's eyes bulged. Marco bounced him into the high grass. And turned on Tom. He yanked the man's arms behind him, bent his head towards his chest. and struck the back of his neck. Tom fell, gasping for breath.

Noel grabbed Marco's knees. Marco kicked, hard. Noel tumbled backwards, his arms akimbo. Rain rinsed his bloodied mouth.

Marco turned to Jesu. "Leave them here. I'll meet you inside." He backed off, into the darkness, going around to the back of his house. He went in, down into the herb cellar.

*J*esu *found Marco waiting in the darkness.*

"Soldiers gone," he whispered. "But they'll be back. You must hide, senor."

"Up in my cave, yes," Marco said. "You know where I'll be." He went upstairs, into the living room. Crouching beside the dying fire, he stretched his hands to its faint warmth. "Leave the house dark," he said. "Kick out this fire when I am gone" He turned. "There is something I must do."

"*Y la doña?*"Jesu asked. And the lady? Marco's bleak look told him all he needed to know. "I will bring dry clothes, and food," he said. He touched Marco's cheek. "That wound should be cleaned."

"No time now." Marco lowered his head to his hands. "Eric, the American—he's in jail. The girl thinks I can help—but I can't, you know that." He looked at Jesu. "*Viejo,* old one, I'm scared."

"Every man is afraid," Jesu said.

"But you taught me. Nothing is impossible for a Devil Man!"

"*Si, todo es posible,*" Jesu said. Everything is possible. He was careful to add, "If your heart wants it."

"My heart wants only her," Marco said. "Why is she denied me?"

Jesu touched Marco's mark. "It is she who must dare love now."

Marco pulled the old man close. He took a last look around this room. He aligned a pile of books, straightened a yellow pillow. He fumbled the mail, stacked it, leaving it unopened.

"Take care," he told Jesu. "Lock the doors. No lights. Stay quiet. There's more than one kind of devil looking for me tonight."

"*Vaya con Dios,*"Jesu whispered. Go with God.

"If things go badly," Marco said, "bring the señora here. And see to it that Santo..." he hesitated, unable to say the words.

Jesu understood. "He will have a blessed ceremony."

"How could they?" Marco asked. "Santo had the finest soul…"

Jesu smiled. "But what an angel he will make! Even now, he plays at God's feet."

"You will come later, to the cave?" Marco asked, not wanting to frighten Jesu but if something were to happen, if he should need.

Elizabeth promised to take my stone…

"It is she will care for me," he told Jesu, knowing the old one understood. "She is frightened though—she does not like blood. Things happened tonight. She is afraid of me."

Jesu nodded. "Afraid of love, like yourself, señor."

"Love is larger than death," Marco said. "All men should fear it, as they fear God."

Jesu smiled. "It is you will win this fight, *hijo.*"

Again, Marco embraced his old friend. "You'll be there, if I need you?"

"She will, if you need her," Jesu replied.

*T*he three men had come down the hill, into the church plaza.
"Now what?" Tom asked.

"We'll let the cops take care of this," Noel said.

"And the paintings?" Ralph asked.

"You'll have them tonight, tomorrow at the latest," Noel promised.

He sent Ralph and Tom back to the hotel. "Stay in your room," he warned. "Don't answer, no matter who knocks. Any minute now, all hell's going to break loose."

Noel hurried across the plaza to the island's one pay phone. He dialed Veronica's private number. He let it ring and, when there was no answer, hung up and dialed again. She wasn't there. He'd expected this. He'd fallen right into it. She'd cut out. Just like a woman, there wasn't one alive who wouldn't take that cash and run. But she'd missed out on the big one. Noel grinned. The paintings would soon be his. If he played his cards right now, moved fast enough, he could beat those two queers at their own game. Noel set off for the Guardia station. He needed to get this witch hunt moving.

He found Dierdre and Hank with the police officer. "What happened to you?" Dierdre asked, staring at Noel. He looked down at himself and saw his shirt was ripped, streaked with mud and blood. He saw Hank's puzzled look.

"Rodriguez's dog doesn't like me," was Noel's excuse.

Dierdre gasped. "You didn't hurt those animals, did you?"

"The General's orders," Noel said. "Rodriguez is crazy, a wild man. He'll kill someone if we don't get him first."

Hank frowned. "I don't like the smell of this." From what the girl Dierdre had just told him, this guy wasn't the nicest.

Noel insisted: "Rodriguez set his dogs on me and my guests. We're lucky we're alive. The man's a killer. I'm not the only one will swear to that."

"Who will believe you, Noel?" Dierdre asked. "Marco should have put you off this island long ago."

"But he didn't, did he?" Noel sneered.

"Easy now, you two," Hank said. "Look, it's raining again."

"I'll go see Elizabeth," Dierdre said. "Eric will know to find me there." Hearing the rumble of thunder, she reassured herself: "My man's a good sailor, he's pulled in somewhere."

"Quit dreaming," Noel told her.

Dierdre ignored him. She nodded at Hank. "Thanks for listening. If you hear anything, you know where I am."

She went out into the wet night, and headed downhill for Elizabeth's house. The village was too quiet, like waiting for something about to happen. Everybody's door shut, the houses dark. Everyone holding their breath. Police everywhere, sly as roaches, skittering. Dierdre slipped off her sandals and, holding them high, she ran through the rain.

Reaching Elizabeth's house, she knocked on the door. "Hey, lady, it's me, Dierdre. Open up!"

"Marco's not with you?"

"Just me, come on, let me in."

Elizabeth opened the door. "You're soaked through! Where have you been?"

"Not just this rain," Dierdre said, "everything's coming down hard."

She warmed her fingers on the brimming coffee mug Elizabeth gave her. "Thanks. Where's Marco?"

Elizabeth was pouring her own coffee, and Dierdre saw her hand tremble. "Lady, what's wrong? You look like a ghost."

"I'm very much alive, thank you," Elizabeth said. She did not sit down. "I'm packing."

"Packing? For when, where?"

"Tomorrow morning. The first ferry."

Dierdre blinked. "But you can't, not now. Not with what's happening. You can't desert Marco now."

"Yes, I can. And I will, Dierdre."

"Listen, lady, I just came from the police station. The whole damn army is out there. Noel says Marco is out to wreck this village. He says Marco's gone loco. They're going to hunt him down like some animal. General's orders are to catch the witch dead or alive. And when they catch him, they'll cage him, lady—like maybe...maybe Eric now." Her voice broke on a sob. "Elizabeth, we've gotta do something!" Dierdre set down her coffee. "We've got to find Marco."

Elizabeth shook her head. "None of this is my business. It can't be. Not anymore, especially not Marco."

Dierdre stared at her. "But you love him!"

Elizabeth laughed. "Oh girl, when will you learn? There's no such thing as love. Look at you now—Eric has let you down, he's cut out on you. Take my advice, get out of this while you still can."

Dierdre pushed to her feet, her eyes blazing. "I'll wait for Eric forever, Elizabeth. And you—you owe Marco something."

"Owe him?" Elizabeth was puzzled.

"You love him."

"I came close to losing my mind, if that's what you mean by love." Elizabeth turned her back, busied herself at the sink.

Roughly, Dierdre pulled her round. "Look at me, lady—tell me straight you don't love that man!"

Elizabeth struggled to escape the hands that held her. Her mouth moved, straining to speak her denial.

At last she said, "I don't believe in love."

"Because you're scared of it," Dierdre scoffed. "You're selfish too. You're saving your own skin. That's it, isn't it, Elizabeth?"

"Don't we all—save ourselves, I mean?"

"Not me! I'd give my life for Eric."

"And you just might have to, Dierdre. You'd better wake up, girl, before it's too late."

"Wake up to living without him? I don't want that. And you, lady—what kind of woman will you be without Marco?"

"Whatever I was before." Elizabeth gazed down at her empty hands. "I'll get over it. I'm used to losing."

Dierdre spoke impatiently. "Why must you lose?"

Elizabeth swallowed. She was near tears again. "Dierdre, listen— he never loved me. Flore told me. She's having Marco's baby. She's not lying, her belly's big…yes," Elizabeth continued, struggling to keep her voice firm, "while he was fucking me, he was fucking Flore!"

Fuck—an ugly word and Elizabeth never used it. Now she did, and liked it.

Dierdre ran a glass of water, sipped at it, dumped it and watched the water drain. Noises outside now, people noises. Someone knocked on the door, moved on. "It's a man hunt," Dierdre said. "All I know is—you can't cut out now."

"But I already have," Elizabeth said.

Dierdre put her hands on Elizabeth's shoulders and shook her hard. "You're the most selfish bitch I know! I'd leave you here if I didn't know how much Marco needed you."

"He needs me, yes." Elizabeth was at the window. "I promised," she whispered, her words dragging from her, her forehead pressed against the glass. "I promised him the thing he most wanted, I did. Dierdre. Listen, I know where he is," she said.

Dierdre was at the door. "So what are we waiting for?"

Sudden as thunder then the night ruptured with the clack and whir of helicopters. Spotlights flared beyond the windows; rain beating down like a tattoo.

"More soldiers!" Dierdre cried. "They'll land on the beach near the hotel."

She grasped Elizabeth's hand. "They'll pass here in a minute."

Elizabeth was remembering those other helicopters. They had come for Loco, taken him so quickly. Marco had been angry; she had thought he would never forgive her. Yes, surely, she did owe Marco this.

"Bastards!" Dierdre said. "They'll search the village first."

"Marco won't fight," Elizabeth said. Her voice broke. "Dierdre, he's such a fool, he'll go without a word. Saving his soul, he calls it. Who's to say he isn't mad?"

Dierdre opened the door. "Are you sure he won't come here?"

"He did," Elizabeth admitted, "but I wouldn't let him in."

Dierdre shook her head. "Oh, lady…we'd better hurry. Maybe we're too late."

*T*he street was crowded, everyone heading out of the village.
Rain drizzled. People carried lanterns, flash lights. Faces bobbed,
slick as carnival masks. Elizabeth saw Juana, barefooted, her umbrella
open above her head. Flore ran past, and Noel then, and his two guests.

"It sure ain't New York!" Ralph shouted. Noel flourished his pistol
and laughed.

The high tide pounded the wall on Elizabeth's right. A palm frond
snapped and fell, scraping her shoulders. Dierdre kicked it aside.

"Hurry!" she cried, grabbing Elizabeth's hand.

People bumped each other, stumbled, cursed the dark, and ran on.
A soldier flourished his gun at Elizabeth. Jesu called from behind her,
and she waited for him.

"Marco?" she asked.

The old man clutched at her. "Hurry, he needs you…"

Elizabeth came to a halt. *I can't do this, I don't want to see it …*

Dierdre tugged at her. "Move, lady!"

Pulled, bumped, stared at, Elizabeth stumbled through the nightmare. A man swore at her, held his torch near her face.

"Puta!" he shouted: whore!

Elizabeth knew they blamed her for what was happening. And they
were right. Marco would be safe in her house tonight if she had not
locked him out. She wheeled, straddling the path, facing the soldier
police behind her. "You don't need guns," she shouted, in English,
forgetting they did not understand. "Go back," she cried, gesturing
fiercely.

Dierdre cheered. "Go on, lady, kick some ass!" She wished Eric
could see this.

Flore gave Elizabeth a brutal shove, sending her to her knees. Elizabeth stayed where she fell. People moved past her, not a hand stretched to her. They had forgotten her. And forgotten their prey. Caught in the excitement of the hunt, both chase and victim were anonymous.

Elizabeth stumbled to her feet. Now was her chance to turn back. Nobody to remark her cowardice. She peered ahead of her, straining to see through the rain and dark. She smelled the rank odor of the dripping forest.

"What's keeping you, lady?" Dierdre was pulling again at her hand.

"I can't," Elizabeth said.

A bove the village, Marco was following the river to the top of the falls.

The rain and wind were strong against him, and he stopped to rest. Setting his back against a fallen tree, he raised his knees, let his head drop to his crossed arms. If he could make it along the edge here, then ford the river, he would be near the waterfall.

Bone tired, he closed his eyes, willing himself to relax, to dream backwards to a better time. Just a boy, he had climbed here—straight up this cliff to the top where he huddled now, the highest point on the island. He had lain for hours on his stomach here, in the blowing grass, watching the pelicans feed their young. They nested, hundreds of them, on the seaward side of Taboga.

Marco remembered jumping rock to rock across this river, his cicada wheeling on a string—it whirred, singing, above his head. He had carried mangoes and salt, and sat here, gorging himself, through the blue afternoons.

Happiness—that was all he had ever wanted. Uncomplicated pleasures: his feet on island ground, his own roof over him; carnival, and a pretty girl in his arms. The schoolroom, and his boys mimicking the English sounds.

Easter was near. The keys to the church were in his pocket now. What would this Easter be, Marco wondered, without Loco marching behind his Virgin? He had wanted Elizabeth to know the island's Easter ceremonies. He had dreamed of dancing in the plaza with her, under the Easter moon, when the church reared white as ivory and all the girls paraded new gilt sandals and lace mantillas. The glass sides of Christ's coffin reflected the trembling torches. Drums moved even the old to dance.

Elizabeth. Just her name filled Marco with an intolerable loneliness. Did she know they were hunting him? He had given her the care of his soul. What more could a man give a woman?

I will need her. A chill shook Marco. *I am nearer death than ever I have been.*

Not death, it was Elizabeth he must hold close now. Reaching for her. He waited for the whole of his vision. And saw her there.

"I can't," she said.

You can. Marco stretched his hands to her.

*I*t *was the voices below, clearer now, that called Marco back from dreaming.*

He looked down at the canvas bundle beside him, set his hand on it. Because of this, an old woman lay dying. Because of this, Santo would not run again through the high grass. Because of this wretched bundle here he and Elizabeth had turned on each other, creating, each of them, a stranger opposite.

Marco lifted his face to the darkness. Near him, the swollen river ran strong. He heard the gurgle and rush of the falls, just ahead now.

A rattle of stones to his left, and Marco tensed, his flesh crawled. He had seen the Devil full, once only when he'd taken the Stone. Larger than life, yes—he had told Eric that. Marco had never been able to describe the face of Evil. The coldness of it, he would swear to that. And the hard stone weight of it, crushing the soul.

Someone, something, behind him now. Marco held his breath, swallowed hard.

"Time you showed up," he said.

You are scared, boy—Papi's voice.

Marco stumbled to his feet, faced the whirling dark. "Mine is a different world, Papi. Soldiers and guns—it is death to stand against them."

And the truth then—wrung from him. "I am only a man," Marco said.

Lightning flashed, shuddered a tree. Marco heard the Devil laugh. Far below, a gun blazed. A dog barked. Marco hunkered back on his heels, watched the black water slide, faster and stronger now, dragging a tangle of roots and debris toward the boiling white lip of the falls.

Marco? Elizabeth's voice, thin as a bell struck. He answered her, from deep in himself: *Be my love.*

He must cross here, now. He would not have another chance. From here, he could climb down to the cave.

The canvas slung across his back, Marco stepped forward, into the roiling water. Stones rolled under his feet. His breath short, wind in his face, Marco halted midstream. Half crouching, he hauled on the clumsy canvas. The plastic wrapping had come loose. Strings dragged, tangling his feet and knees. The plastic pulled free, unwound. Several large squares of canvas floated loose. Marco saw the colors of his island bleed, the canvases dragged to catch at the edge of the falls.

Marco pushed forward, slipping, taking hold. One step more, and he was across the river, clutching at rocks, reaching for the canvas. He was hip-deep now, dangerously near the edge. If this damn rain would let up.

Marco did not see the branch sweep down upon him. It caught him from behind, whipping his shoulders, tearing savagely at his arms and legs. Clutching at the bank, Marco's fingers closed on fur and flesh. A claw raked his wrist.

"You!" Marco shouted. Grabbing hold of the creature's rough hair, he shoved the animal into the main stream. He saw the rolling whites of its eyes as it slid, over the edge of the falls.

Marco's chest was near bursting. Pain was a fist striking. Shreds of canvas and Marco reached for them. He fell, dragged over the falls' edge. Down, down into the bruising dark.

*E*lizabeth saw Marco fall.

Terrified, she fell to her knees, hid her face in her hands. She must not look. Scrunched down into herself, Elizabeth shielded eyes and ears, and self.

Flore, too, saw the hurtling body. *Dios!* she prayed, *it was not this I wanted.*

It was Jesu pulled Marco from the pool. He put his ear to Marco's chest, afraid to listen—listening, hearing at last the faint irregular beat of Marco's heart.

Jesu lifted his head, crossed himself. "He lives!"

"Marco!" Flore beat on the still shoulders.

Jesu pushed her away. "Don't touch him." He stripped off his shirt, folded it, and placed it carefully beneath Marco's head. "Find someone who can help us move him."

Marco's eyelids flickered. "No," he said. He plucked at Jesu's arm. "Elizabeth..."

He had strength only for her name. And the power to stay until she came. He could not feel his arms or legs, but his thinking was clear, and his vision. He was aware of soldiers gathered near him, guns pointed at his head. He heard harsh voices, the squelch of boots through mud.

"We'll take him now," an officer said, snapping open a tarpaulin, spreading it near Marco. "Move him," he told his men. But they held back, afraid to touch a Devil Man. What he died of—some said such evil would spread like the plague, carry them off to Hell.

The villagers gathered closer, pressing in a tight circle. The soldiers swore, and shoved the people back.

"No lo toque!" Jesu ordered. Do not touch him. He pulled a knife

from his belt, brought the blade of it near a soldier's face. The crowd tittered. The rain died then, streaming from the dark trees.

Dierdre leaned above Marco. Opening his eyes, he recognized her. "Sorry..." he whispered, not remembering why he must tell her this, knowing only that her face was like a flower.

"Please—Elizabeth?" he asked again.

Noel pressed close, Ralph and Tom behind him. "The canvas?" Noel said. Marco turned his head away and shut his eyes.

Jesu addressed Noel: "Fetch the señora." Noel did not move.

"*Cabron!*" Jesu hissed. He-goat!

Noel jumped as if struck. Tom giggled. "Hell, this is primal stuff," he said, and took Noel's arm, and Ralph's. "Let's watch from a safe distance."

"Rodriguez is done for," Noel said. "You don't want to see this. Let's go back to the hotel, wait it out over a couple of drinks." He needed a stiff one. What the hell had Rodriguez done with those canvases? "If I had my way," Noel said, "I'd kick the truth from him!"

"I'm staying," Ralph said. "If it's his last words," he nodded at Marco, "he's going to tell me where he hid our Gauguins."

He made a move towards Marco, but Jesu barred his way and knelt again beside his master. He straightened Marco's scarred left arm and lifted his knife. He prayed his hand strong now, to take the stone.

Marco saw the knife and, with enormous effort, touched it. "Elizabeth," he said.

Jesu stared into Marco's eyes. He saw the years there, the years he had served this man. And now another, a stranger, would take his Stone. A woman, a foreigner, would lift Marco's soul to Heaven. Tears spilled down Jesu's cheeks. Would the woman cut surely, quickly? He knew she would not—a frailness to her, a shadow of doubt. The Stone must be removed fast; swiftly as his soul leaves a man, so must the Stone slide free.

Jesu touched Marco's chest, wishing he had something to cover the ruined body. Because the *gringa* would turn her face away; she was like that, frightened of the truth.

Marco spoke again, his voice a whisper. "Jesu, remember..."

The old man nodded. "It is she will take your stone."

Dierdre covered Marco. Her small shirt lay like a bright handkerchief across his chest. She wanted to straighten his legs but was afraid to move him. Jesu began to pray, his voice high, keening. It was raining again, and Dierdre leaned close above Marco, protecting his eyes with her hands. She looked behind her for Elizabeth. *Lady, don't fail him now...*

It was Juana who found Elizabeth on the edge of the crowd. "Señora, only you can finish what began with you. Make us a proud ending now." Juana's voice broke. "He is a prince, señora—we believe so. Give him what he most desires."

Elizabeth held tightly to Juana. "I can't do this. You don't understand. I don't like blood—or death."

Juana nodded. "None of us do, señora."

Taking Elizabeth's hand, she led her, gently as she would a child, nearer to Marco. "See," she said, "El Brujo lies quiet. Nothing is ever quite as bad as you imagine." Juana released Elizabeth's hand.

Marco's eyes opened. Kneeling to him, Elizabeth saw herself there, deep in his gaze. Someone set a torch near her. And another. The light paled Marco's face.

Turn out the light. Let him sleep now...

"Señora..." Jesu offered his knife on the flat of his hand. "You have promised. Cut now, he hasn't much time."

Elizabeth stared at the knife. It winked in the torch light and Elizabeth recoiled from it as if it threatened her own flesh.

"Take it," Jesu insisted, knowing the woman did not understand what she must do. He spoke again: "*Doña*, he cannot stay much longer. It is you only can give him Heaven."

"I?" She could not cut, not with that knife, not into Marco's arm.

She saw his hair wet, plastered to his forehead and she smoothed it back. A certain quickening of his body told her he knew she was there. She thought his lips framed her name. "Yes," she answered.

"I am so sorry," she began. But knew immediately that was not important, not anymore.

An enormous effort, she felt it in the rise and fall of his chest, he slid his arm across her knees. She saw his Mark gathered tight as an angry mouth, and she lay her palm flat across it. A healing gesture.

Jesu touched her shoulder. "Yes," Elizabeth said, and accepted the knife he offered. She tested it, it was not as heavy as she had thought it would be. *As she imagined it, so would it be.* Marco's words.

She leaned close above him. "I am here," she whispered.

An officer prodded her with his booted toe. "Tell him Adios and be done with it."

Rage choked Elizabeth. "Damn you bullies," she hissed, "you, and your rotten guns!" She touched Marco's arm with the knife blade. Behind her, the crowd hushed.

Hank knelt beside Elizabeth. "Sorry I'm late, ma'am. We'll get you out of here right now."

Elizabeth shook her head. "I don't want out of this."

Marco. She felt his impatience within herself. But he must wait, there were things she must tell him. So much to explain. Elizabeth stretched herself on the ground, the length of her body close to Marco.

Placing her lips on his, breathing into him, she kissed him as he had kissed her once...*Breathe, love, breathe...*

*H*er breath was sweet, it filled his lungs.

*Stay, love…*He wanted to hold her. *Where are my hands, my arms?*

He was floating. Figures came and went. An angel, spread-eagled on a table, kicked her silver legs. St. Peter dangled a key, just out of reach. A black dog flicked his tongue at Flore who was sweeping shadows like crumbled flowers from a house where Marco knew his mother waited. He began his climb up the long green hill…

A stone weighed heavy on his chest, settled above his heart. Marco moaned, lifted his arm from Elizabeth's lap, let it fall there again.

He was standing above a blue sea, Papi beside him. "Horizons," Papi said. He was wearing new slippers. "Come now," he urged, pulling at Marco's hand.

Then—it was Elizabeth's voice: "I love you," she said.

Gently, she kissed Marco's eyes closed. "Heaven," he begged, the word rushing from him.

She must do it now…

And Elizabeth lifted the knife.

"I love you," she whispered. Holding her breath, she set the blade's edge to the center of the scar. She saw the skin split under the blade, and the welling blood. Pressing her fingers into the wound, Elizabeth felt for whatever was the Stone. It slipped from Marco's flesh, warm in her palm.

"I'll take it," Jesu said. Hadn't he set it there himself, long ago?

"I must see it," Elizabeth insisted. Because if she could see it she would believe it. She let the cross lie a moment in her hand. A warmth to it, and Elizabeth put it to her lips.

"Yes," she said, "I understand." She gave the cross to Jesu.

Gently then, with her fingertips, she closed Marco's eyes.

Dierdre was kneeling beside her. "Lady, come away now."

"No, I must have all this ending." Elizabeth said.

"It is dawn, *doña*," Jesu said.

Light was sliding over all. The soldiers leaned, dumbly, on the their guns. The villagers waited in silence, sensing an ending nobody had dared to imagine.

"*Un milagro*," Juana said. A miracle. Those who heard her would repeat her words. Telling this story, they would embellish it. The blue-eyed gringa—some would swear her eyes changed color—green as the pool there, they said, and her soul looked right out at them, you could see it, yes.

"A miracle—more than one!" Dierdre's voice, so full of joy it startled Elizabeth and she turned.

Eric stood above her. Tears coursed down his cheeks, but he managed a grin. "I saw it all, lady. Dierdre and me, we're proud of you."

Elizabeth stood to embrace him. "How did you get here?" she asked. "We thought...Noel said..."

"Noel is a devil of a liar." Eric reached out an arm to draw Dierdre, and Elizabeth, too, into his embrace.

"Do you know what they are saying, lady?" Dierdre asked. "The Devil has left the island, that's how they tell it, that it was you, lady, who chased him away. It is you who gave Marco his Heaven."

Dierdre smiled. "They will not forget you, lady. You and Marco—I mean, you two are big time, the island's love story. They're inventing you already, Elizabeth. By tomorrow you'll have a halo and wings!"

Eric leaned and touched Marco's shoulder. "I'm no good at speeches. How to say goodbye? I mean this guy—what he said—he gave me back my self. I wish he knew I'm safe."

"He does," Elizabeth said, with a certainty that surprised her.

Hank joined them. "Ma'am, I've never seen anything like what you did! I couldn't have done it myself."

"It's very simple," Elizabeth said. "I kept a promise."

She was aware now of the sky's dawning. She could see to the dark bottom of the pool.

"Look!" Dierdre pointed. "All that canvas—like a sail come down the river."

Elizabeth saw the twisted sheets. She went to them, and lifted a sodden corner. Other pieces floated out of reach. "Whatever these were," she said, "we'll never know."

But we never did know...

A rough hand gripped her elbow. "Damn! Is that what's left?" Ralph asked. He waded into the pool, snatched at the shreds of canvas. "Shit! There's nothing left."

He turned on Elizabeth. "Do you know what you've done? What that bastard did? He threw away a fortune—damn his soul!"

Elizabeth stared at Ralph. His strained face, the tight lips and hard eyes reminded her of someone she had known. "I was like you, once," she said.

Tom spoke: "Don't mind him. God, I'm sorry." He gestured at Marco's body. "We didn't mean for this to happen."

"Yes," Elizabeth said, "we never mean for anyone to die."

Jesu was covering Marco with a tarpaulin. "Let me do that," Elizabeth said. She tucked the heavy cloth around Marco. She would not cover his face.

Seeing real remorse in Tom's eyes, she pitied him. "Gauguin is an old story here. Gossip is truth, sometimes. Like Marco's story—his Devil Stone. People wanted to believe it and so, for a moment, it was real."

Tom stretched a hand to Elizabeth. "I'll believe anything, after tonight. What you did—you were something else!"

Elizabeth was looking at Marco. "Not I," she said softly, "he was." She was aware she stood on the edge, the abyss of an enormous sorrow.

But there was another side. She would get there.

It was then Noel saw Eric. He blanched, reeled backwards. "A God damm ghost! What the hell are you doing here?"

Eric laughed. "Man, you'd better believe I'm here! What you gave me? I wasn't born yesterday. When I figured what *Gull* was carrying, I dumped it quick. I never saw that dock. I hope they aren't still waiting for me?"

"So that's what happened?" Dierdre said, her eyes wide on Eric. "I should have known you—"

"Are one helluva lot smarter than you imagined!" Eric hugged her tightly.

"You never got to the city?" Noel asked.

"Hell no! I ain't your delivery boy." Eric laughed. "Know what? There's lots of stoned fishes in the ocean now."

Dierdre slid her hand into Eric's. "Let's take our lady home."

"To the señor's house," Jesu said. "He wanted that."

Noel stood, stunned, staring at Marco's body. Nothing left now. Rodriguez, and his Devil, too—erased. The gringa had guts, Noel had to admit that. What a scene she'd given them. Better than a late night movie. Noel kicked at a pile of sodden leaves. Whatever luck he'd been born with, the Devil Man's curse had soured it. But now, with Rodriguez gone, maybe things would pick up? The General had what he wanted: this island was his. Best thing he, Noel, could do now was offer to take the load off the man's back. He'd handle the Columbian drops, see the stuff on its way. If he played it right, things might work out. Veronica? He was well rid of the bitch.

Something caught Noel's eye. "Hey, look!" he said, pointing at a black shape at the edge of the pool "So who pushed that one over the edge?"

Jesu stared at the drowned dog. Crossing himself, he said, "The creature cannot haunt us now."

Juana nodded. "El Brujo did that for us."

Noel laughed. "It's what you want, isn't it? Your Devil Man turned saint." He turned to Ralph and Tom. "I don't know about you two, but I need a stiff drink."

*E*lizabeth *watched the men leave, trailed by the villagers.*
One quick shy glance at her, they did not look back. Flore slunk away like a fox. Juana laid a white lily on Marco's chest. The green trees closed over him like a chapel roof. Elizabeth smiled, seeing the new story shape itself.

This magic puzzle of an island, she thought. Tin cans and tomato sauce, yes, but a church too, its tower inlaid with mother-of-pearl. Whiskey distilled in the ruined convent garden where the walls were made of bulls' blood, honey, and the whites of eggs. Elizabeth determined to bring jasmine from the house to Loco's Virgin. She would light one last candle.

She remembered something else: "Jesu," she said, "that loose nail on the cross in the church. It should be fixed for Easter."

Jesu shook his head. "We wait for His arm to drop. It is then Christ moves. When He does, we are frightened. Only then is the story real."

"Ah, yes," Elizabeth said. "Only then is it real." She was beginning to understand.

*R*eaching the path that led uphill to Marco's house, Elizabeth told Jesu to go ahead of her, she wanted to make this climb alone.

As she had done, that first time.

Because she must fix all this in memory. The pitted path, the golden spills of mangoes and coconuts. Dark banyans. The scarlet birds of paradise. Pelicans sketched the sky above her head. The tall grass then, and Marco's house. Like long ago, like yesterday, his dogs barked, ran out to greet the visitor. Jesu walked towards her.

"Santo?" she asked.

Jesu shook his head. "Señor Noel shot him."

Dierdre and Eric were inside. Just as before, that first time. Elizabeth sat on the couch, where she had sat that first time.

"Who will live here now?" Dierdre asked.

"I've been thinking," Elizabeth said. "What Marco wanted for the village was an English language school. Why not here? It mustn't be too large, that will attract attention. If it is financed by a gringa, the General won't complain. Jesu could remain here as caretaker. We will give it Marco's name. He would like that."

Dierdre sat cross-legged on the floor. "I don't want to talk, let's just remember."

Elizabeth could not sit still. The Frida Kahlo there, yes. She picked up a yellow pillow and hugged it close against her cheek. It was then she saw the carved walking stick resting on a table. It had a card near it, and she reached for it and read what was written there: *For my love.*

She took the cane into her hand. "He must have known what was coming."

Dierdre was beside her. They sank together to the couch. Dierdre holding Elizabeth close, rocking her gently. Eric stood at the window, watching the clouds on the horizon. Once again rain threatened. Eric blinked, rubbed at his wet eyes.

At long last, and feeling an immense relief, Elizabeth lifted her head. "I haven't cried like that in years." Her hands fumbled her hair. "I must look a wreck."

Dierdre smiled. "Always our lady Elizabeth. You needed to shed those tears. We all do. They wash away all kinds of junk."

"Laughter follows tears," Eric said. "My mom said that."

Elizabeth looked at him. She could not remember when she had not liked this man. She touched the stick in her lap. "Marco knew I loved this."

"Hey—look," Eric pointed at the fireplace. Bright white wings fluttered above the charred logs.

"That's my butterfly!"

Carefully, Elizabeth approached the insect. "Come," she whispered, "come." It alighted on her wrist. She carried it to the open window and released it, and watched its flight until she could no longer see it.

"Souls with wings—that's butterflies," Dierdre said. "That one acted like it knew you."

"It does." Elizabeth smiled "That one was here from the beginning."

"May I?" Eric took the walking stick from Elizabeth. "You never told us you were looking for Gauguin's paintings."

Elizabeth smiled. "Perhaps because it was something else I needed?"

Eric understood. "I've done that too. It's a game we play with ourselves."

Dierdre spoke softly: "Lady, I don't know another woman who would do what you did. That rain, those cops with their guns. The mud, that creepy jungle. And you with that knife. I mean, you're a real lady. I bet you never handled a knife like that?"

"It was not as bad as I imagined it would be," Elizabeth said.

MARCO'S GIFT

"You had to cut him," Dierdre said. "You had to put your fingers right into that bloody mess and find that Devil Stone—something you didn't even believe in, for God's sake—and pull it out. My God, woman! You're what I call a warrior."

"He knew I loved him," Elizabeth said. "At the end, he knew."

Dierdre smiled. "Marco knew you loved him long before you did. Like the whole world knew, Elizabeth."

"The whole world?" Elizabeth sat straight. She sensed a new self, the swell of pride filled her.

Heaven could be anything: place or person. Her paradise had been Marco's embrace. Now her Heaven was knowing she had kept a promise. Yes, Elizabeth saw it all so clearly. Loco's Heaven was in the moon. Jesu's Heaven was the place where God lived. Santo's Heaven was a field of pampa grass. And Marco's Heaven?

He said I was his paradise. She would forgive him for leaving her. Truly, he would never leave her.

His school, she wondered. It must be. Certainly she would return here.

"I love you," Elizabeth said. *Speaking to this room, to this house, to the Guayacan tree. To the convent, the church, the Virgin there. And to the man who had given her love.*

She must do something about Loco. Could he forgive her?

Elizabeth felt the weight of years slide from her shoulders.

CPSIA information can be obtained
at www.ICGtesting.com
Printed in the USA
LVOW08s1601280317
528762LV00002B/291/P

9 781432 791179